The Bliss of Your Attention

Johns Hopkins: Poetry and Fiction
Wyatt Prunty, General Editor

THE BLISS OF YOUR ATTENTION

STORIES

David Borofka

JOHNS HOPKINS UNIVERSITY PRESS
BALTIMORE

This book has been brought to publication with the generous assistance of the John T. Irwin Poetry and Fiction Endowment Fund and the G. Harry Pouder Fund.

Printed in the United States of America on acid-free paper
9 8 7 6 5 4 3 2 1

Johns Hopkins University Press
2715 North Charles Street
Baltimore, Maryland 21218
www.press.jhu.edu

Library of Congress Cataloging-in-Publication Data

Names: Borofka, David, 1954– author.
Title: The bliss of your attention : stories / David Borofka.
Description: Baltimore : Johns Hopkins University Press, 2025. |
Series: Johns Hopkins: poetry and fiction
Identifiers: LCCN 2024013759 | ISBN 9781421450544 (paperback ;
    acid-free paper) | ISBN 9781421450551 (ebook)
Subjects: LCGFT: Short stories.
Classification: LCC PS3552.O75443 B55 2024 | DDC 813/.54—dc23/eng/20240415
LC record available at https://lccn.loc.gov/2024013759

A catalog record for this book is available from the British Library.

Special discounts are available for bulk purchases of this book. For more information, please contact Special Sales at specialsales@jh.edu.

For Deb, once again and always

In the bliss

   of your attention,

I burst into

   blossom: the

   metamorphosis of our twinned

souls' intention.

—CONSTANZA DE FIORE,
"*In the Darkness of the
Solarium*"

CONTENTS

The Bliss of Your Attention

Domestic Arrangements: Live with It

LEARN TO LIVE WITH YOUR DISAPPOINTMENTS. This is what I tell Alan, newly retired middle school English teacher and my would-be-novelist husband. I mean, I could give him the Campbell party line, you know, follow your bliss, etc., etc., but that's where the disappointments come from, don't they? I mean that's where bliss leads if you're no good at the thing that you think makes you happy.

Take Georgette Cartwright (*please*). A choir director for the past forty-seven years, Georgette is a local institution and something of a spiritual dominatrix. She has been in the front row of our sanctuary for thirty-five of those forty-seven years, and since I've only been on the ministerial staff for twelve and the senior pastor for a little more than eighteen months, she often uses her years of service as a blunt instrument when disagreements over worship occur. The congregation of the Church of the Open Door is non-denominational and as liberal as the Progressive platform will allow, but we use the Methodist hymnal, a nod to our mainline past, so she refers to me as "that Unitarian" because I've attended workshops at Starr King. All of which is beside the point. What you should know is that for all of Georgette Cartwright's years, she is a mediocre choir director at best, and her own voice is terrible, which means that every Christmas and Easter and at various holidays in between, we are treated to some of the most cringe-worthy solos I have ever heard. *Ave Maria* as dental drill. Her voice breaks, the pitch is imperfect, her instrument is out of tune and has been for the decade-plus that I've known her. Not that I could do better. But she loves to perform, and she loves having an audience, no matter how captive we all are. She presses on, delighted with herself, and no one has the heart to stop her, an autocrat of the first order: she follows her bliss and she does what she wants while the rest of us suffer. We talk about it later, though, over dinner amongst ourselves. Unkindly. Ruefully in some cases, spitefully in others. Which makes us all feel smaller by half. And makes the roast taste like ash in our mouths.

When our older son set off for college the first time, he asked me (because he wanted to be good so desperately) what he should study, and I gave him the Campbell line. "Follow your heart," I said, "and satisfaction will come." To which he shook his head and said that of *course* his ministerial mother would say that, with no regard for money or long-term sustainability. How "satisfaction" might play forty years hence with no retirement at hand. We were just that feckless; that's what he seemed to be saying. On the other hand, Alan said that Josh should study finance and get into investment banking so that he could take care of his aging, infirm, and spendthrift parents when the time came. He was kidding. A little. Mostly. Josh knew that his father was joking, at least in part, but he looked worried nonetheless. Josh did start as a finance major, but then he was back home before the end of his second semester. He was that miserable. "I thought I needed to take care of you," he said, much to Alan's chagrin, "but I couldn't open one more textbook with dollar signs. Those fat books are the image of death." He shivered as though from a cold wind. He stayed at home for the next two years working at a Best Buy where he used his employee discount to buy computer parts for his brother, who never thought twice about his purpose in life, just started making money hand over fist as the sole proprietor of three different companies. Cole designed software for restaurants and bars. He built custom game systems. He unlocked cell phones for the police, but only in cases that passed his own private sense of conscience. I don't know where he got his gifts, that boy, or his sensibility; one day Cole was thumbing a Game Boy, the next day he was tearing apart a leftover Trash-80 unearthed from his grandfather's closet, and the day after that he had a sleeve of business cards, an accountant, and an assortment of phones which were always ringing. If I wasn't constantly tripping over cords and wires, I might have concluded that my son had become a dealer.

"Who are you?" I said.

To which he shrugged while taking another call from the technologically desperate and afraid.

"Do you like this?" I was puzzled and astonished; how else can I say it? I had a fifteen-year-old nerd-savant on my hands, and I had no idea how that had happened. "I mean, does this nourish your spiritual being?"

He covered the cell phone with one hand. "Mom," he said, not unkindly, "I'm busy all day long, my computer science teacher asks *me* questions, but I never know what you're talking about."

He had no disappointments that I was aware of, but if this was bliss, it had taken a form for which I was completely unprepared. When his brother had had enough of wandering in the Best Buy wilderness, he packed the car for college once again with a plan that he said he'd share with us once he was sure that it was going to work out. We didn't hear from him for fifteen weeks, and Alan and I were in agreement: we would give him the freedom to make his own decisions and we wouldn't pester. We received texts now and again letting us know he was alive. He said he was happy.

He made his announcement over the Christmas break after he had unloaded the car. He had shaved his head and he wore a cashmere scarf around his neck even though it was sixty degrees.

"Mom, Dad, Doofus," he said addressing us and his brother, "I've come to certain conclusions. First, I switched my major to theater. Don't worry: wardrobe and costume design, not acting.

I like to draw, I like fabric, and I like to pretend. Second, I don't give a shit about money, but I'll figure it out. Third, I'm gay, and I finally had to admit it to myself. There. That's it, that's what I needed to say."

We were silent for a moment.

Until his brother said, "Like you being gay was such a secret."

Sure, we'd seen all the signs, stereotypical as well as intuitive; maybe we had taken civility to the extreme in thinking that Josh needed to be the one to broach the subject first. That wasn't the biggest surprise, though. Theater? I mean, we'd taken them to plays, but neither boy had seemed particularly interested, not when they could go see the latest dystopian thriller at the IMAX. Sitting in bad seats in a drafty auditorium while two people yak about their sins when they could be lolling in recliners and watching half-dressed female androids carrying phasers? Not a tough choice, apparently; they yawned and asked for popcorn, and I never was successful at making the argument politically. About their intellectual enrichment, about what they ought to watch. Although, given my ministerial lens, that should have been my first clue about their disinclination: the word "ought."

But now, whether they chose to admit it or not and whatever term they might have used, Josh and Cole were both following their bliss, they were doing what sparked joy (to use yet another cliché), and they were finding their way.

Alan, on the other hand, Alan is the one I need to talk about.

◎ ◎ ◎

When I proposed to Alan thirty-one years ago, he looked at me a little vacantly, as though I had disturbed his calculation of pi to the thirtieth decimal place when, in fact, he was only grading vocabulary and spelling quizzes. *Piquant. Reptilian. Trapezoid. Mercurial.* Check. Check. Oops. Check. We had been living together for a couple of months in his over-the-garage apartment. He was five years older than I was, my brother's best friend, and he was already working at the middle school. He had a responsible job, a tie, and a briefcase, while I had homework and Jung and a rich imaginal life, one that didn't include a retreat back to the trailer park that I had once called home.

"Why?" he asked.

"Why not?" I said, as smartly as I could. To be honest, I was worried that it all might blow away—this camping site of momentary stability—before I had a chance to hammer the tent pegs as firmly as possible in the ground.

"Oh." He looked up and rubbed his eyes. "I guess. I mean, I suppose we could do worse."

"Right," I said.

He was pudgy and abstracted, and when he wasn't abstracted, a bit bad-tempered, which no amount of coffee could cure, and I had psoriasis and a limited bank account dwarfed by student loans and a mismatched thrift store wardrobe that I called bohemian but that was really just the best I could manage. Neither one of us was destined for a magazine cover, is what I'm saying. So we were not in thrall to any huge upsurge of hearts and flowers and nonsense; I knew what I was getting, and I think he did, too. In my mind, the trade-off was clear, and the garage apartment with Alan won hands down over the cramped quarters of a trailer and my mother, especially after my brother left and the boyfriends started moving through like the wind.

If I'm honest, though, I didn't entirely reckon with what marriage meant for Alan. All along, he had said that he was going to work at Garfield Middle for no more than five years and then quit to work on fiction full time. But then we got married, and then we got pregnant without really intending to, and, well, that's the oldest story in the world, isn't it? In most cases, it's a story that results in recrimination and bitterness, but I didn't see that at the time.

Instead, Alan soldiered on, a little more resigned each year, while I finished seminary and then worked for a succession of more and more liberal congregations, churches further untethered from their denominational origins. On Sunday mornings in the adult spirituality class, I talked about dream work as a pathway to the divine. Alan never came to church if he could help it; instead, at night and on weekends when he wasn't grading bad middle-school writing, he dreamed up plots and characters imprisoned by language and mired in the mess of reality. He had boxes of typewritten manuscripts that he hadn't looked at since our days above the garage and then files on a computer that were foldered under the title "Old Shit"; I had taken a peek at some of it, and I understood well enough the reason for both parts of the title. I encouraged his continued employment at Garfield, and I confess that this was due in no small part to aesthetic as well as economic reasons. He commandeered the garage for his writing space, and if I have any memories of the last twenty years, it's of parking both cars in the driveway no matter the weather and taking the boys to soccer practice and band practice and swim lessons while Alan fumed and fretted behind a roll-up door. At the time, I thought I was making a sacrifice in the name of equity, and like any state of compromise, neither of us was getting what we wanted.

We could hardly afford for him to quit, though, but even more importantly, I didn't know if he could withstand the onslaught of rejections that he was sure to receive. In my humble opinion. As a fulltime minister of the modern gospel and in my spare time a reader of fiction that real people actually buy and consume. He wrote about people who were down on their luck, but even though I could have told him a thing or two, he never asked. Then again, what do I know about fiction? About the tastes of publishers or the book-buying public? Year after year, he tried and tried. One novel was a finalist at a no-name publisher for a $500 prize; the editors kept him on tenterhooks for eight months before sending him a form letter thanking him for his interest and his patience, not to mention the entry fee. They had received so many quality manuscripts. Blah, blah, blah. He had come close—he was in the final five—and yet so far: no publication, no check, no cigar. For three months, his name appeared on a website that no one ever viewed and then winked off again. He had a tough time with conversation for a week or more, and then most of it was in grunts of one syllable or less. Myself, I couldn't make heads or tails of it, that novel. There was a murder, and various characters assumed identities not their own; the time went back and forth, and by the second chapter, I was lost, and I didn't care enough to figure it out. He also had short stories that didn't seem to end and others that had no beginnings; nonetheless, he called them all complete. I would have called bullshit if there had been anyone to listen.

I wasn't his ideal reader, I guess.

We had some tense times. One Saturday afternoon, the boys were off somewhere, and the house was quiet while I rattled around from kitchen to bedroom to living room while Alan worked away at his job-away-from-the-job. I suggested obliquely that he could try another hobby. Other husbands in the neighborhood had taken over their garages, but instead of a desk, a file cabinet, and computer they had installed Shopsmiths or AUTOLifts.

When I said something to that effect, he looked at me over his glasses. "A hobby. Something a little more manly? A little more in keeping with the middle class?" he said. "Something that costs three or four thousand dollars and adds to environmental woe. Is that what you're saying?"

"No, no," I said, backtracking for all I was worth. "I just don't like to see you unhappy."

"Who says I'm unhappy?" He looked as puzzled as he was irritated.

"I thought that was obvious," I said. "Every time you get a rejection, your eyes glaze over, and you wander around like a member of the lost battalion."

"Unhappy?" he said. He was genuinely mystified. "I want to write. It's something I have to do, not something I do to occupy my time. I don't want to make birdhouses or bookshelves. I don't want to change the oil. So shoot me."

"But no one wants it!"

I lost it, and I yelled. I admit it. I lost my ministerial reserve, affect, and understanding. "No one fucking wants it." He seemed so intransigent. "It's not like you write something fun to read."

He shut down his computer and removed his glasses; he put a dustcover over his monitor because he was just that fastidious about his tools. This was a garage, after all, and even his lawn mower was clean.

"That may be true," he said. He was quiet and measured in the wake of all my noise. "Speaking of fun, I'll admit it's no fun to read yet another email saying thanks but no thanks, but that's not why I do it. Maybe no one ever wants anything I write. Maybe no one enjoys a word. Maybe no one reads it except me. I've had to make my peace with that. I'm the tree falling over in the forest. But, at the risk of sounding too full of myself, I do hear the sound of my own demise even if the forest is empty of all else. If I have to be my own reader, so be it. I'll know I did it."

"Okay," I breathed. "Okay. If that's how you feel."

"That's how I feel," he said. "Now, if you'll excuse me."

After such an argument, another husband might have gone to a bar to drink beer after beer and yell at the television with the rest of the pickleheads; instead, Alan picked up his laptop and went to the silence of his classroom to continue working on the next novel that no one would ever want. I mean, if you were me, what would you prefer?

◎ ◎ ◎

I was worried, then, when Alan announced his date of retirement. He said he was doing what he wanted. He'd put in his years, twenty-four more than he had originally bargained for, and he put me on notice: no party and absolutely, under no circumstances—no ifs, ands, or buts—was I (or anyone else) allowed to utter the words *Mr. Holland's Opus* within range of his hearing. He was sensitive, I guess: to the thought of committing a lifetime's effort to a transcendent quest but being rewarded instead for the grudging toil at the salt mine. He couldn't stand the thought of having the quest treated as some kind of sideshow, a kind of lifetime joke, celebrated and given an epitaph. To be honest, I doubted whether he was any better a teacher than he was a writer, more taskmaster than counselor and consoler, but did I say that? I'm not that stupid. It wasn't worth the discussion or the inevitable argument.

Instead of a party, we went out to eat the day after he turned in his last grades. I told no one of our plans, I swear, but wouldn't you know that there were half a dozen of his younger colleagues there anyway, having their own end-of-year celebration in the bar, and I could see his face freeze in a rictus of fear that he would be forced to engage in social niceties and unwanted chit-chat with others who knew how to laugh and have fun. The hinges of his jaw turned into golf balls, a good trick for a man who looked like the Pillsbury Doughboy otherwise. How, I wanted to ask him, could he write about people when he plainly didn't like them?

Still, we settled into something like a new routine. The boys were gone. Josh was working at his first job for a regional theater in Idaho, and Cole had an apartment in town and a revolving door of roommates and his share of surfable couches. Alan stayed at home, primarily in the garage since he refused to use one of the newly freed-up bedrooms as an office. Meanwhile, I was at church, doing my own work and fending off my own set of frustrations. Georgette Cartwright's hymn selections. The monthly leadership committee meeting. Annie Bengsten, church administrator, who believed that she truly was the final arbiter of all church business. The parishioners who had suggestions for my hairstyle as well as my sermon delivery. For a congregation of thoughtful, well-educated souls, I had no shortage of ill-informed opinions, suggestions, and criticisms to absorb.

Then the pandemic happened.

And like everyone else in America, I came home.

To Alan. Our echoing rooms. And the dog.

◉ ◉ ◉

I didn't mention the dog, did I? So first, I have to make a confession. I once got a dog without consulting Alan. Well, it wasn't that simple. You know how ministerial work goes: you're one quarter spiritual leader and with the other three quarters and a half, you're social worker and psychologist, food bank administrator and community organizer. It's not a job for the faint of heart or the inflexible. At the Church of the Open Door, we had our share of the homeless and the psychotic, those who had been abandoned by the society that should have cared for them, and we had a name to live up to, even if our best efforts were only as a referral source. But now and again, we also saw those of the middle class who had fallen on hard times for one reason or another. Job loss, divorce, domestic violence, alcoholism, gambling. The reasons were as many as the supplicants who came and just as prosaic.

Not long after I started working at the Door, a young woman came to the office with her suitcase and a Jack Russell on a leash and a choke chain. A bark collar was fizzing on its neck, and he looked like he was poised to launch into outer space. She had been living with a man twelve years older than she was; her partner had kicked her out for reasons she didn't specify, but the right side of her face was several shades of purple and green from a black eye that looked to be at least a week old, and it wasn't hard to read the signs. She didn't seem daunted, however. In fact, I would have called her downright chipper, given the circumstances. She needed to get home to her parents in the Midwest.

"Terre Haute," she said. "Tea and sympathy, pity and gossip. It's all in my future. At least I'm not pregnant."

She needed money for a bus ticket, a ride to the station, and one more thing.

"It's the dog," she said. "I can't take him with me, and I won't take him to the pound, but I don't know that I have any other choice." She paused, and I waited for the next ball to drop. "His name, by the way, is Bastard. Sorry. That's just the way he came."

We asked around, and there weren't any obvious or good choices. The no-kill shelter had closed a couple of years earlier, and no one in the office was looking to adopt a dog that appeared to be needy in the extreme. If we took Bastard to the pound, there was no guarantee he'd ever get adopted, no matter how many pit bull mixes would be there to make him look benign. And if he didn't get adopted, well, you know the drill. The senior minister, Reverend Smithson, called a meeting. We sat in a circle while Bastard quivered at the end of his leash. As the newest member of the staff, I volunteered to take the bullet. It felt like the thing to do.

Alan was not thrilled. And the boys were less than impressed. For years they had asked, begged, and pleaded. They had had their hopes pinned on a Labrador retriever or a Golden, one of those beautiful dogs with a doped-up personality. Instead, they got a twenty-pound psycho who required dog park runs morning, noon, and night. He couldn't lie down; he paced and he twitched, even in sleep. He chewed the legs of our furniture, and it was not uncommon to find a pile of Bastard's leavings, embedded with wood chips, by the laundry room door. As a watchdog, he let us know about every leaf that fell as well as any suspicious visitors, no matter how high we turned his shock collar. If he couldn't discriminate between threat and a moment of benevolent nature, that was our problem.

We lasted six years as dog owners, and I have to admit, the majority of the burden fell on Alan since the boys were as good at avoiding the dog as they were the rest of their chores, and I was usually at church until the early evenings. One afternoon, when Alan came home from school, he opened the back door, and Bastard shot out as he was wont to do. But instead of running in frantic circles in the back yard, he found the side gate ajar and was off. The end result was as inevitable as it was, at least on an unconscious level, desired. From two blocks away came the squeal of brakes, the bleat of a horn, the sound of breaking glass and accordioned metal, and then silence. Alan jogged toward the sound and found Bastard inert in the southbound lane of Armstrong Boulevard, the only time that dog had ever been still. He had barreled headlong into an oncoming Humvee, and when the driver tried to stop, the Honda Accord behind him couldn't brake in time, its hood wedging itself underneath the SUV's back bumper. While the drivers argued, Alan picked up the bits of what was left of Bastard and carried him home. When Cole and Josh came home from school, they helped him dig the hole and buried the dog in the backyard. They marked the grave with rocks that, over time, sank into the ground and were covered over with bark (hah!). By the time I got home, the deed had been done, but I'm not sure that Alan ever forgave me. Or the dog. That poor, demented creature.

So our tenure as dog owners did not go well, and there were no pleas by the boys to try again. We couldn't even use the word "bastard" in a fit of anger since the very word made us feel complicit in a failure of compassion and vocabulary.

Surprise, surprise, then, when a month after Alan retired, I came home to find a monster asleep in the garage on Bastard's former dog bed, which was positioned next to Alan's table and computer.

"Who or what is this?" I said.

Alan and the dog looked up at me simultaneously and with the same expression. Something like passive-aggressive victory.

"Dorothy," he said.

"And the Wizard of Oz?" I said.

"No," he said. "More like your aunt from Topeka."

Here's a side note: my great-aunt Dorothy, who was single her entire life, had hair on her chin that she treated with pride. She made a mint from writing accounting texts back when textbook publishers were the only game in town and thought nothing of gouging students' and their parents' wallets. Her books are probably among the reasons why Josh went to college twice. She wrote accounting book after accounting book, new edition after new edition, and when she retired, she had enough in the bank to purchase a mansion in the Rockies. Bought it outright without batting an eye. Oddly enough, she never skied and had never cared for the outdoors, so her choice of location was surprising, and when her car was caught in a snowdrift one frigid night in December a year after she moved, she died with her bank account more or less intact, but with none in the family either named in the will or surprised. My mother, her niece, could have used some of the cash but never saw a dime. Make of it what you will, but thirty years after her death, her textbooks are still available online on various used-book sites, making money for others. I say it's a story with a moral attached.

I looked at our new-old dog Dorothy, named for a cautionary tale as she was, and she looked back with intelligent, if indifferent, eyes. She crossed her saucer-sized paws across each other and then let her black-and-white snout rest upon them. I had no idea what she was breed-wise, but she was like a triple-sized terrier, Asta on steroids. Lying on the dog bed, she made it disappear, and when she stood up, the top of her head hit my ribs.

"You named this thing after a mean old lady who froze in her car?"

"It was either that or Grendel," he said. "Or Kali."

"Oh, good one," I said, "a gender-fluid list of monsters."

◎ ◎ ◎

But let me back up for just one moment. Dorothy and the pandemic can wait their respective turns.

Friends sometimes ask, Why church work? And given the social moment in which we live there is also buried within the question another subtext, Why *liberal* church work, of all things? Can there be anything more irrelevant in this age of literalized faith? It's a good question and one I don't always know how to answer, especially when I drive by those hotel monstrosities and monuments to the Prosperity Gospel. Given my trailer-park background, you would have thought I'd be the one to go to B-school in order to learn the mysteries of capitalism and get a piece of the pie previously denied my family. And if I had ever been the beneficiary of some illuminating, evanescent moment, you might have thought me grist for the Evangelicals, Charismatics, and Fundamentalists. But no, and no. One day I was a psych major reading Jung, and after that, all the cognitive stuff seemed like warm tea and dry toast. From there I walked into religious studies with all the free will of an orphan in an Irish convent. But don't think me unhappy. Bliss for me was having a place at the table without comparing paystubs. I could have gone into social work, but that seemed like a job, while the church reassured me of a sense of calling.

One of the advantages of growing up poor was that I knew how to adapt to situations; I knew how to be a chameleon. Before I came to the Door, I had jobs at other mainline churches, mostly in the area of youth work. Since I didn't really stake a claim on any particular dogma other than a need for goodness and introspection, I could finesse the doctrinal stuff and become what was required. I worked for some pastors who looked at me a little askance when I hedged my bets, but since I was a woman and they were happy and oblivious in their misogyny, they figured what harm could I do? Besides, these associate slots paid so little, they were happy enough to let it go. In their own calculations, I was a risk that they were willing to take for the sake of someone willing to do the work for next to nothing. I developed the Sunday school curriculum, set up programs for summer camps and retreats and festivals, and made sure to cultivate the power brokers, both male and female, of each congregation. In a sense, I was everyone's wife. If my activities skewed toward service and social action, self-actualization and pizza, and away from Jesus and verse memorization, no one ever faulted me. I made myself just that indispensable as well as likeable and non-threatening.

So when I came to the Door, I found myself at home without any need of pretense at last. I could take the high schoolers to temples and synagogues and churches alike in the name of comparative spiritual experience, and none of the parents questioned my choices. The senior pastor, Reverend Smithson, was gruff and crusty, but he told me the truth, which was a far cry from some of the others I'd worked with and for. I was happy there for ten years or so, and then Smithson retired, and since the congregation was dwindling and aging and young families were coming but mostly going, the leadership committee decided to hand me the job as his replacement, no interview needed. They eliminated my former job in favor of college interns. A promotion, a new title, twice the work, the same pay. Because the church knows how to take care of its own.

A year and three months after my ascension, the pandemic sent us all home, and I had to figure out how to conduct a person-to-person job over the internet and listen to the same tired jokes about our faith community as the Brady Bunch. I also had to figure out how to negotiate being at home with Alan, whose encampment in the garage had become permanent. And Dorothy, who now could not remain at Alan's feet in the garage but felt the need to pace back and forth from the garage to Josh's old bedroom where I had set up shop; back and forth she went, making sure we were both in our appointed spots.

I practiced giving my sermons into a screen and conducted meetings and worship over Zoom, and it was not uncommon for Dorothy to join us at the most inopportune moments; she put her paws on my shoulders, set her muzzle against my cheek, and peered into the eye of the camera along with me. There was no denying her. There was also no denying the fact that whenever she made an appearance, she was better than the best visual aid as far as attracting an online audience's attention. Much better than I was on Sunday morning, for sure, no matter how practiced my rhetorical flourishes. They might be eating their breakfast or painting their nails while I spoke about Needing to Listen to One Another in a Time of Plague, but once Dorothy took a bow all eyes were forward. They still weren't listening to me because they had their own worries and concerns, but they were entertained by the dog, and I could at least pretend otherwise.

One dark Friday afternoon in November, Dorothy started barking and barking, a hound's baying that I had never heard from her before. It was during that week just after the election when the outcome was still in doubt, and my first thought was that Dorothy was merely joining that chorus of anxiety that seemed to have us all in its grip. I finally got up and went downstairs and found Dorothy near the door to the garage. She was hopping on all four legs as though possessed by Bastard's spirit, and for such a large, ungainly creature, hers was the oddest depiction of panic I've ever seen. Alan was on the floor on his left side. His glasses were a few feet away and his face looked to be a shade of blue. But then he'd always harbored his own set of angers, and besides, I could see his lips moving, so I didn't leap to any level of concern. I'm not uncaring, but you wouldn't be wrong for believing me that way. Even I can't quite fathom my reactions. Call it shock. For some reason, I could only think that we'd had another of our usual earthquakes, one that I hadn't felt, and he had fallen off his chair.

"Oh, Jesus," I said, "what happened to you?"

"Call 9-1-1," he whispered. "I think I've had a heart attack."

"That's not possible," I said because, after all, we were both too young for something like that, weren't we?

"Don't argue with me." His breathing was shallow, and his eyes were squinting and strained. "I know what I feel."

"What are you on about?"

"Do you realize," he whispered, "that I worked all my adult life at a school named for a president who was killed by a religious lunatic? Ain't that something."

"What you won't do for attention."

So I made the call despite my own misgivings, no matter my disbelief, and it seemed that within seconds a fire truck was there with enormous firemen who filled the garage with their shoulders, their equipment, and their competence and began to ask Alan questions. And then there was the ambulance with two exhausted EMTs. Each took a deep breath outside on the driveway as they unfolded the gurney and maneuvered it between our parked cars.

"I can't believe it's anything serious," I said. I still wasn't processing the situation; I couldn't see myself as a widow, grieving or otherwise. "I mean we've been in lockdown for months."

"You'd be surprised," one of them said through his mask. "It hasn't been easy, being at home. Fewer car accidents, more falls."

"More domestic violence," the other said. "And with chest pains we don't mess around. No matter what's going on otherwise."

"It's not like we fight." Not for nothing, I felt as though I needed to say it. "It's friendly banter, maybe a little aggravation. We pick at each other, but it's all in good fun."

"Okay. Look," the first one said to me, "we're going to get him into the ambulance and do an EKG. Then we'll determine which hospital to take him to. If there's anything he should have with him, you better get it now. You can barely make it into the parking lot much less through the doors."

"Right," I said. Such were the strictures of our virus-wary world. "Okay."

I followed Alan and the gurney and the EMTs, and after they'd pushed him inside, I stuck my head in.

His phone and charger, Alan said when I asked. They had put one of those nitro gizmos on his chest, and his eyes and forehead were a little less clenched. The EKG monitor was spitting out numbers and charts.

"And a favor," Alan said. "Walk the dog, would you?"

"Fine. Me and Ms. Sasquatch. What about clothes?"

He thought for a moment.

"Nah. It's not summer camp."

"Your laptop?"

He thought for a moment more.

"No," he said. "What the hell. I'll take a vacation day."

"You're retired," I said. "What do you know about vacations?"

He lay back on the airplane pillow on the gurney. "Huh. Call it a vacation from my life, then. A vacation from my vocation."

"Oh, boy," I said. "The monk on his holiday."

"Go ahead, laugh," he said. "Cruel woman."

He said it, but the tone was kind. At least, I think it was.

◎ ◎ ◎

For the next two hours, I did what needed to be done. I called the hospital, I called the boys, I let the leader of the pastoral care committee know the situation even though it was the pastor and her husband who needed the care and not some unlucky member of the congregation. The boys reacted in ways that surprised me. Josh ran through a list like a diagnostician while Cole started to cry. For a theater major, Josh seemed to know his biology, and for a computer nerd, Cole seemed more friable emotionally than I would have expected. When I called the Emergency Department, a harried nurse told me to call back in an hour, that Alan had not even been entered into their system yet.

So then I called Alan.

"What are you doing?" I said.

"Lying here having a heart attack," he said.

"No, you're not."

"Maybe not now. But I was."

"You probably ate something you shouldn't have," I said, because that was something that Alan was liable to do, eat some questionable chicken that had been in the refrigerator for three weeks or spoon out some yogurt, the skin of which was thicker than it should have been.

"I know heartburn. It wasn't heartburn," he said. "You won't be laughing when I'm gone. And I'll bet you haven't walked Dorothy yet, either."

He had me there on both counts.

"I've had a few phone calls to make, you know," I said. "Given all the drama. I told you I'd do it, and I'll do it. She hasn't been lunging at the door or anything."

"Okay," he said. Then, "You wouldn't believe this place. It's crazytown."

He was still on the ambulance gurney in a non-virus hallway, surrounded by the demented, the aged, and the insane, all of whom were shouting and yelling something about how bad they felt, how they were being abused. He now sounded more than a little rueful about sounding the alarm.

"You could have a heart attack just by walking through the door," he said.

"If you didn't already have one," I said.

"True."

"You did the right thing," I said, replaying the EMT script. "You did the right thing, making me call. You don't mess around with chest pains."

"Helluva way to spend a Friday night," he said.

"It's no great entertainment," I agreed. "Not exactly dinner and a movie, which we couldn't have gone to anyway, things being as they are. Listen," I said with the force of revelation that sounded to me as something like the truth: "Don't you dare die on me and leave me with this damn dog."

He promised to text me in the next hour, once he was again sure he hadn't died, and then I searched the house for Dorothy before I found her in the garage; she was curled up into a dog-doughnut underneath Alan's desk. You would have thought I'd look for her there, wouldn't you? Well, I did, but she wasn't there the first time I checked. All I can figure is that she waited for me to leave the garage before she resumed her place. As large as she was, she could be a sneaky bitch when it suited her.

So I got a jacket and poop bags and hooked the leash to her collar, thinking she'd jump at a chance for a walk, but she only looked at me as though I was kidding. Which gave me a moment to look at Alan's computer, and his email that had remained open from when he'd fallen off his chair. Line after line of political screeds, product ads, and magazine offers of various kinds. Buried in their midst was an email from a journal in the most flown-over of flyover states, with the subject line, "Congratulations!" A story, written at least five years earlier, a story about a depressed minister and an absurd, politically correct congregation, had been selected as the runner-up in a contest. Two hundred dollars, publication, and consideration from an agency in New York.

"Well," I said to Dorothy, "he better not kick off until I have a chance to tell him."

The dog was unmoved and seemingly unimpressed by this turn of good fortune.

I texted Alan, in case he hadn't checked his email from his phone.

"Guess what?" I wrote the news with my thumbs. "You're almost famous, thanks to me."

And almost immediately, came the response: "That's great," he wrote. "Better than a sharp stick in the eye."

He didn't have much to do except nurture his usual cheery self while he was lying on his ambulance gurney, and I suspected he had hours to go before they got to his turn in the queue.

"You can thank me later," I wrote, "since you co-opted my life."

So, the dog. The night had turned wet and sloppy in this place where the merest threat of rain seems to be judgment from above, and I could hear the wind and water against the metal of the garage door.

"Come on," I said. "I'm not cleaning up puddles and landmines."

With that, she began to move, albeit grudgingly. But then, once we were outside in the wind and the rain, she began straining at the leash, and no matter how hard I tugged, it seemed that nothing could hold her back.

"What do you want?" I shouted at her. "Where are you going?" Because it seemed that she had a destination in mind.

And as it turned out, the destination we found was three blocks away from the house: the parking lot of the Door, and my office that I hadn't visited except briefly in the last eight months when I needed certain records or office supplies. There was a canal that ran by the church property, and Alan often let the dog run there to snuffle along the canal bank when the season was dry. And although that was not the case this evening, she was running for all she was worth, and my arm was about to come unhinged at the shoulder.

"Whoa, Dorothy," I yelled. "Slow down, you dumb, fucking dog." Hardly ministerial. Still, she pulled.

There were lights on in the church, which didn't really register with me as odd since Friday nights had often been filled with activities in the past, before concerns over our public health had put groups and gatherings at an end. I wasn't thinking, I guess, trapped in a time from before. I heard "O God our help in ages past" on the church organ, and I was thinking that this was the hymn that our boys had once called "The Stormy Blast Song" since that was the line that they bellowed whenever they were given the chance. At the ages of nine and twelve, they were like frat boys with a musical expletive. Dorothy pulled on. And then we came to a curb that was hidden by wet leaves, and I guess I slipped or tripped or fell while trying to hold Dorothy at bay with the leash. I don't know. I'm only grateful that I didn't take a header into the fast-moving scum of the canal that was only three feet away. But I did take a header into something hard, the ground, if nothing else, and I blacked out momentarily. Blessings small and large.

I have the sense that I went back to that moment when Alan and I were first living together, when I first heard the no-tone sounds of my so-called calling. I had come to Alan's apartment above the garage to visit my brother. When Alan and I looked at each other, I knew that safety lived there. With him. I don't know what he saw. He wasn't looking for a roommate or a wife, I knew that, even then. And I wasn't looking for bliss because I didn't have unrealistic expectations, no matter what Campbell might have said about it to others. Safety, stability, that was as far as I allowed my mind to drift. My brother left our mother's trailer and our mother's life with her erratic succession of less and less possible boyfriends, and I was just that envious and desperate to make a move of my own. Because I had no desire to bear the consequence of choices our mother made with, you know, those boyfriends. Gary moved in with Alan, and then he took off with his engineering degree and his desire to make his own life in another state altogether, which is when I moved in, and I couldn't do it fast enough. I couldn't even be certain that Alan noticed the change when it happened, he was so intent on teaching and writing his unpublishable stories. Did we talk? I guess we did, but I couldn't tell you whether we understood each other or were merely responding to our own needs at the time. We lived together and we had absent-minded sex, we got married and we got pregnant. We worked, and one of us retired to follow his own interests, no matter what anyone else might think of the result. *Things have worked out.* I guess that's what I should have said to Josh or Cole. Or Alan, for that matter. Lives work out however they can. You can call it bliss when it's over, but it's nothing to follow. I was thinking all this, dreaming all this, and that moment when Alan looked up from his typewriter and saw me, really saw me, for the first time. That time when I proposed. He saw me through glasses that were opaque from the reflection of the overhead light.

"We'll get along okay," he said, "so long as you don't mind . . ."

He gestured toward the typewriter on the kitchen table. The manuscript pages with penciled cross-outs, corrections, and bubbles of insertions.

"As vices go—" I said, but I admit it: we both left our sentences unfinished and circling in the air.

"Just don't die on me," I said.

"What?" he said.

"Just don't die on me." I might have shouted.

"Who said anything about dying?" Wearing a rain coat and a hood that made her look like something out of a medieval pageant, Georgette Cartwright bent over me with a flashlight that made me go blind.

The rain fell so steadily I had to keep blinking. Somewhere nearby, Dorothy was running along the canal.

"Godzilla was barking, and I couldn't even hear the organ. So I came out to see what was the matter."

"I fell," I said, "and I must have hit my head. And then you found me."

"So I did." She switched off the flashlight, and even though she was in her seventies and not the most robust person I knew, she helped me to my feet, and the world and the parking lot came back into focus. That was when I told her about Alan, the 9-1-1 call, the firemen, the EMTs, and the rest. The worry that I hadn't allowed myself to believe, much less feel, which now was like a pressure in my own chest.

"Oh, honey," she said, putting a hand on my arm. "There, there." Which is all anyone can say. There, there. "He'll be fine, or he won't. One way or another, you'll get through it."

"Things will work out."

"Exactly."

"I've been thinking," I said, although it wasn't entirely true; if I had been thinking at all, it was straight from the top of my head, which was already throbbing. "I've been thinking we ought to sing something together some time. A duet. 'Amazing Grace' or the one you were playing a while ago. One of the standards. I'll ditch the sermon, and we'll make a joyful noise."

"Sure," she laughed in her strained senior citizen register. "Noise. We'll make them cover their ears in the safety of their own homes."

"We'll be fools," I said, "but we'll be human."

"That's all we can be," she said. "None of us will ever be more. And they can laugh all they want while muted."

Dorothy had returned, her muzzle visibly muddy even in the dim lights of the parking lot. She trailed her sodden leash like a criminal record.

"Miserable, wet, windy, and cold," Georgette said with no small measure of triumph. "Don't you love a night like this?"

◉

The Surreal Nature of
Money and Marriage

I. The Garden

In this town the name of Linden Hempstead might get you a drink and ten minutes' reminiscence; in my case—since the name is mine—it got me a quarter interest in a beverage distributorship and a lifetime sinecure as club pro at the Oakwood Racquet Club. I'm forty-four years of age, assured—so I thought—of love, financial security, and general well-being. The leg that I broke twenty-three years ago no longer causes me pain except in memory and in the twelve hours preceding a storm front, and the residual effects of that other period in my life—when I imbibed too freely—are apparent only to me. There were certain indiscretions committed then, but they are not the issue now.

Married for nineteen years to the same woman, whose every movement in our walk-in closet still commands my respect and admiration, I have been fortunate beyond reason. We met at a party following a football game my junior year in college. I was in attendance at the party—wearing the cast on my recently shattered leg and watching as my crutch was used as a limbo bar; Candace was outside, protesting the fraternity system as an anachronistic symbol of male chauvinist attitudes and directly responsible for American foreign policy in southeast Asia. She had read enough Mailer to know. She was dressed in a parka, thermals, and snow boots, and her placard was painted in smears, the sentiments unoriginal, but there was no disguising the forward thrust of her carriage, which to this day reminds me of a frigate pounding through heavy seas and threatening weather. I retrieved a bottle of Scotch, offered her a nip, and two hours later we were throwing snowballs at cars on Route 223 and making snow angels on top of one another. One's political idealism runs only so deep, Candace said, when the temperature is hovering around zero. By the end of the evening, we were wet through and through, my cast was the consistency of oatmeal, and Candace was alternately moaning German obscenities and vomiting in a ditch outside her dormitory.

◉ ◉ ◉

Although we were not married until four years later, the moment we each said I do, it seemed that we had finally obeyed a long understood, albeit delayed, destiny. We were, as the clichés would have it, made for each other, made in heaven, made for love. And yet, what does the lover know of the spouse indefinite years into the future? The football player whose playing days are done? The would-be activist with a low tolerance for cold? Who knows what the other will become? At the time, we might not have had our ideological or social credentials in order, but as rational creatures, deliberate and imaginative by turns, Candace and I have grown in many ways. We share the duties of the household and both of us pitch in when it comes to the children. We've taken pains that those roles associated with gender not dictate our actions, but let our interests and inclinations be our guides. Candace has been known to don overalls and crawl underneath the cars; last summer she drywalled the rec room. I bake hot cross buns at Easter and play Barbies with our daughter. In matters of household finance, we take turns paying the bills, rotating the duty every three years. For fifteen years the arrangement was satisfactory, but in the sixteenth, seventeenth, and eighteenth years of our marriage—during my wife's watch over our checkbook—our life turned to chaos. It started when Candace, recently laid off from her job teaching foreign languages to junior high students, began taking piano lessons. A bond issue failed, two hundred seventh-graders were denied a wonderful experience, and Candace was devastated. The lessons seemed to help, but she desperately wanted a piano at home for practice. Madame Tanamarenko recommended the discipline of daily exercise. According to Madame, scales not only developed one's awareness of fingering and tempo, they fortified the soul against trouble. I said that we could work something out. We could find a used upright, or maybe an electric keyboard. She held out for a baby grand at the least, insisting that a piano should be furniture as well as instrument. You can't just throw it into the closet like a tennis racquet, she said. I said that there was no way; we were strapped as it was. Had she forgotten our recent decline in income? Referring as it did to Candace's recent loss of employment, our precarious existence, and the limitation of our possibilities, this last remark bordered on accusation. We had already decided upon no vacation that summer; the children would have to make do with fewer extracurricular activities. It's all my fault, she said, sniffling quietly. All my fault. Now, now, I said. We were in our bathroom at 11:30 at night. The children had been asleep for hours, and we spoke in whispers. My wife had just come from her shower and her skin was dewy, a sight which often causes in me acute confusion—sexuality as of that night we first met, mixed with the innocence of Ivory and childhood—and yet the effect this night was undermined by her shower cap, a disposable one lifted from some hotel a month before. To be truthful, my wife's hair is her glory, but when it is hidden, she looks a bit like a child not invited to the party. It was impossible for me to be too stern. In fact, my heart went out to her. Hadn't I promised—in wedding vows which I had written myself—to provide her with all good things, that I would sacrifice myself for her? Wasn't her desperation proof of my own failure? The shower cap was the final straw. We would work something out, I said. There might be some creative solution. I could talk it over with Stassen Metzger, my employer at the Racquet Club and my partner on the beer route. He might have some suggestions. Candace sniffled, said that all she had ever wanted was to be good at something, that she thought that something had been work, and now that had been taken away. If she was going to play the piano, she said, she was going to learn to play well, and not on some water-marked, wood-scarred upright from the church basement. A day later I came home to find a Steinway the size of an aircraft carrier gleaming in our front room. And how did this get here? I wondered. I was creative, Candace answered, no payments due until July and interest-free for ninety days. Well, I said. Well, well. Candace was beaming, there was no question about that, and I could see that it would do no good to point out the booby trap that is deferred billing. If it made her happy, etc., etc. Our lovemaking that night was passionate, Candace breathed obscenities into my ear in French, German, Italian, and Portuguese, and I was willing to overlook certain realities. Three weeks later I came home and found workmen installing new hardwood floors in the living room, dining room, and den. Candace was working on the fingering to "Eleanor Rigby"; she was humming the melody and seemed genuinely oblivious to the commotion around her. What is this? I said. Did we win the lottery? Don't be a silly, Candace said. It had taken some doing, but she had found a way to arrange payments that were still within our budget. When I asked how that could be, she said that I should not pester. That it indicated a lack of trust in her judgment and management skills. In the months to come I was to be greeted by more surprises: new suits for me, gold and diamonds for Candace, a new roof for the house. In retaliation against the public school system which had disemployed her, the children were enrolled at Oakwood Preparatory; and in accordance with our new social status, invitations for charity functions began rolling in. Of course, one could not attend such functions without writing two checks—one for the disease *du jour* and one for the Oakwood Prep library. I perspired rivers while my dear Candace patted my arm and in perfectly enunciated English whispered huge sums into my ear. What? I would say, aghast. Have you gone out of your mind? But she never failed to win out in the end.

You might think me terribly naive, but I resisted the temptation to ask how we were to pay for all this, although every day there were fresh indications that our situation was growing perilous. Bills arrived daily in stacks, and more and more of them came in envelopes marked Final Notice. We took to unplugging the telephone in the evening to forestall those creditors demanding payment. Although I had not smoked for a decade or more, I went through a pack of Camels one afternoon, waiting for a collector to leave our front porch. I sat in the bathroom lighting cigarette after cigarette, and by the time I left, I could have cured a ham. Even Stassen Metzger had grown concerned; he called me into his office one day after Bereniece Miller's racquetball lesson. The poor woman is fifty-seven years old and seventy pounds overweight, but she huffs and puffs and flails at the ball as though each point is seriousness itself. She has a temper, too, which explains why I was nursing a lump the size of an egg above my left eyebrow; she'd thrown her racquet in disgust and when I saw the graphite Ektelon spinning toward me, I lost whatever agility I normally possess. Her racquet retails at two hundred and fifty smacks unstrung, and in that moment when I saw it flying toward my head, I wondered whether or not I ought to stop it from hitting the wall behind me. An idle preoccupation, as it turned out, since I was her first good stroke all afternoon. She wrote out a check $500 over the usual hour's rate, hoping to settle accounts immediately. Her husband is the president of Oakwood Community Bank, and he's good for it, but it was one more indication of the gaps in my education by public schools. How the rich think they can buy their way out of trouble, indulging their desire to make trouble for others when it suits them, I don't know. I should have been insulted. Even so, I folded her check into my pocket with a relief that bordered on giddiness, and I wondered what else she'd like to do to me and for how much. Which was precisely Stassen's point when he spoke with me in his office a few minutes later.

"Do you have any idea," he asked, "how goddamn stupid you look?"

"I've got an idea," I said, trying to staunch the trickle of blood running down my cheek.

"You look like a goddamn beagle. You wag your tail any harder, Bereniece'll be beating you with a sledge hammer. The old girl has lots of hostilities to vent. And you're cheap."

"I'm easy. And cheap. Cheap and easy."

"Listen, son," Stassen began, "I'm serious, dead serious. Bereniece can beat you all she wants, but it sure as hell won't cover the damage you and Candace are doing."

"Candace has it covered," I said. "You don't have to worry about us."

"All I'm saying is, a person loses her job, it's bound to make things a bit unsettled. You don't want to start looking for comfort from a credit card. It takes the sting out for a little while, but the injury only runs deeper. Believe me, I know."

It has been my experience previously that whenever Stassen wants to give me advice—especially when he believes that I've been acting like a baboon on roller skates—the usual strategy is to say that for him this is nothing new, he too has been a baboon on roller skates—*oh, granted, this happened years and years ago*, he'll say, and while the incident might have some interest from an historical perspective, it would not be something he could ever recommend.

I rose from my chair a bit unsteadily, knowing from previous experience that Stassen was about to claim kinship with my dilemma, that he knew what one might do to please a fractious, acquisitive, social-climbing wife, that he was about to pledge his support out of love for my dead father, for me, for Candace, for our children, and for his memories of that time in my life when I could soar across grass so green it could hurt your eyes.

Even now he was holding a business card for me to take, one with the serious mien and black lettering of a financial planner. "Talk to your wife, then call this guy. You won't regret it. I don't call him twenty years ago, I wind up working out of the back of my car instead of having a job to give you." His eyes had the strange, faraway look of someone seeing the backdoor view of the past, and I tried—as gently as possible—to ignore his outstretched hand.

"Thanks for your concern," I said as formally as I could muster. "I appreciate it, but it's really not necessary."

Lies, of course. And, as it turned out, an illusion only for my benefit.

⊚ ⊚ ⊚

Stassen told me to put my affairs in order—sell the house, rent the children, do what had to be done. He was right, I had known it all along, but how often does a person act upon the dictates of conscience? I cornered Candace in the bathroom that night. She had ordered new den furniture that morning, a team of landscapers was due the next day, and she offered to share her shower, her Vitabath, and the loofa. She had a notion of what needed to be scrubbed. She murmured endearments in Russian; she enticed me in Japanese. I told her that this couldn't continue, and although my sweet wife was advancing on me frontally and the earth promised to move, I held my ground and her shower cap.

"No, you don't," I said, "not this time."

"*Cara*," Candace said. "*Leibling. Cheri.*"

"I mean it. Every merchant in town is talking, Stassen is passing out business cards and free advice, and Bereniece Miller seems to think I'm fair game for target practice." I pointed to the swelling above my eye. "We have become a laughingstock."

"Oh, baby," Candace said. She was sincerely overcome. She slumped against the side of the tub, and since she had recently included a tanning salon in her beauty regimen, her outline was warm and brown against the white skin of the tiles. "You don't need to tell me what I've done," she wailed. "I know better than anyone."

The measures of austerity are neither happy nor hopeful, and our discussion that night must have seemed to Candace like a bell tolling doom. The alternative, however, was not pretty; underneath her sink in the bathroom I found half a dozen bottles of liquid antacid, evidence that our financial burdens had become too much to bear alone. We could sell the house, the cars, refuse that which was ordered but not yet received, we could withdraw the children from private school, and we could still lose everything, our dignity included. We drew up lists, totaled figures, but our net worth never rose above zero.

"It's no good," Candace said at three-thirty the next morning. Her skin, so brown in the bathroom five hours earlier, had turned sallow underneath the kitchen fluorescents.

"We'll hope for the best," I said. "It's all we can do."

Such hope is better left to the political candidates of fringe parties and coaches of enormously overmatched teams, and I experienced the out-of-body sensation that occurs when one talks through one's hat. Still, in the next three days we did what we could: ads for the cars and the piano were placed in the classifieds; a "For Sale" sign adorned our front lawn. Yet what had really changed? I went to the club and flinched every time Bereniece Miller took a swing. Candace managed the house and the children, but she did so in a soiled robe and a short temper. I also knew that while she was alone, she continued to practice "Eleanor Rigby" and—in some abstract way—heard only borrowed time, our one debt accruing no interest. Each evening I came home to hear that desultory, made-for-Muzak melody as it drifted through the screens. And each night, while the children and I made ourselves scarce, she worried that one tune until bedtime. During the dark hours of early morning, I seemed to hear the notes of "all the lonely people" in my dreams.

Quite frankly, I was worried. Worried that my dear wife's faculties had become unmoored, that she now faced the gray swells of some uncharted and malevolent sea. On the fourth day, thinking to call her doctor, I reached for the phone a dozen different times, and each time, I refrained, hearing that inarticulate whisper that counsels patience, stoicism, and forbearance. That night, my restraint seemed justified. The children had been fed and bathed. On the table, dinner beckoned from the good china, a red wine sparkled in the crystal. In a red sheath and high heels, her hair curled and hanging past her shoulders, Candace looked equally inviting.

"Sweetheart, *cara mia*," she said, my face framed by her fingers, "it's the most wonderful thing. We now have our very own financial advisor, Mr. Dunwoodie. Mr. Dunwoodie is taking care of everything."

"Oh?"

"And the best thing of all," she said, "we don't have to sell a thing. The kids can stay in school."

Too good to be true, I thought. Too, too good. I had done the math with a calculator. How could I be so far wrong? But what did I care, wrong or right? What did I care in the presence of veal piccata, a Petite Syrah, and a woman with a light and happy heart? To question her glad news so soon would have been an expression of cynicism, a slap in the face of joy and good fortune.

I would have to meet with Mr. Dunwoodie, Candace said. I would have to meet with this marvel. Of course, I would. But I put it off for three weeks, a month, and even in that short a time our finances improved markedly. I can't explain my reticence, my reluctance to meet this man who was doing us so much good. Perhaps to meet him would have been to admit my own failure; that a stranger could perform such miracles on our balance sheet seemed like a sort of cuckoldry.

◉ ◉ ◉

Candace had given me Dunwoodie's card, and my first thought was that Stassen never could mind his own business. I imagined a man in his fifties with silver hair, a designer suit, and an office in one of the bank buildings west of the river. But when I looked at the card again, the address was in the heart of our industrial section. His office was located in the rear of a bowling alley, next to the cocktail lounge and across an access road from an auto parts warehouse, and no amount of acoustical tile could muffle the crashing of the balls and pins or the roar of forklifts. Over the phone, Mr. Dunwoodie had sounded wary, consenting to meet with me only after I had assured him of my identity, but then on the day of our appointment, I arrived to find his door locked. A hand-lettered sign had been taped below the nameplate: "Sick in bed. Lousiest cold I ever got. I don't wish it on nobody. A.B.T. Dunwoodie." I shook the door handle again, for what reason I couldn't say, there was obviously no one about.

At nine-thirty in the morning, the cocktail lounge was empty. The only bowlers were members of a senior citizens' league sponsored by a downtown mortuary. One of the machine mechanics came in, turned on one of the coffee makers and the stereo, but when I asked what he knew about Dunwoodie, he merely shrugged. "I thought he died. I never seen him for a long time. Nah," he said, thinking further. "He's gotta be dead. Unless they rent the office, the name stays, you know?"

"But I talked to him," I said. "He does our finances."

"I wouldn't know about that. Except even a dead guy would probably be better than my Uncle Larry, the family CPA genius because of whom I owe the feds $900. You find this guy, you give him my name and number too, okay?"

Sure, sure, sure. The mechanic left, but not before giving me his address, phone number, and a copy of his most recent 1040. "I'm in trouble all right," he had said, "so if your friend isn't so dead as I thought, it would be a big favor if you could mention something."

So it was not just Candace and me, I thought. The whole world might be crazed. There must be some, I realized, who were in even deeper trouble than we, a thought which caused gooseflesh to appear on my forearms while the second hand of the beer clock above the bar swept the moments away.

"You Hempstead?" The voice, raspy as a metal file, came inches from my right ear.

"Yes?"

"I been waiting half an hour already. I don't have nothing else to do with my life, if you pardon my meaning, but to wait around for you?"

"You're Dunwoodie?"

"I waited this long account of your lovely wife. A lovely woman. Who knows what it is to go without. Who doesn't buy that Puritan borrowers-and-lenders nonsense, she buys what her wants tell her to buy. I know I'm old-fashioned in these things, but that suggests a real classy lady to me."

"Your note said you were sick," I said.

He waved one hand in the air, a cigarette glowing between his fingers. "Ah," he said, "it gets rid of the street traffic. When I'm with a client, I don't like to be bothered, you know what I mean?"

He didn't like to be bothered. That must have applied to many things, for his physical presence cancelled the last of my original expectations. Tall and thin, he managed, nevertheless, to appear as flaccid as tapioca. Bald but for a few tufts of white fuzz that dotted his skull, he also sported ears and nostrils that grew hair like shrubbery. His shirt was tailor-made with French cuffs, but the collar was brown with grime, and one of his cuff studs was missing. Cigarette ash dusted his trousers and a wrinkled blue suit coat with lapels at least two decades too wide. When he took a breath, the air rattled in his chest like dice. I had the impression that I had awakened him from a potentially fatal nap.

He seemed to know what I was thinking, for he said, "Looks ain't everything, kid, and sometimes you got to be around for a long, long time before you can be of any use."

"This has all been very confusing for me. Candace said you could explain everything. I would have come sooner, but—"

"But if it works, what's it matter?" Dunwoodie sighed, coughing, finishing the thought.

"Right," I said, feeling as though I had been found out. "If it works."

"You see anything to tell you different?" He led me to his office, unlocking his door with three separate keys. "I am too cautious maybe. Who comes to a bowling alley to rob an office?"

No one I knew would have been interested in this office, that much was certain. Nothing more than a cubicle, the office of A.B.T. Dunwoodie was filled by a wood desk and two chairs, each of which was as scarred as if it had been carried over the Himalayas on elephant. A mound of paper tottered upon the desk. An ashtray overflowing with charred filters was used as a paperweight. A smaller pile of paperwork, moved from the extra chair, threatened to send the whole ramshackle mess sliding. One mistake of a match or an ember and this tinderbox of an office would explode.

"Behind on your filing?" I said.

"Please, Mr. Hempstead. Don't mock. I make certain sacrifices to serve my clients better. I don't ask for much, and this is what you see."

In that moment, the true horror of what we were doing was suddenly revealed. This teetering empire of uncatalogued paper was our foundation, and it could topple at any time, taking Candace and me along with it. It was then that another question made itself known:

"What are we paying you?" I asked.

"First comes the explanation, then comes the cost."

"I don't mean to sound distrustful, but I've yet to see a bill or a statement, and we're already in a terrible bind."

"Let me assure you, I appreciate your dilemma. But I have learned to do things in a certain order."

Waving away my protests, he proceeded then to outline the steps he had taken and planned to take in unravelling our financial knots. I can't pretend that I understood all of it since it dealt with matters well beyond my expertise. But even a rank novice such as myself could recognize tactics that were certainly questionable if not illegal: acquiring new low-interest credit accounts to pay off older high-interest debts, then obtaining even more accounts in an expanding pyramid scheme of balance transfers, special introductory interest rates, interest-free grace periods, and lines of credit larger than the mortgage on our first house. Our indebtedness grew larger month by month by month, but as long as there was more credit available, we were always covered. There was no danger unless there were no lenders looking to make a buck, and that, Dunwoodie claimed, would never happen. The mounds of paper were evidence in support.

"Let's be honest," he said. "Does anyone really want you out of debt? Who wants you out of their pocket? Are they so anxious to lend you money just so you can pay them back? Of course not. They only want to lend you more so that you pay back more and more and more. And for what? To enjoy your life? Is that so much to ask that good people—such as yourself and your lovely wife— have to carry such enormous burdens?"

As to the possibility that the scheme might unravel through an audit of our burgeoning credit report, Dunwoodie provided a less philosophical answer: his nephew, his sister's boy, a bright young fellow from some blue-blood college back east, knew a thing or two about computers; as a favor to his favorite uncle, he had pressed two or three buttons, and—*whaddya know?*—certain indictments of our past and present situation disappeared. Late payments, missed payments: gone. Accounts grown impossibly large: diminished, the numbers shaved to something manageable, believable. If such information could be so easily deleted or revised, then maybe it never really existed. But you didn't want everything to disappear, Dunwoodie said. That stirred up too much scrutiny. All he knew is that one week we were a terrible risk and the next week we had a credit history tidier than a Swiss banker's. This nephew was prepared to sanitize our paper every six months or so. Bankruptcy without penalty or stigma.

"But that's illegal," I gasped. "Definitely."

"Only in a technical sense. In a people sense, you deserve to have what you been promised in the magazines. No one should live with less."

◉ ◉ ◉

In the end, I drove away from the bowling alley in a daze, forgetting to ask his price, but knowing somehow that when it came, it would be impossibly high. Our house, our retirement, our insurance policies, our power of attorney, our reputation. A child, a home, a soul. Mr. Dunwoodie had offered Candace and me consolation, and we had gladly taken it. We would deal with the cost later. You might think us foolish, and you would be right, but who are you to judge?

Although Candace expected me, I could not go home. I drove to the Racquet Club to pick up my messages, and I watched Stassen as he gave a tennis lesson to Bereniece Miller's daughter Melanie; the old bugger looked natty in his whites, his brown knees glistening in the slanting, fragile sunshine of spring. Melanie hated tennis, she hated the lessons, she was as thin as her mother was fat, but Bereniece lived in mortal terror of reproducing herself, so Melanie indulged her mother. Stassen had his arms around her as though they were about to mambo. I wanted to see in the gesture the stirrings of an old man's harmless fantasies, but after my session with Dunwoodie, realizing that Stassen too must be on the hook, I could see only a perverse prelude to seduction.

I drove to the beverage warehouse, but as a partner with no managerial responsibilities, there was little for me to do except gab with the drivers as they loaded their trucks. I had no real business being there. They knew it and I knew it. The sound of their voices had floated out the warehouse doors on a breeze but hushed the moment they saw me. They were pleasant and cordial—although my very presence was making them late for their afternoon rounds—because, technically, I was their employer. That didn't mean they were happy about their day lasting twenty minutes longer on my account. There was nowhere else for me to go, but still I could not make myself go home. Instead, I drove along the ridge that skirts our city, home to millionaires and the over-extended. Here the fog still drifted like spun sugar, sunlight was bending through the bare branches of trees, and the moisture in the air glittered like diamonds. The natural world is full of such treasures, I thought. There must be such benefits by the thousands, if only one has the eyes to see. And yet even that thought did not cheer me; with a backdrop of pseudo-Gothic turrets and towers and faux Tudor fronts, I could only assume that even the sunlight must be a counterfeit of itself.

If this kept up, I realized, I would soon lose faith in the notion of honesty altogether. I drove back to the bowling alley determined to make a break from Dunwoodie, take back our tattered financial records and deal with them conventionally, and if necessary, at substantial cost. But the door to his office was once again locked, the note was gone from his door, and the mechanic whom I had seen earlier in the cocktail lounge reported seeing no one. He thought I was putting him on about Dunwoodie, about meeting him earlier, that it was somehow part of an elaborate practical joke at his expense.

"No, really," I said. "He met me here. I sat in his office. I looked at his paperwork. We had a long chat."

But it sounded like a story, even to me, and later, as I sat in the parking lot across the street from the bowling alley, I wondered what sort of specter might visit me next. I could be losing my mind, and Dunwoodie might be just a missing piece come back for a visit. But then, how to explain the mysterious uptick in our finances? Or the meeting so recently concluded? What dark power had we enlisted to our aid? My thoughts might have continued in this vein indefinitely but for the sight of a fellow crossing the street toward the bowling alley. Dressed in a natty three-piece banker's suit and tasseled dress shoes, he seemed out of place in this neighborhood of geriatric recreation, auto parts, and economic occultism. He whistled the opening measures of "Jesu, Joy of Man's Desiring," and the notes carried aloft on the breeze. As he stepped onto the sidewalk, I saw him kick an empty Budweiser can with those immaculate shoes. Then to prove it no mere accident, he kicked it again, once again with the form of field goal kickers of thirty years ago, toe first, with none of the effeminate swank of the soccer style. I heard him grunt as the can went skittering past my view.

This seemed, at last, to be the assurance I needed, that not all was deceit, that the joys and innocence of childhood could be regained if one were pure enough of heart. I would eventually track Dunwoodie down. Maybe not today. Or tomorrow. But eventually, we would be responsible for our lives once again.

I planned to tell Candace all this when I returned home—my meeting with Dunwoodie, my unspoken misgivings, my inability to find him again, my resolve to cut ourselves free—but she had invited Madame Tanamarenko to lunch and they had just finished their salad when I opened the door. Madame wore stirrup pants and a bulky sweater like an aging ski bunny on the prowl, and while Candace filled their glasses from a carafe of chardonnay, the old maestro picked alfalfa sprouts from between her teeth without a shred of modesty or decorum.

"What a morning I've had," I said, collapsing into one of the dining room chairs.

"Yes, well, it can wait an hour, can't it? You can tell me later?" Candace said. "Go to the garage and fix something. Go. Go."

I went to the backyard instead. There the landscapers were taking their own lunch break at our patio table. The outlines of a terraced garden had already begun to take shape in place of our patch of struggling grass. Boulders had been lifted in by crane, a row of fruit trees still in their buckets lined the back fence, a miniature bulldozer waited to scrape and mold our spot of earth. When it was finished, we would have our own spot of unpaid-for paradise. Four men for eight hours. The plants. The equipment. The costs soared higher and higher and higher. At this rate, despite my earlier optimism, we would never be free of Dunwoodie. My ears filled with the sound of roaring. One of the crew offered me his chair.

"Here," he said. "You better sit down. You don't look so hot."

"I don't feel so hot all of a sudden."

"Better take a knock of this." He held out a blue thermos cup filled with rum and Coke, easy on the soda. It would be a wonder if they didn't run over one another during the afternoon, I thought. Speed trials with the bulldozer. "One more. One more nice long one," he said, holding the thermos cup in front of me.

"Yes," I said. "It hits the spot, all right." And I was reminded of the last time I had drunk rum and Coke in quantity. This was just after I had broken my leg. Actually, I did not break it; it was broken for me by Kyle Mendoza, whose weight during the season usually settled around two-eighty. Kyle didn't mean to break my leg during a particularly violent one-on-one drill, but he had meant to hurt me, so he felt guilty about it for weeks. He had slipped Grady Clark's block as though the fat slob hadn't even tried—and come to think of it, maybe he hadn't—so all of Kyle Mendoza was waiting for me when I came steaming up Grady Clark's backside. I don't remember much: only that Grady Clark's hip pads and pants had slipped dangerously, disgustingly low, and then a pain more horrible than I had ever experienced before. A pain that seemed to have less to do with physical sensation as it did with knowledge, the certain understanding of what had been done to me—my leg had been snapped, and I assumed that were I to stand, the rest of my leg from just below the knee would remain on the ground in protest. Intolerable. I lay with my facemask pressed into the earth, my fingers clutching the grass, a ladybug sauntering just past my chin, unaware of any suffering other than its own. I wound up with a cast from my toes to mid-thigh, my career was over, and my draft status in either the NFL or Vietnam reduced to nothing. Two weeks later I met Candace, and two days after that Kyle Mendoza came to my apartment offering to buy me drinks. Why not? I had just gotten over my binge with the Scotch; for all I knew Candace still had a headache, and my future seemed bleak at best. My leg throbbed, and movement seemed preferable to moping. We must have visited half a dozen bars and taverns, the last of which was next door to the train station. One thing led to another. I don't know how it was decided, but one of us came up with the idea of boarding the next train that stopped. For emergencies, Kyle had a checkbook with his father's name on it and oodles in the account. I remember that we kept saying to one another that a train was just the ticket, a fine place to drink and see a little scenery. We said this over and over again with the sense that we were being very original and witty. Kyle bought a bottle of rum at the last tavern, and for the next five hours we settled into our compartment and drank and played cribbage on a board that the bemused porter brought to us. We tipped him like crazy for the cribbage board and the Cokes, and he would have brought us anything short of a camel. By two in the morning, we were gliding into Klamath Falls. The snow was deep, the lights of the station were orange, and the outlines of the trees were only a deeper darkness. The slowing motion seemed to signal something in both of us, and before the train could come to a complete stop, we were both hanging over the half-door, throwing up onto the railbed in the Klamath Falls station. Observed, as it turned out, by an entire wedding party waiting to board, their faces registering neither shock nor amusement. The bride wore her dress and the groom his tux. The wedding was to be performed in the club car, but they had not counted on being greeted by two drunks, one of whom was crippled. They were a big-hearted couple, however, and we were invited to the ceremony. The bride danced with Kyle in spite of my warnings about the clumsy ox, and the groom's mother wouldn't be satisfied until, hopping on my one good leg, I had danced with her. Five days later we found our way home, out of money and credit—Kyle's father pulled the account when he saw what we were up to—otherwise we might still be traveling. But the memory of that wedding party would not go away, and I asked

Candace then if she would have me. She had answered emphatically: she most certainly would *not* have anything to do with me, not with the alcoholic that she saw me to be. The story of our odyssey had become common knowledge. It took me four years to prove myself worthy—four years of meetings and confessions and failures and more meetings—but that was the best thing that Candace could have done; I would have used up all of her power to forgive me otherwise.

Now, as I stood in the beginnings of what would become our garden, drinking a rum and Coke of memory and time, I looked into the faces of the landscaping crew and listened to the opening notes of "Penny Lane" as they drifted out the back door. They watched intently as I downed my drink, and in that moment, they seemed as impassive as that wedding party from Klamath Falls. And just as generous.

"Drink up," the one with the thermos commanded. "There's more in the truck. Relax, take a load off. If you're worried about how this is going to look, don't. We're gonna make it gorgeous."

II. Words from Another Time Zone

The first anonymous note reached Crawford's desk on a Friday afternoon. It was spring, sunshine beckoned from every corner, and because the building was old, windows were open and a gentle, god-kissed breeze turned the office blinds into a chorus of chimes. The building was nearly empty. He had gone down the hall, looked into Magruder's darkened office, drank half a cup of boiled coffee in the deserted lunch room, and then came back to his own cubicle to find the plain white legal-sized envelope propped up against his picture of Susan. The note itself was typed—badly, by someone with little practice, it seemed—on standard bond paper.

JACK CRAWFORD,

YOU ARE A CLASS "A" CHEAP SHOT ARTIST! I KNOW WHAT
YOU ARE UP TO AND DON'T TRY TO DENY IT BECAUSE I
KNOW. MORE PEOPLE THAN YOU WOULD LIKE TO KNOW HAVE
FIGURED YOUR FUCKING LITTLE GAME TO THE PENNY AND
KNOW THAT YOU ARE STILL A BIG JOKE (A JERK). SO IF
YOU THINK THAT YOU CAN JUST GET RID OF ALL OF US
YOU'VE GOT ANOTHER THING COMING!! GETTING RID OF
FEASTER MIGHT BE EASY BUT NOT US, YOU ARE A TOTAL
ASSHOLE!!!

He read it four times in rapid succession, the meaning of individual words escaping him more completely with each reading. The syntax was clumsy, the diction crude; the tone, however, and the meaning of the whole were unmistakable. Rereading it a fifth time, he tried to laugh. Whoever had written it—obviously stupid, although somewhat compulsive, witness the orderly escalation of exclamation points, the capitals—whoever had written it did not count.

Still. . . .

Water sprang to his eyes unbidden, a reaction to this dislike emanating from an unknown quarter. He had always known that he might not be universally loved or approved, but faced with this letter and its expression of definite and specific dislike, he recoiled. Who could do such a thing? Who hated him this much?

That Feaster had been fired was not his fault. Not entirely.

He'd just been used.

You are a Total Asshole!!!

From an office down the hall he heard Arlene Steinhauer singing "Blue Skies." A fly battered itself senseless against the screen. It was still spring. The air still tasted of angels.

But when the phone rang, he answered it, sniffling into the receiver, forgetting to say anything.

"Jack?" Susan's voice.

"Jack? Hello?" She began to whistle into the phone. "You spaced out on me again?"

"Yes," he said, "I'm here."

"I'll be ready at six. Dinner here or when we get there?"

Outside, a tow truck was pulling a new Porsche away from the red curb in front of the building's main entrance. The car's front wheels dangled uselessly, and the sight of it, somehow, went to his stomach.

"Jack!" She was now hitting the phone with something. Possibly a set of keys?

"Sure, dinner's fine," he said.

"Never mind," she sighed. "I'll see you at six. Let's see if we can't rediscover the home planet by then."

He stood with the letter in one hand, the phone in the other, the dial tone insistent in his ear. When had she hung up? Why had she called?

He wandered out of his office, holding his letter as if it were an organ that he himself had excised. Magruder's office was still dark. Rosemary, his secretary, looked up guiltily from her latest Danielle Steele as he stumbled in then out.

"He's in Turlock this afternoon, Mr. Crawford," she called after him.

One by one he looked into other darkened offices, only to find himself standing in the doorway of the last office in the hall, spying, listening to Arlene Steinhauer sing.

The director of marketing, Arlene Steinhauer held a foxy, triangular-shaped face out to the world, her nose often twitched in a gesture of suspicion, her gray eyes were as skeptical as glass, and she could sing a song such as "Blue Skies" so facetiously as to sound like an expression of cynicism and disbelief. The arch of her back reminded him of clipper ships, inclement weather, and choppy seas.

He had heard several stories about her: that she had been the on-again, off-again mistress of Arthur Brennan, CEO of Tri-OptiCor, for well over two years; that she had driven the former director of marketing wild during a tempestuous six-month affair ending with herself installed in his job. One found her name inscribed in the stalls of the men's bathroom, her feats described in terms bordering on the heroic. And so on.

Crawford had once propositioned her himself—at a Christmas party a year and a half before—an act so out of character as to fill him yet with chagrin. He had gotten drunk, and under the influence of the alcohol and the memory of such unsubstantiated gossip, he approached her. Facing her hostile stare, he had withered within thirty seconds. His testicles tingled yet with the memory.

Now, while she sang, her posture in no way moved by the currents of spring, she peeled off mailing labels, licked stamps, and affixed both to envelopes. Her secretary was among the early weekenders, and she sang as though she were alone, punctuating each bar with her work: *Blue skies*, lick, *smiling at me*, stamp, smirk, *nothing but blue skies*, peel, *do I see*, press, sneer. Her blonde hair turned to ash in the afternoon sun.

"Well?" she said. "Or do you just like to hear me sing?"

"Look," he said, offering her the note, failing as he did so to keep the tragedy from his voice, "look at this, will you?"

She looked up, stretched out one hand. She read the note, laughing once—at which part it was impossible to tell.

"What a surprise." Her upper lip curled. "The fact that there's no name, I mean," she said. "I wouldn't worry about it."

Then why was this lovely spring day such a mockery?

"I can't believe that someone's this nasty."

"What did you expect? Medals?" She fixed him in the eye with a look reminiscent of that Christmas past, securing them together with this reminder of his foolishness and her rejection. "You are a bit of an asshole."

She handed the note back, tore off another stamp, positioning it near her mouth.

He had been dismissed.

"I don't mean to be," he confessed, hoping for some form of absolution. "An asshole, that is."

And he realized with an almost pleasant grip in his bowels that she was the only person on this side of the building besides himself, that they were alone together, that she could be the author.

"You can't be nice all the time." She was not being unkind now. "Besides, no one will care, even if you try."

◉ ◉ ◉

The Feaster business had occurred seemingly by accident. One of the first employees of TriOptiCor, George Feaster had managed the Manufacturing Division for thirty-two years. When he was forty, his personality could have been described in polite terms as prickly; when he turned seventy—and no one had dared suggest retirement—prickly had long since been replaced by volatility tempered by dementia. At ten-thirty each morning, production ceased, and the workers were led in prayer followed by a group rendition of the "Hokey Pokey." He insisted that all Hispanic women who worked in Manufacturing wear Carmen Miranda hats on their birthdays. The vats filled with chemical wash were christened Adolf, Benito, and Idi Amin, in honor of those "fine, fine gentlemen." When the cafeteria ran out of ham sandwiches one day, he brandished the red-hot tip of a soldering iron, threatening the manager with anal cauterization. The list went on.

As the assistant director of personnel, Crawford had been the one to suggest at a staff meeting, half in jest, that Feaster be fired for cause, but since no employee complaints had ever been filed and because Manufacturing was demonstrably the most efficient and productive division within the company, he never dreamed that anyone would take the idea—obvious as it was—seriously. However, word got out. The president of the employees' union called to offer her informal, off-the-record encouragement. Mr. Brennan invited him into his office, offered him a drink, told him that he—Mr. Brennan—personally sympathized with Crawford's desire to make the company a progressive employment environment, that it took bright, forward-thinking, correct-thinking young men and women to make such things happen.

Filled with such puffery, Crawford typed out the notice himself. "This is to inform you that your services will no longer. . . ." He had practically hummed with the work of building the company's case, ending with a magnanimous option of retirement or separation with forfeiture of benefits. After reading Crawford's catalog of Feaster's errors and indiscretions, Mr. Brennan had promised him a paid weekend at TriOptiCor's conference suite. He intimated the prospect of further reward. Dangling a set of small gold keys at arm's length, Brennan had winked, "I've seen that picture on your desk. And what I'd do is take that pretty gal along, open the liquor cabinet with this little ol' key here, and celebrate. And then I'd celebrate some more, if you know what I mean."

Four weeks later, Crawford saw what had happened: in charge of his fiefdom, Feaster had been a powerful icon among the older, more heavily involved investors, too entrenched for major power plays or high-level bloodletting, something of a genius albeit a practitioner of dubious method; exposed and disgraced—at the hands of a junior executive, no less—he was just an old crank who had outlived his usefulness, an old crank with one hell of a pension.

A retirement dinner was hastily thrown together, and the old man sat at the head table, sandwiched between Brennan and

Arlene Steinhauer. He looked alternately stricken and enraged; Crawford avoided making contact with Feaster's unremitting stare, feeling as though he had sharpened a blade he'd never intended for use.

Mr. Brennan stood, saying how much he regretted accepting the resignation of such a valued member of the TriOptiCor family, and then one by one, his employees from Manufacturing stood and recited stories of kindness and good will. No mention was made of the "Hokey Pokey" or Carmen Miranda or soldering irons, and Crawford wondered whether, like Alice, he were looking into the mirror from the wrong side. What had he done?

And now just this Friday, this Friday filled with springtime and promise, while locking his car at the curb in front of his condominium, he had been made to realize that the sidelong glances received in hallways and in meetings were reserved for the executioner, the villain, the man with the hatchet. And the price for that was to be unloved, to lose that last delusion of youth: that one could possibly remain aloof, untouched by the injuries of ambivalent circumstance and fickle human nature. He would be wiser for having endured the experience, but in the process he seemed to be drifting farther and farther away from that pleasantly vague, no-fault image by which he had always defined himself.

He stood in front of his door, rifling through the mailbox crammed with bills and advertisements and petitions for charity. One envelope in the box was not addressed or stamped. His name only, printed on the outside. He tore it open, reading as he jiggled the door unlocked.

HELLO FUCKHEAD!

SO YOU THINK YOU CAN TAKE OVER. WELL YOU LITTLE SON OF A BITCH HERE'S THE WAY THINGS ARE YOU'RE NOTHING BUT PISS AT THE BOTTOM OF THE WELL. YOU AND YOUR

WHOLE CROWD, THE STEINHAUER SLUT, AIRHEAD MAGRUDER,
YOU'RE ALL PISSANTS AND FUCKHEADS. AND DON'T THINK
YOU AND LITTLE MISS PIECE OF TAIL ARLENE HAVE GONE
UNNOTICED. NO SIR.

He half fell to his knees on the welcome mat, thinking he
might be sick, this newest letter a death's head in his hand.

"What is the matter with you?" Susan's head craned from
behind the front door. "Here I use your secret key, sneak in like a
petty criminal just waiting to give you a little surprise, and all you
can do is act like some Arab on his rug."

"I've had a bad day." It sounded lame even as he spoke.

"Get in here, cowboy, before I rope you."

He crawled through the doorway, seeing first her bare feet
then her brown legs topped by the dark tangle of her pubic
hair. Her breasts bobbed above him. A rope dropped from her
hand.

"Surprise," she said. "Happy weekend. Big deal."

"A real bad day," he said, pulling the lasso from about his
shoulders. Susan believed in variety as the spice of most everything, but her timing, regrettably, did not always match her
intent. Her ex-husband had often complained of her interfer-
ing, although, she insisted, he was way off base, confusing interest for interference. Susan's ex-husband's judgments were often
suspect in any case.

"So what's your bad day?" She had dropped onto the couch,
crossing her legs and putting a pillow into her lap. "I saw thirty-
eight kids for flu and Mr. Parkinson came back in for his genital
rash. I swear I think he cultivates it."

"I got hate mail." He handed her the letters. "One at the office, one just now."

"Well, shit. This is pleasant." She bit her fingernails while she
read. "You got yourself a real friend here."

"Friend."

"Still," she said, throwing the letters onto the coffee table, a movement which dislodged her pillow, "still, it ain't nothing but words. Anyone who could do you real damage would have kicked your butt by now."

"Thanks."

"Seriously. If your best shot is passing notes like some fourth grader, then you don't have leverage, you only got nuisance value."

"Fine. So now I'm getting bit by a Doberman without teeth. That's great. I feel a whole lot better."

"Beats real teeth."

She stood up, moving towards the stairs and the bedroom, all hips and flanks and reproof.

"I'm hungry," she said, "and if you're not gonna play the game, then you're damn sure gonna buy me dinner."

◎ ◎ ◎

The TriOptiCor suite balcony overlooked Monterey Bay. In the midnight darkness, the water was black and roaring, and Crawford sat with his feet propped on the railing and a tumbler of the corporation's Glenfiddich balanced on his stomach. A thin fog had moved in, making a gauzy curtain of the air, distorting the sound of the water below. Susan slept. Her legs were tangled in the blankets and she was snoring as though pleased with herself. Crawford was sure that if he looked in on her he would see her mouth open and her fingers curled around the edge of her pillow as if she were riding it or taking its pulse.

He had known Susan for six weeks. He had met her in the buffet line at the TriOptiCor spring picnic when she was loading up her plate with ham and potato salad. He had seen women who were voracious eaters before, but Susan ate hugely and talked hugely and gestured wildly to accompany both activities.

She held the contract to do health screenings for new Tri-OptiCor employees, and she genuinely surprised people when she walked through the examination room door: a tall, big-boned woman wearing blue jeans, a silver belt buckle the size of a small purse, and cowboy boots with three-inch heels. The dark riot of her hair plunged beyond her shoulders. Her accent and mannerisms were reminiscent of a Texas rodeo groupie although she had grown up in Newport Beach amid women in silk scarves and men in blue blazers and Topsiders.

Crawford had never understood the process by which she had rejected these roots only to assume something so foreign, and Susan would not talk about her parents. But she would talk about her ex-husband Bud, who used a welding torch, a freezer, and an ice pick to make specialty ice sculptures—banquet centerpieces that featured miscellaneous car parts frozen inside the figures of dolphins or mermaids. It was incredible how many stupid people there were who would pay good money for such things, Susan said. Bud sometimes drank a lot and when he was drunk he sometimes became belligerent or else he talked at great length about ice and auto parts as media for art; she finally figured out that she no longer needed to be counted among the stupid, bailing out after three years in spite of Bud's threats that she would fall into despair without him.

At the picnic, her natural expansiveness was even more exaggerated, the result of finalizing her divorce. He thought from the moment he met her that he would do well to know such a woman if such a woman would allow herself to be known; she might counteract his own inhibitions and desire for others' approval with her Here-I-am-take-it-or-leave-it attitude. Wasn't there something to be learned here?

But now, holding Mr. Brennan's liquor cabinet key, his glass of company Scotch, and watching the fog-shrouded stars, he was not so sure that it had worked out after all: she fascinated him with her energy, and her athleticism during sex exhausted him, but that only made him feel smaller, even more constrained.

While he worked on Feaster's removal, he had felt determined and assured, but he also knew that Brennan's accolades had been largely responsible for his sense of well-being, and it further saddened him to think that his own fortunes might be built on the failure of another. The moment he'd received the first letter, the illusion, being a brittle one, had crumbled.

Water broke on the rocks in the darkness. The fog had brought with it a cold and dampness that made him shiver inside his robe. He heard laughter from other balconies below his own. From one balcony he heard a man and a woman, their voices raised above the din of the ocean.

"I will not have you making a federal case out of this," the woman yelled. "It was your choice, your mistake, and you'll have to live with it."

"There's nothing to live with," the man pleaded. "Pookie, please." His voice held a note of urgency, and Crawford thought that the woman must have some sort of advantage, some leverage, either moral or financial, to wield. She should use it judiciously, he thought, otherwise guilt—whether or not it was justified—would be the only result. And what was the point of feeling guilty even when you're right?

He sat looking out into the blackness at the end of the earth even after the couple had retreated, taking their argument and turmoil back into their own suite.

The glass door opened behind him and then Susan was sliding onto his lap, naked and glowing, breathing into his ear. "Kinda cold out here, don't you think?"

Crawford raised his glass of Scotch. "I'm warm enough."

"Well, I'm not." She snuggled closer and stole the glass. "Better. Now if I could just get my biscuits out of the sea breeze."

Her fingers went underneath the robe.

"Am I an asshole?"

"What?" She raised her head from his chest.

"Am I an asshole, a pissant, and a fuckhead?" he said.

He was not unaware of the irony. Had it come to this—that he could sit with a beautiful and naked woman in his lap, a woman of wit and intelligence, a woman who obviously cared for him, that he could sit thus in earshot of the gentle sea that begged one to think of eternal truths and the fidelity of one human to another and think only of a letter that had named him an asshole? Had he become so abstracted, so narcissistic . . . so in love with his own guilt and self-importance that the clumsy anger of a crank's letters held more reality than Susan's sweet flesh and his own involuntary bone?

Susan gripped the lapels of his bathrobe, pressing her lips against his ear:

"One of these days this little boy-child's gonna grow up, I think." She smoothed back his hair, touched his nose with her own. "Prob'ly not this weekend. But one of these days."

◎ ◎ ◎

Crawford received three more letters during the next six weeks. All typed, all in the attention-getting shout of capital letters, profanity, and exclamation points. Each one was delivered on a cheery Friday afternoon, as if the writer's intent was to disrupt his weekend as well as his happiness. One came through inter-office mail, one was deposited on the dashboard of his car, and the last was posted on the lunchroom bulletin board for all to see. No one claimed to have noticed the person with the thumb tack.

Each letter affected him less than the previous ones. Identifying his mystery correspondent no longer mattered; the letters were nothing more than words from another time zone, another life. Dull reminders of human frailty. When he removed the last one, he pushed it through the swinging door of the lunchroom trash can, forgetting about the file folder with the previous four letters.

Susan was picking him up tonight so that they could drive to Anaheim. She had not been to Disneyland in years. On Sunday they would stop in Newport Beach so that he might meet her parents, see the house in which she had grown up. He had insisted despite her grim-lipped reservations. He couldn't know her otherwise.

Since the weekend in the company suite, they had talked about moving in together, and Susan once even used the word "marriage," although she quickly clamped her hand over her mouth after it had dropped out. She was not yet ready for that, not after Bud and his car parts. And neither was Crawford. He couldn't decide if his hesitation was due to a reluctance to part with his privacy, or if there might not be a deeper cause—the fear that living together under the obligations of contract might become a breeding ground for insult and injury, his fear that he might come to despise her tough good humor if he were to see it in slumber each night.

He was finishing a report on health benefit options, very nearly finished with this day and this week, when Arlene Steinhauer came through the door.

"I heard about your latest love note."

She shook her head, pulled her hair back away from her neck as she sat in the extra chair.

"I took it down," he said.

"There are some very mean and nasty people out there," she sighed, "who wish others nothing but ill."

She stood and closed his door.

"Fuck them," she said. "Fuck them up, down, and sideways. Fuck, fuck, fuck them." She pronounced the words deliberately, with care but without relish.

"I suppose so."

She pulled her earrings off, a gesture that confused and intrigued him with its reflection of intimacy, and he remembered that he once thought she might have been the one.

"It'll stop soon," he said, "at least I think so. He seems to be running out of steam—repeating himself, that sort of thing. I don't think he's very interested any more. It's some sort of obligation now."

He prattled on, unable to stop himself from reviewing everything—how devastated he'd first felt, how he'd had to evaluate his life to make sure that there had been no grain of truth in any of it, that maybe he was, at least sometimes, a bit of an asshole, he had been Brennan's hit man, and maybe, too, he was just too malleable, that he was too willing to be defined by others. *Blah, blah. Blah, blah, blah. Blah, blah.*

She had begun to pat his hand, and she kept patting it until he wound down, until he stopped talking abruptly, knowing he had spoken too much and ashamed of that breach. He was confessing to Arlene Steinhauer, a woman who already knew at least one of his worst humiliations, and the thought occurred to him that she was fully aware of human hostility, and that she had known it for a much longer time.

III. (The) Only Lie

I once knew a man who was conventional in every respect, except for his belief that he had flown jets over Hanoi in 1968. Other than a few short trips from Los Angeles to Phoenix to care for his aging parents, he had never flown in his life. He had never been in the Air Force or Navy; he had not served the military in any capacity whatsoever. A trumpet player in his high school band, he had stepped into a gopher hole on the practice field and destroyed the anterior cruciate ligament of his left knee, his military career terminated before it could begin, much to the envy of other males his age.

After high school he moved away, went to college, but made few friends. After school, he went to work for an established bank, bought a house in a neighboring village, and married. His parents died within six months of each other. In his thirties, while he made fistfuls of money in real estate ventures and the stock market, he began to drop broad hints about the rigors of military life—the discipline, the regimentation, and so on. For his fortieth birthday, his wife arranged a surprise party, and while drinking, he alluded to the missions he had flown while hung over on Singapore Slings. Ten years ago, as though some wall inside himself had crumbled, he suddenly turned effusive about his military career and, in the manner of aging veterans, described in detail the missiles he dodged over Hanoi, the payloads he dropped, and the guilt he carried with him as constant as his keys or his wallet. He limped, he claimed, from the time he was forced to eject; he had landed awkwardly thirty kilometers northwest of Saigon, then walked six hours on a moonless night to an aid station. He woke two or three nights each week, on average, with nightmares. He blamed Agent Orange for his inability to father children. He drank in VFW halls with old men wearing campaign hats, he marched every July in our small town's American Legion parade, then one night last November—the Friday after Thanksgiving—he hanged himself from the rafters in the garage. He stepped off the roof of his Audi and flew into the unknown. Dora, his wife, found the body. A note was never discovered, and investigators remained confused. What was his emotional state? Were there problems in the home? At work? Was he in debt, having an affair, addicted to gambling or drink or an illegal substance? Nothing could be found, and at his funeral, the minister's remarks focused on the lingering trauma of war and the inscrutable aspects of human nature. We are all a mystery.

Sometime later, our newspaper ran a story about local veterans, and the facts emerged. The trumpet, the gopher hole, his knee. The implication being that the duplicity of his life was the cause of depression and remorse. Truth be told, however, it could have been the effect just as easily.

Dora grieved afresh. She had not known the facts but would have loved the high school trumpet player just the same as her war hero.

"What makes a man do such a thing?" she asked her sisters.

She asked girlfriends from grade school and the waitress from the Cupboard Cafe and the plumber from Vern's. She asked her question of Jehovah's Witnesses who backed away from her door and pedestrians waiting for the light to change at Main and Fourth.

"What makes a man do such a thing?"

She had cut down her husband's body from the ceiling of the garage, but the deception had cut her far more deeply.

"What makes a man do such a thing?" she asked me, who (once upon a time) had been her boyfriend, whose past betrayal ought to have given me insight into the stupidity and cruelty perpetrated by men.

"What makes a man do such a thing?"

What indeed?

◉ ◉ ◉

As it happened, Dora worked on the same floor as my wife. Sister nurses of the oncology ward. Dora worked days while Joan worked nights. Dora gave the patients their chemo, and Joan cleaned up the vomit. The running joke concerned their role reversals since Dora, all softness and rounded edges, administered the poison, while my wife, who was made of sterner stuff, rubbed backs, breathed encouragement, and mopped up the mess. Because of our past history, Dora's and mine, we were not in the habit of socializing as couples—it somehow seemed too complicated even thirty years after the fact—but I knew Frank casually, we had passed through the same living rooms and dens at hospital parties, and he seemed a nice enough sort, though in general I have felt that bankers are not to be trusted.

Dora first read the newspaper account of her husband's fictions during her lunch hour; she became aware that her colleagues in the hospital cafeteria were staring at her over their salads and bowls of chili. "When is a life not a life," the article began, "and when is a hero not a hero?" The reporter sketched the outlines of her husband's life, real and imagined, and as Dora pored over the details, she questioned the depth of her gullibility. Her husband's boss, a veteran of the lies of loan applicants and himself a participant at Khe Sanh, had his own misgivings about Frank's biography. "It wasn't my business, one way or the other, you understand," he said. "Frank Baxter was one of my top people. But whenever he talked about Vietnam, there were too many discrepancies, too many times when I was convinced that I was being told a story, not the truth." Near the end of the article was a quote attributed to Dora, although no reporter had ever contacted her: "I never knew," she was reported as saying. "Twenty-four years of marriage, only to find out that I never knew the man I was living with." She never said it, but curiously enough, if someone had taken the time to ask her, she would have. Those words exactly. On paper, they had the force of fact, and she wondered if she had simply forgotten the conversation, if she had spoken to the reporter in a dream.

As it turned out, her husband's stories were nothing more than a minor footnote to everyone but herself. She endured a month of downcast eyes and those commonplaces meant for sympathy but which border on spite. She went back to work, determined to put her life back onto an everyday footing, and then— *surprise, surprise!*—found routine all around her. News of her husband's fabrications, like the news of his death, was the briefest of interludes. The story blazed in the fire of gossip and faded just as quickly. Within five minutes of coming back to her place on the ward, her life returned to the cycles of chemo, radiation, surgical intervention, and their aftermath. Some patients responded well to the ministrations of such well-intentioned sadism—they went into remission and grew confident of life's hold—while others lost ground despite the best efforts of doctor, nurse, or technician. No one, in a condition of such necessary self-absorption, cared that her husband had carved his own identity out of the air.

◉ ◉ ◉

One of those patients was me, as it turned out. I myself, post-surgery, the failure of which I was only dimly recognizing, in an adjustable bed on the third floor, sharing a room with an eighty-four-year-old emphysema case and his oxygen tank hissing day and night. After six months of delay and paperwork, rescheduling and authorization codes, they had opened me up, then sewn me back together, little different for the experience. Dora had visited with me during the day as she made her rounds, lingering to chat with the sick husband of a coworker, an old flame still dopey from anesthesia. And then Joan, of course, who as the wife of a patient had waited all day for the results of my surgery and now at night was in her more familiar, more comfortable role of nurse. Which lately had erected a more formidable barrier between us. The distinction between the sick and well, caregiver and cared for, not to mention her own natural reserve, a professional distance consciously cultivated.

"Why don't you crawl in here?" I asked. "It's dark and Wheezy's asleep." I nodded toward the other side of the curtain and my lung-labored roommate.

"Aren't you the mean one," she said.

"Just a little cuddle," I said, indicating the IV lines that extended from my arms, "that's all I need. That's all I could handle in any case."

I don't know what I expected. For the past fifteen years, we have lived in the familiarity and detachment of siblings. We have known one another as well as we desire and have called a truce in the conflict of intimacy.

In her starched uniform smock, Joan was a black outline framed by the light from the hall, and only my imagination let me see the gray in the blunt cut of her dark hair. The balloon bouquet sent over by my third-period American History class bumped against the ceiling in the currents of the air conditioning.

"You must be sore," she said, "with all that rummaging around they did. I could get you something. He left orders for Demerol."

"No," I said, "enough of that."

"Well, then," she said, "try to get some sleep. I'll check back in a little bit."

"Okay," I lied. "Good. I could use a little R & R."

The day before, I had been preparing my classes for the substitute they would have the next day, a girl fresh out of college named Tina Green. "Go easy on her," I said. "For god's sake, don't be lousy kids and make us all look bad."

"Is she a babe?" one of the football players asked. Titters bubbled and broke throughout the room.

"She'll break your heart. She'll chew you up and spit you out in tiny pieces. Especially you, Garcia." I had never set eyes on Tina Green. For all I knew she could have had three eyes.

"Any other questions?"

A girl in the second row, pale Virginia Mayhew, a little mouse with a perfect GPA, raised her hand. "How long are you going to be in the hospital?"

"Three days. I'll be out for at least a week. Longer if I feel crummy. I've got about two years' worth of sick leave, it's time

I used some of it." Ever since the district had prohibited the use of accrued time toward years of service and retirement, I had contemplated the benefit of catastrophic illness. Be careful what you wish for.

Virginia raised her hand again. "So does that mean that our Reconstruction papers won't be due next week?"

"Yes," I said. "Let's call them postponed. Thanks for your concern."

Virginia blushed to the roots of her translucent hair. I had thrown a cheap shot and embarrassed a good but shy kid, and I felt like dirt for doing it. She probably hated me now. They all do, at some point, in any case.

So it wasn't that surprising when Cheyenne called that night, expressing at a distance her concern for my health and well-being. "Don't worry, Dad. You'll be okay. Mom says it's a pretty routine deal these days."

"I suppose it is." Routine for everyone except for the one on the table, I might have added, but after Virginia Mayhew I knew that silence was my only safe response.

"I'm in kind of a bad spot with my job right now, otherwise I'd be there."

"Don't worry about it."

"I just can't take any time off."

"Don't sweat it, honey."

"We had a couple of things go sour this past month and I'm not in a very good position to take personal leave."

"The only person who has to show up is the doctor," I said, "and like you said, it's routine."

There have been times in my life when I would have chosen another life altogether if the option had presented itself. Every March, with twelve weeks of the school year left, the dread of waking up in the morning is nearly overwhelming. For the last twelve years, Joan has worked nights, so—since she is loath to disrupt her schedule—we sleep together but rarely, and our sex life seems prompted by duty more than desire. Our daughter lives in another state and has declared without words that we are people she is embarrassed to know. That's the worst of it.

Don't get me wrong. I am nothing special and my circumstances hardly extraordinary; many must have it so. But I have not been able to dissuade myself that in another world, I might have made different, more successful choices than those made in this one, that circumstance might have been kinder, more golden. There would be other circumstances and other mistakes, too, no doubt, possibly with even more devastating consequence, but isn't that the risk that Frank Baxter had taken when he exchanged a gopher hole and anonymity for the danger and notoriety of a parachute in a war-torn foreign sky?

◉ ◉ ◉

My history with Dora was nothing to be proud of; she had every reason in the world to be wary around me, and each time I see her, even so long after the fact, I am moved by guilt and tenderness in equal parts. I met her in our senior year of high school. Her parents had come to town from some place back East—New York, I think, maybe Pennsylvania—and she looked lost that first week in a school year when one should rule the roost. Her blond hair was a butter-yellow beehive and her arms were golden in a sleeveless blouse. She looked lost because she was new but also because she refused to wear the black, rhinestone-studded glasses that she absolutely loathed yet absolutely needed. How could I not be smitten? We dated all year, and during Spring Break, two months before we graduated, her parents took an anniversary cruise to Acapulco, and we set up shop like newlyweds. And, like newlyweds, we forgot to take the necessary precautions. My induction notice and confirmation of Dora's pregnancy came within a week of each other in late May. We argued. Predictably and at length. So I fled: I enlisted in the Navy and left for San Diego in June. Dora cried, and over the phone I said that it was impossible, there was no way I could get leave for a pregnant girlfriend. Panic-stricken, Dora found an accommodating OB-GYN, then had a miscarriage before she could get to the office. At the hospital, things went from bad to worse: the D&C did not go well and Dora bled and bled and bled some more. Her father and a sympathetic pastor convinced the powers that be that my critically ill "wife" needed me desperately. I was given emergency leave and a bus ticket, then drank cheap whiskey in my seat until I couldn't see straight, stumbling off the bus at 12:30 in the morning over the objections of the driver one hundred miles south of home. Instead of calling Dora's family, I went to a bar and drank some more. I can't begin to understand, much less explain, my actions. Had I felt trapped by the possibility of marriage or fatherhood? Who knows? I was in boot camp, my head was as smooth as an egg, and I couldn't face another new life. I walked out of the bar half an hour later, lurched into the street to vomit, and was mugged by men whose faces I never saw. I woke from a concussion six hours later in a hospital bed, with three cracked ribs, some busted teeth, and a shattered patella, but no wallet or pants to show for my night on the town; those gangsters had been angry that I had only fifteen dollars to offer and they had expressed themselves. They had offered me a fresh start. I called Dora's house from the hospital and spoke to her father, but I could tell he didn't believe me. Why had I gotten off the bus? I was back in town three months later—my knee would never be right, and the Navy had no use for cripples—but I could never face Dora, it was all too complicated to undo. Then Dora met Frank (more heroic than I), I met Joan (less emotive than Dora), we found jobs, bought houses, and made lives for ourselves in the midst of other choices, other possibilities, well on the path toward middle age if not happiness.

⊙ ⊙ ⊙

I prepared myself for surgery by consoling myself with the thought that if I died, I would not have to correct the last batch of tests, sure to be lousy, from my US Government classes. What is the two-party system? A heavy weekend. Very funny stuff. Lying down on the operating table sounded like a vacation. Which it was at first. The anesthesia dropped me into the deepest sleep I have ever known, a sleep from which I woke too quickly and found myself standing against the wall of the operating room while a team of doctors and nurses proceeded to open my guts to the air.

"About time," I thought, though I already knew the futility of their task. They would find the evil in residence in the lymph nodes, its migration toward bone and brain well under way.

"Ah, shit," said Dr. Moore, the surgeon, behind his mask. "Shit, shit, fucking shit."

"Preach it, brother," I said from my position on the wall. "Testify. The glory that is managed care."

Although the procedure was now pointless, they took out tumor and prostate anyway; they had the knives out and everyone was gathered. If I were left incontinent or impotent or both, the death that would surely follow wouldn't seem so bad. Modern medicine and a thing of beauty.

While the butchers continued their work, I walked through the automatic door of the operating room into an evening of my old neighborhood and the life I could have lived. My life as though lived by a better—no, let's say *different*—me. The neighborhood was not the same, some indefinable alteration having been inscribed in the air, so that I knew it was not merely the difference that time makes. I have lived in this town all my life, and although it has changed in fifty years so have I; I wear it like my skin, but my skin was as itchy as though I were being scaled. The grassy square in front of city hall was greener, the theater marque brighter than I had ever seen before. The streets were cleaner. In a house I had never owned, I knew that Dora was waiting for me like a scene out of *It's a Wonderful Life*, for this was our anniversary and our children, gathered from the four corners of their lives, had planned a party. I knew that as I approached the front door, I would see Dora framed in the living room window and illuminated by lamp light, already dressed for the party and touching the back of her butter-colored hair. A moment of quiet before celebration. And although she has worn contacts for years, she retained that myopic gaze, that intimation of the lost that threatened to drop me to my knees.

I stepped onto the front porch and opened the screen door, an Appalachian waltz drifting from the front room.

"I have it," I said, holding aloft the bottle of Moët that until that moment I didn't know I had.

"Wonderful."

Dora brought glasses for the wine, the cork flew, and bubbles sped upwards inside the flutes.

"Dance with me," she said.

"I still have to shower and shave and get dressed," I said.

She set her glass down on the coffee table and held out her arms. "We have time."

Our children were not due for an hour, the evening was a milestone of love, and in front of me stood my fragrant and inviting wife.

"We could do more than dance."

"No, you don't," she said, laughing and swatting at my hands. "After the kids leave."

"A quickie," I said, "an appetizer before dinner."

"No thanks. I'll end up asleep and drooling on myself. Dance with me now, and I'll wrestle you later."

She held up her hands again, the CD spun in the player, and in three-quarter time we moved slowly and carefully about the room, my hand alive to the shift of her hip underneath the silk of her dress, two partners tied by the mystery of our souls' connection. I buried my face at the golden conjunction of her shoulder and neck, drifting along the current of fragrance toward her breasts. "God," I said, "you smell so good."

"Go on," she said. She pushed me away, laughing yet again, her power over me so unambiguous as to be a source of her amusement. "Go on," she said again. "Take your shower. Make it a cold one."

And then, dressed in unfamiliar coat and tie, I stood in the side yard, raising the garage door, peering into the murky twilight, weak sunshine filtering through dust-coated windows. What was I doing here?

◉ ◉ ◉

My sense of the past is more precarious than the dates and names and places of the textbooks, and in my classes—much to my students' chagrin—I prefer to talk about the what-ifs of the past, the speculation of what could have happened. What if Douglas had beaten Lincoln in 1860? What if the Nazis had been successful in their quest for atomic power? What if Oswald had stayed in the Soviet Union, keeping house with his Russian wife and daughter? These are the kinds of questions that tease us, they are ghost stories, giving us the horrors we have not had to face and the balm we have not experienced. But I had never imagined that the greatest what-if would be my own. How would we be different now? And how many lifetimes are we given? The conventional answer is that of life we have but once to experience it. And yet can we be absolutely sure that while we are sitting on the patio drinking a glass of iced tea and watching the sun set, in another, skewed version of reality we might not be in another country entirely, weeping for the loss of a doomed, yet divinely ordained love? Our lives are littered with such possibilities, an infinite set of railroad switches leading to territory uncharted and unnamed. Is it so hard to imagine skipping to the next set of tracks? One life with layers of lives. What we dream, we do—and what we imagine, we live—in another sphere simultaneous with our own. The shadow of Walter Mitty, a hint of things grander and finer, falls across our way, and one hopes that neither choice nor circumstance conspires to rob us of our dreams. All is possible. And the only lie is the one we refuse to tell.

I woke in recovery with a feeling of irrevocable loss, then woke again in my room on the third floor as Dora wrapped a blood pressure cuff around my arm.

"Hey, sweetheart," I mumbled.

"Tsk, tsk," she said, "you're healthy enough for now. There's no need to start that old thing."

"I danced with you," I said.

"Yes," she said gravely. "You did. Once upon a time."

"For our anniversary."

"Of course."

"The kids were throwing us a party."

She took the cuff from my arm, placed her stethoscope around her neck. "Joan will be here in a minute."

Joan? Who's Joan?

I knew quite well, of course, and later that night I would attempt to draw her into bed, an attempt doomed to failure from the start. In the meantime, the curtains had been parted, and while the poisons of my own body bred and manufactured more of themselves, I saw the tatters of ragged clouds scudding through a hazy afternoon sky. What was keeping me from that murky twilight garage, my life with Dora, our children, and the celebration of life as it can be imagined? I closed my eyes, hoping to will my way back to them, envious of Frank Baxter and his gift of dreaming: his ability to construct a mirage and believe it wholly.

◉ ◉ ◉

I once knew a man.

IV. Financial Planning in the New Millennium

Here's the thing: my wife and I went through something of a bad patch. The cars broke, the house needed a roof, all our cards were maxed. Every debt came due. Our investments—tech stocks and startups—went out like candles at a four-year-old's birthday. Our accountant couldn't believe our luck. Forget the petty stuff. Baby needs shoes, not a chance; our babies needed braces, while my teeth were falling out faster than my hair. We were swamped. Every big ticket, punched, just like that. A happy suburban family at Christmas, we were bankrupt by June, pariahs, unable to look our neighbors in the eye. When the movers came, we were grateful to have it over and done.

"Take every stick," I said, "and burn it in the fireplace of hell."

I was a little theatrical. Maybe a little crazed.

"My God, my God, why hast thou forsaken me?" I said, pulling at my hair.

The moving guys had seen it before. They rolled their eyes, flexed their knees, then hoisted our bedframe and dresser into the truck. It wasn't the first time, you could tell, that they had seen a family go from bad to worse.

"You had yourself a nice place here," one of them said. He stood in what had been our kitchen drinking tap water. "But a place is a place, and there's always another one."

So we moved across town to an apartment complex that had seen better days.

"Wonderful choice," Suzi said. "Why would I trust you? Why would I do that? What was I thinking?"

I admit, there was something a little Third World about it. The loose plaster, blistered paint, and so on. Our attorney had suggested it, that bastard, and I hadn't bothered to inspect it, my head was in such a whirl.

"You're punishing us, aren't you?"

"I don't know," I said. "You could look at it as a kind of adventure."

Our daughters drew close to our legs. When Suzi saw the two hookers unlocking an apartment upstairs, she started unpacking boxes looking for something to drink. She never takes more than a glass of white wine with dinner, but when she found a bottle of vodka, she tipped it up like an old lush.

"I can't do it," she said, wiping her mouth. "I'm thirty-six years old, and my life is over. There are the girls to think about."

"Poor Mommy," said the four-year-old.

"What has Daddy done now?" Our seven-year-old was patting her mother's shoulder and giving me the glare from the metal in her mouth.

"I didn't do a thing," I said. "Honest."

"This will not do," Suzi said. The door of the upstairs apartment remained open, and the laughter of sex drifted out. "This absolutely will not do."

She took the girls to the pay phone in front of the corner liquor store, and an hour later I was driving them to the train station. She had the money her father, the not-quite-Orthodox rabbi, had wired for tickets. The old sharpy could pull ten thousand from the front pocket of his pants and wonder what had happened to the rest.

"This is awfully sudden," I said. "Isn't it?"

"On the contrary. I was too slow by half." She bit her lip. "You're welcome to come, you know."

"Oh, sure," I said, "wouldn't that be pleasant—having coffee in the dining room with the Prince of Egypt himself. 'Moses, have a little more kugel?' No, I don't think so."

"Your choice," she said, her mouth a grim line.

"Look," I said. The train had rolled to a stop next to the station and the girls were fascinated, edging toward the conductor and his little step, their father no longer of much interest or note. "Look," I said, "I admit it, I've been a little depressed, and I guess you know the reasons, but this is still America. Land of the free, home of the brave. God blesses the righteous and prospers the faithful. Where the only failure is the one who gives up."

"If you say so." She was climbing into one of the cars, following the excited trail of our children, but she turned to me one last time. "I think you need to rethink a few things. Alone."

And she was gone. I waited on the siding until the train pulled out. The girls planted their faces against the window like a pair of suction-cup car toys, but Suzi refused to look at me. She stared straight ahead, and all I got was the edge of her profile, sharpened by bitterness and disappointment.

"Okay," I said, "if that's how you want it." I sucked my cheek where I could feel a molar beginning to crumble along with my resolve. "I'll go it alone then."

◉ ◉ ◉

You're probably thinking that it couldn't have been that bad, that I'm exaggerating. No one can go from prosperity to the poorhouse that quickly. Or maybe you think we were lavish spenders, victims of our own desires. But no and no. It was that bad. And yet I never had cable, never had a TV as good as the ones in a cheap motel! I can't begin to tell you how it all happened. One minute we had a mortgage and the next we had a lawyer. But my plan was to work hard, pay the leftover bills, reestablish our credit, and buy a better house than the one we had been forced to leave. Once everything was settled, I would give Suzi a call, tell her the good news, and—*happy ending, fade to black!*—wait for the hero's reward. Suzi could be very grateful. She could also be inventive. How long could it take? When I said to Suzi that in America only the failures give up, I meant that America is a place where you can reinvent yourself every morning, and if you can't reinvent yourself in America you're just not trying. This wasn't God's country for nothing. I could be as positive as the next guy, especially if I was just pretending, which is the definition of faith. So I went to work each morning with a smile on my lips but an ache in my heart that grew wider and deeper as the hours wore on. I came home late at night to my empty and suspect apartment, ate beans from a can, fell asleep to my cracked TV set with the picture that rolled and the programs I hated, only to wake from a dream in which I wore a T-shirt captioned "God Bless Chapter Seven. At least I have a shirt to wear." And on and on.

◉ ◉ ◉

It wasn't all bad news, of course: I had a job. Some of the best bankrupts I know have been steadily employed with a surprising income but, like Suzi and me, ran into bad times. And since our financial troubles, I've had two jobs, can you believe it? By day I teach second grade at Dryden Elementary, and then, Wednesday through Sunday, when the day is over, I change clothes and wait tables at Carmazza's as though I have been thrown back into college and my twenties all over again. My principal, Mrs. Nedney, was not impressed.

"Nicely done, Mr. Walters," she said as I lowered a tray of food to her table. "You look as though you have a future after all."

"It's just for a little extra money," I said. "You know what I've gone through. I'm trying to cover my expenses."

Her blue helmet of hair bobbed above her plate of penne. "So long as it doesn't interfere with school duties, I don't suppose it really matters." She arched her eyebrows, as though something had just now occurred to her. "Still, it's not entirely *professional*, now is it? I'm not sure how it *looks*."

"You'd like a little more Parmesan with that, wouldn't you?"

"We have to consider what the parents of your students will think. The reputation of the district is at stake."

"Maybe a complimentary glass of Chianti?"

"It's wonderful to see you grasp the situation so quickly."

So now, when I am leading my charges to the playground and I pass Mrs. Nedney in the hallways, she sniffs the air as though there is garlic and tomato paste clinging to my skin and clothes, and maybe she's right. I can count on seeing the foxy old lady at least two evenings a week when she bellies up to her free plate of pasta, her free glass of wine—all in the name of district policy— my one-dollar gratuity already on the table. She has tipped off most of the trustees as well, so I have become a model of industry and the school board's favorite faculty member. Each night I saw one or another of my employers and I found another tooth floating against my tongue, ready to be swallowed. Proving that America may be the land of opportunity as I had once proclaimed, but it is also, if you have no money, the land of blackmail and emotional thuggery.

And yet, despite Mrs. Nedney's occasional extortions, I nearly doubled my income, which you may see as a sad commentary on our educational system. I sent a small check to Suzi each month, but the bills seemed to be expanding exponentially, and I wondered if I would have to claim bankruptcy in the midst of insolvency. How does it happen? What did God have against me? I never bought a thing, nothing I could recall. At this rate I would have to take a third job, forego sleep, and pray that

Mrs. Nedney and the school board president were not on the prowl at three in the morning.

◉ ◉ ◉

So I sank and I sank, and although I never knew a moment's peace, I pretended that it was only a matter of time before my luck would change. Then Suzi called. Her father had been very gracious, the children were fine, and she was working part-time in a warehouse bookstore. And then the pleasantries ended.

"Loren," she said, "I don't know how to tell you this."

"But you'll find a way," I said. "You always do."

"Don't," she said. "Don't be that way, please."

"I suppose you need something extra this month. What is it? Opera tickets? Sixty-dollar sunglasses for the seven-year-old?"

She inhaled deeply, her breath audible two hundred miles away. "I know how much you've counted on the two of us getting back together again."

"Uh-oh," I said. "This has an ominous ring to it. Who is he?"

"I'm so sorry," she said. "I can't tell you how sorry."

"One of your father's associate schmoozers, I bet."

"I feel so horrible. I never thought it would turn out like this."

"I can't believe you'd fall for one of those Old Testament types. You know you can't stand beards."

But it was even worse than I had imagined: a realtor who had made his millions in the East Bay hills, then cashed out to enter rabbinical school. He was virtuous, sensitive, and kind, and he knew when enough was enough.

"He says there's more to life than accumulation," Suzi said, "and it was time to work on his soul."

"Spoken," I said, "like a man who has plenty stashed away."

"Oh, I knew you wouldn't understand. How could you?"

"Good question."

But I understood all I wanted to. Suzi and the kids would be cared for, they'd never want for money again, and her father would be dancing in his handsome alligator shoes so happy would he be. Against such compelling arguments in her favor, what chance did I stand?

"Don't hate me, Loren," she said. "I didn't plan for this to happen, but now that it has, I think it's all for the best. These things happen for a reason."

"Of course," I said. "You can hear the happiness in my voice, can't you? Congratulations. *Mazel tov.* Whatever."

I can't tell you much of the rest of the conversation. She had the details pretty well figured out, wanting neither assets, of which there were none, nor alimony, which I couldn't have paid. The divorce would be a snap. And I was free to visit any time. But, she said, given my current economic situation, joint custody would be out of the question. I had no time to spend with the girls anyway, did I? Of course not. I was never home, working stiff that I was.

"Just say the word, Loren, and you're welcome to stay here at the house, stay as long as you like. Aaron insists that the girls need to know their father, that you continue to be a part of their lives. It's just that I would like it to be in a more appropriate context."

"One bad housing move," I said, "and it's never forgotten, is it?"

"It was a bad day," she said, "and it lasted six months, but now it's over. I can get on with my life. And so can you."

I didn't tell her how grateful I was. How could I?

"Your father's second banana is Aaron," I said. "Why am I not surprised?"

◉ ◉ ◉

This last bit of news sent me reeling. Although, as I said, I wasn't surprised. Her father hated me, the lapsed Baptist who had stolen his only daughter, carried her off to the dry plains of disinterested Christendom. His sugar plum! His *latke*! He hated me the first time Suzi brought me home, he hated me when we were married at the courthouse, and if his animosity toward me has diminished, it is only since the divorce papers were filed and signed.

Suzi and I met in college, and while I can't say it was love at first sight, it didn't take more than a second or third glance before we had swapped roommates. She wasn't the prettiest girl I knew: there was the faintest down above her upper lip, her ankles were a shade too thick, her laughter caused heads to turn, but she had recently lost twenty pounds, she was energetic and funny and warm, and she invited me to bed with a whoop and a holler, unacquainted with the Protestant guilt that dogged me like a stalker. Decent lives have been constructed of flimsier stuff, and let's be honest, I was no matinee idol myself. I understood my luck. We had our moments of sweetness anyway: sitting with the children at the breakfast table during an unexpected hail storm, for instance. Suzi held my hand. We watched our children, the products of our coupling, dancing outside in boots and umbrellas, while the heavens showered white upon the new spring grass and the swaying fronds of our backyard palms. Our girls looked back at us framed in the kitchen window as though we were the safe haven in the midst of storm, and Suzi put her hand in my lap to give me a squeeze of things to come. We had no idea how tenuous a thing such stability was.

But I suspect now that as much as Suzi once loved me, once loved the life we had created, I was merely a supporting actor in a drama of her own construction. And when our bank balance and credit were ruined, our hedge against misfortune destroyed, she was willing to admit that she might have been wrong, that her life was an illusion after all: she went back home to her father, to marry the one selected for her and lead the life of her father's choosing. The rebel returned to the fold. But it's a fact that Hollywood never tells the story of the character who's left behind, and I had no idea where to turn.

◎ ◎ ◎

You will recall that on our first day in the Villa Tropicana, Suzi took one look at our surroundings, after which she found her way to the hootch packed away by the movers then packed herself and the kids off to the train. Remember the hookers in the apartment upstairs? Cassandra and Monique led regular lives, as it turned out. Their door opened at ten each morning, and their customers—furtive, embarrassed, faces hardly above the pavement—arrived throughout the day. Their lights were seldom extinguished before three in the morning, and it was a rare evening when either of them had time to step onto the balcony for a smoke or to watch the lights flicker on the surface of the swimming pool. Oh, but their business was good! They met their customers at the door in hot pants and halters, inviting them inside as if they had waited, and waited longingly, for this moment to arrive.

After Suzi's phone call, I thought it might be nice to be wanted once again. It was the least I deserved, that was my reasoning. So I stuffed my pockets with a week's worth of restaurant cash and trudged up the shaky flight of stairs, only to be met mid-flight by an old guy in blue blazer and gray flannel trousers, the two women having bid him a fond farewell.

"You're smiling, I see," I said. "But when there are two of them and one of you, I suppose that's as it should be."

"Oh, they're very resourceful," he said, and there was no doubt that he had a bounce to his voice if not his step. He was gripping the handrail so tightly his legs must have been turned to rubber. "They're very thorough."

"I bet they are," I said. His cheeks and forehead were flushed, and perspiration dotted his upper lip. "Though you always have to worry about heart attack or stroke."

"Oh, no. It's very gentle. You're in good hands. I shouldn't worry too much." He began to edge around me, but I admit that I blocked his progress.

"One last thing," I said, "and then I'll let you go. You come here pretty often, I take it."

His mouth spread into something like a leer. "Whenever I need to," he said, and then he turned serious. "It's best not to let these things fester too long. That's where the damage gets done."

"Of course," I said, stepping aside.

Monique, the shorter of the two women, greeted me at the door, pulling me inside with both hands.

"Finally, you arrive. We almost gave up," she said.

Monique wore a halter and a matching pair of hot pants made of some sort of iridescent lime green fabric. Her belly was flat, a gold chain encircled her waist, and a diamond stud glittered from her navel. A tattoo of Benjamin Franklin fluttered above her left breast like a flag. "We've been watching for you, but we'd just about given up. Isn't that right?"

Wearing much the same uniform, Cassandra lounged on a chintz-covered sofa. She wore reading glasses while leafing through a vintage copy of *Cosmo*. "Oh," she said, measuring me over the tops of her glasses, "there wasn't much doubt."

The front room of their apartment (two apartments, actually, since the adjoining wall had been knocked out) was more spacious than my own, and walking up the shabby staircase and through their door was not unlike facing a warehouse only to find the Casbah inside.

"This is quite a place," I said.

"We're happy here," Monique said. "It suits us."

"Well," I said, "judging by the foot traffic, time is money, isn't it? Do I pay you now or later?" I pulled a wad of bills from my trousers.

"First things first," Monique said. "Your checkbook, please."

"I prefer to pay by cash," I said. "No offense, but there's no reason to leave a paper trail, is there? Would you be surprised if I said that I'm not completely comfortable being here? I'm something of a novice, after all."

"Oh, comfort is what you want," she said. She put her arms around my waist and moved in close enough that Ben Franklin rubbed against my ribs, and I could smell her perfume, a complex scent from the base of her throat that brought to mind bank vaults and stacks of currency, safety deposit boxes and stock certificates. "I'll give you comfort, but I need your checkbook. I can't help you otherwise," she breathed.

"I'll get it back?"

"Of course, you will," she said. "Getting it back is the whole point."

◉ ◉ ◉

Our rendezvous was not remarkable. I might have called it perfunctory, notable only for its brevity, and five minutes after we were through, I couldn't have been sure it had taken place at all.

"You see," she said. "That didn't take long."

"Well, as far as the factory model goes, you're efficient as they come." I looked underneath the bed for my clothes. "So I suppose I should get myself together and go. Make way for the second shift."

"Stay put there, mister," she said, putting her finger against my lips. "We haven't even started yet. I am going to take you places you've never been."

"That's very kind," I said, "but I should probably warn you that I've had my share of stress recently, and I don't know about my powers of recovery."

She put one finger against her own lips in the universal signal to shut up and listen. We were in a room at the back of the apartment in which an enormous bed was the only furniture. Now that we were finished, she sat cross-legged next to me, a pillow in her lap, as she riffled through the carbons in the checkbook.

"Good lord," she said, pointing to a purchase of CDs and videos.

"Be still my heart," she said, holding out a reminder of my latest splurge at the florist, my one idea for winning Suzi back.

"Uh, uh, uh," she said. "Pete's Meats?"

A dwarf of a man had come door-to-door, selling boxes of frozen steaks. One leg shorter than the other, he was limping from apartment to apartment, up and down our dilapidated stairs, hauling around his built-up shoe like penance, and I had bought thirty pounds on the monthly plan. It had seemed noble at the time, like a good idea on my part.

"Hopeless," she said, shaking her head. "Your retirement plan has 'street corner' written all over it. And I'll bet your credit cards are melted around the edges. And this after a bankruptcy."

"I've seen worse," she said at last. We had moved to the kitchen table in matching robes, so that she could work a little more easily. "Not many. But a few."

"I came here for guilty pleasures," I said, "and I certainly have gotten what I came for. Comfort me anymore, and I'll go ahead and shoot myself."

She squinted at me from across the table. "Self-pity is not an admirable trait."

"I couldn't agree more," I said. "Is it any wonder I hate myself?"

"Now look here, here's your problem," Monique said. She was holding an old book of checks, one that I hadn't gotten around to balancing. I guess it had been several months.

"There's just one?" I said. "I thought there must be at least a dozen."

"Oh, at least that," she said. "Maybe dozens and dozens, but when you come right down to it, they're all the *same* problem."

"And that would be?"

"You want stuff. But you don't want to pay for it."

"There's a news flash," I said. "Who doesn't?"

"You gonna be a bank robber?" she said. She punched me on the shoulder, but I felt it in my groin. "You think you're Jesse James or something?"

"No, of course not."

"You don't think you buy anything, do you?"

"Just the necessities," I said. "I live simpler than most. I have a lot of bills."

"Guess what? The bills come from somewhere. That's what I'm saying. You want; you pay. No free lunch, no free ride. I ask you, Cassie, what's the matter with these people?"

"Goodness knows," said Cassandra, whose perusal of a month-old *People* magazine had taken on the intensity of research.

Monique said: "No one seems to know the meaning of thrift anymore."

◉ ◉ ◉

Monique set up a ledger system for me with all of my expenses identified. She cut up my credit cards, impounded the checkbook, and gave me forms for direct deposit.

"We help those who can't help themselves," she said, "and you qualify in spades."

Each month she paid my bills and gave me a small allowance. "But when it's gone, it's gone," she said. "Don't even think about coming to me for extra. You haven't had an ounce of discipline, and your only hope is tough love. You've heard of tough love, haven't you? Well, in your case it's only going to be tough."

Each week I climbed their rickety staircase for counseling. After that brief first session, sex was no longer part of the equation, if it ever was. My eagerness, instead, was for their kitchen table, where most of our time was spent cataloguing the sins represented by my receipts: spending too much for a pair of shoes, a CD I didn't need, processed food that was too expensive not to mention unhealthful.

"When are you going to grow up?" she said.

"I don't know," I said. "It's ridiculous, isn't it?"

"I mean, my god in heaven, what in the world do you need with *NSYNC? You're not a twelve-year-old girl."

"No, but I have one who'll be that age soon enough."

"Her stepfather can buy it. He's rich. You ever hear of quality time? Beats buying crap like that. I suppose you're going to blame your daughters for this register tape full of Twinkies and Cheetos? You're a bad boy, and at the rate you're going I don't see you getting better any time soon."

I hung my head. "You're right. Absolutely. I'm a mess."

"I rant and I rave, and nothing seems to get through. What am I going to do with you?"

"You should probably yell at me for the loafers. Nugent's was selling them for twenty dollars less."

"Keep talking," she said, "and I'll get the whips and chains."

In the months that followed, order was slowly restored: my debts were repaid dollar by dollar, and Monique set up savings goals, a retirement account, and an investment portfolio. She recommended mutual funds for security and blue chips and commercial real estate for speculation. "Just remember," she said, "old money is safe money." Monique took twenty-five cents of every dollar saved and fifty cents of every dollar earned as interest or dividend, and she was ruthless in our mutual self-interest. So even after my finances had turned the corner and I could see my way clear to something like comfort, I maintained my weekly appointment. I confessed my sins of commission, and then, when my spanking was through, I went back home to my apartment filled with a virtue I had never known previously. Even Suzi noticed the difference. We were arranging a visit for me and the girls, and I offered to take them to the boardwalk at Santa Cruz.

"We'll be out of your hair," I said. "You and Aaron can catch a movie or go to dinner. You could make love without being interrupted. I remember how they are."

"You're not taking anything, are you, Loren?" she said. "I mean, you haven't gotten into anything illegal, have you? Or is this the Prozac talking?"

"Not unless pay-as-you-go is illegal in a country run on credit," I said.

Maybe I had sold my soul, and all of us who trudged upstairs to see our angels of mercy were deluded. But if it's true that one cannot serve both God and mammon, then we were on God's side, weren't we?

Yesterday, as I made my way downstairs from my weekly session—I had purchased one hundred shares of Microsoft even after their latest troubles, so my knees were buckling from shame and Monique's disapproval—I nearly fell into Mal McBride, our attorney who had, once upon a time, recommended this place.

"Mal," I said, "you old panderer. What a surprise to see a horse trader like you haunting the Tropicana."

"Ah, it's not good, not good," he said. And it was true, he did not look at all well: his ruddy Irish face was gray and the pouches underneath his eyes were as blue and puffy as garden slugs. He was climbing the stairs with difficulty, a wheeze attending each step.

"To be honest, you've got the look of a man in crisis," I said.

"It's bad, all right. Worse than I ever thought."

"There's nothing that can't be fixed," I said. "I'm living proof of that."

I gave him my newly restored smile. You know, these dentists are such magicians nowadays. They can screw teeth back into your jaw.

He gripped my forearm with surprising strength and looked me straight in the eye. "After twenty years of the straight and narrow, I couldn't talk myself out of it," he said, nearly to the point of tears. "I bought a boat. I knew better but I did it anyway. It was so beautiful, and I couldn't resist."

I put his arm around my neck and shoulders, my arm around his waist, and then together we climbed one stair at a time toward the doorway of our salvation.

◉

My Fresno Book of Death and Disposal

Kill your darlings.

—ANTON CHEKHOV (*maybe*) or
—WILLIAM FAULKNER (*possibly*) or
—ARTHUR QUILLER-COUCH (*unfortunately*)

Alive one minute and dead the next.

—WILLIAM SAROYAN,
"The Man with the Heart in the Highlands"

YOU LIVE A LIFE, YOU MEET ANY NUMBER OF PEOPLE. All with their life stories and their generational histories and family contexts. Their flaws and failings of character, as well as their private braveries and hidden virtues. Here is one example: my Fresno neighbor, Henry Carlyle, once taught a young man who was extremely bright but terribly naïve and unable to handle abstractions. He struggled with Raskolnikov's moral journey, for example, incapable of seeing any connection between Dostoevsky's fictional dilemmas and real life. While still in his early twenties, this former student went to work as an assistant for a woman who was a chemist and owned an agricultural research lab. By all accounts, she was no great beauty—she looked like a Russian jail matron, in fact—but she was smart and energetic and ambitious. She exuded a powerful and formidable presence, call it charisma or pheromones, and Henry's former student, Jason, found himself powerless to resist.

Her husband, on the other hand, was resisting. The marriage had deteriorated. Over the years, she had heaped abuse upon him until he could take it no longer; he filed for divorce and he sued for custody of their children, and the judge was leaning in his favor. When it appeared that he would get his way, she enlisted Jason's help. They went to the front door of the husband's apartment and used a stun gun to subdue him and then drove him, barely conscious, to a storage facility in an industrial park where they dumped him into a barrel filled with acid. The police found her estranged husband—or the pieces of him that hadn't entirely liquified—five days later and only because Jason broke almost immediately under questioning. Was his involvement a matter of employment, love, or sorcery?

Henry visited him once. Was it compassion or prurient interest? Jason told Henry that he feared for his own life if he didn't do as she expected. But he also acknowledged that fear wasn't his only motivating impulse. She had called him *dearest* and *sweet cheeks*, she had intimated that a new life was about to be theirs together, and as embarrassing as it was to admit it, he confessed that such endearments and promises had had their effect upon him.

During her trial, however, she claimed that the murder and disposal of her husband had been entirely Jason's doing, a result of his obsession with her, that she had been horrified at what he had done but had been terrified by what he might do to her if she objected. This despite the fact that she had ordered the stun gun in her name as well as the vat of acid, which she claimed was for "business use." She deflected and demurred and denied. She refused to take any responsibility for her estranged husband's death. She blamed her young assistant for everything, and despite her lack of cooperation, she received a life sentence, rather than the death penalty, due to her gender and the fact that she was a mother. Jason, on the other hand, answered all of the detectives' questions, he pointed them to the storage facility where they found the drum and the bits and pieces of the husband that hadn't dissolved, and he readily confessed his involvement because, after all, he really was a good person at heart, and his conscience would not allow the untruth to continue. And yet, for all his cooperation, he, too, received a life sentence.

"I don't think that's fair, do you?" he said. "I mean, you don't think that anyone really believed her, do you? About me, I mean."

"I'm not sure that fairness has a lot to do with it," Henry said, "murder being what it is. I see what you mean, but still . . ."

Henry pointed out that with two trials, two judges, and two different juries, anything could have happened. The two trials were not like tests for which they had each received the same grade after providing wildly different answers.

"You're not in school now," Henry said, "and you ought to be able to see fairness for the fiction that it is."

"I suppose."

"Don't you remember anything we read?"

Henry told me how confused Jason seemed; as he hung up the phone behind the glass, he looked about ten years older as he stared into a future that had no more promise than an unfertilized egg.

◎ ◎ ◎

That was not his first experience with a crime motivated by certain passions. At the beginning of his brief academic tenure, Henry had an older colleague who taught public administration and who had made a name for himself by designing communal living spaces for the next millennium. A native of Manhattan who was accustomed to apartment buildings, doormen, and superintendents, Dr. G wanted to buy a place in which to live, but the thought of a yard left him anxious. He believed that renting was for the financially irresponsible, and as there were no apartments available for purchase, he bought a tract house in what was then a new subdivision, but rather than deal with landscaping and maintenance, he had the front and back yards covered in adobe pavers. No grass, no shrubs, no flowers. Once a month he sprayed the gaps between the pavers with Roundup to prevent weeds. His yard was sterile even if he was notorious among the other members of his department for neglecting to bathe. He lived alone, but twice a month, during a sabbatical semester, he drove three and a half hours to West Hollywood, where he picked up willing young men and entertained them in various motel rooms. During one such assignation, his date turned out to be more ambitious than the rest; he threatened to expose him to his employers and the *Fresno Bee* unless G paid him a substantial portion of his annual income. G did not wish to risk exposure, but he was also fundamentally a man of thrift and financial expediency. As a result, G spiked the young man's drink with the roofies he'd intended for another time and a happier occasion, smothered him with a pillow, and then the next morning, he left the inert body in the tub and a "Do Not Disturb" sign on the door to his room while he rented an electric chain saw at a nearby hardware store. He hacked the body into eight pieces while the television blared *Regis and Kathie Lee* at full volume; he washed the blood down the drain, and then returned the rental and reclaimed his deposit. Since the chain saw was electric rather than gas-powered, the noise was never reported to the police until several days later; however, since it was also under-powered for the task at hand, the dismemberment took an hour or more, and despite the Do Not Disturb door tag, G had to answer his door twice: first to assure the housekeepers that all was well despite the television—he claimed he was hard of hearing—and then from his next-door neighbor, who had been trying to sleep off a hangover in spite of what sounded to him like an extraordinarily loud Irish hair dryer.

G transported the pieces of his victim to his car using his suitcase and then disposed of them in various rest area trash cans along I-5 and Highway 99. The pieces were wrapped in newspaper and sealed with duct tape. Suspicions were not aroused until the clerk at the hardware store observed what seemed to be human flesh still caught in the chain and called the police. G never thought of himself as a murderer or criminal; after all, he had used his real name and his Fresno address for the rental and the motel room. When detectives came to the door of the tract house, he answered their questions politely—and more to the point—truthfully. He told them which rest areas they should check before they could even break out the Miranda card. When they searched his house, they found boxes of pornography and the materials necessary to sound-proof the spare bedrooms, where the windows, which faced the street, had already been blacked out. Forensics teams pulled up the pavers, anticipating gruesome answers to other unsolved cases, but their searches yielded nothing new, and the pavers remained scattered in the yard for months as the dirt dried and hardened, the weeds flourished, and the crime scene tape attracted gawkers. The murder, G insisted, was not a *habit*, after all, only a necessity.

As I say, Henry knew *of* G, he knew him by reputation more than he knew him in any personal way. They were colleagues at opposite ends of an enormous campus, and they occupied such different academic strata (he was a full professor and of long-standing tenure, while Henry was a lecturer of the briefest duration, with no job security whatsoever) and from departments so different, they might as well have spoken other languages. But, oddly enough, not long after leaving their previous home in Tempe, Henry and his wife moved into a house two blocks from G's adobe-paved compound, and what they had initially viewed as an oddity (the pavers, the blacked-out front windows) was revealed to be something both more sinister and more innocent. G became legend: the fodder for riddles and the subject of party conversation for years to come.

How many police officers does it take to judge a sabbatical project?

How many reminders does an absent-minded, hygiene-challenged professor need in order to clean the chain?

◉ ◉ ◉

Let me start over. This is actually my story, although it may not appear so, at least not at the beginning. Doesn't every story belong to the narrator? It doesn't begin as my story, but somehow it becomes so all the same. Henry and his wife moved into our cracker box neighborhood, just north of the university and its farmland, driving a U-Haul and towing an ancient, graduate school Rabbit. This was in the Clinton years of the mid-'90s. The sun was still high in its three o'clock position, and the air was hot and still, brown with haze, exhaust, and dust. From a position on my knees in the front yard, I saw Henry and Liz emerge from the cab of the truck. A sprinkler had broken, I was in mud to my elbows, and here was this kid in a yellow polo shirt bouncing up and down in bright white Nikes and sticking out a hand to shake. By kid, I mean Henry Carlyle, and he might have been thirty, but at my advanced age of forty, he was a kid to me. A boy. He *seemed* like a kid to me because he *acted* like a kid, with an adolescent's self-absorption and self-centeredness. He had just finished his doctorate in modern American lit with a dissertation on Dreiser and Dostoevsky, he had a five-year non-tenure-track lectureship at the neighborhood university, and he was excited about this new phase of his life and career, etc., etc., etc. He might as well have been wearing a tie and a blazer with a Greek pin, he was that irritating. That self-obsessed. Lots of chatter. Oh, he was a wunderkind, he was. On the fast track to a tenured position and advanced rank. Maybe a spot in administration and a rackful of suits. Our neighborhood was twenty years old by then, and I assumed Henry and his wife wouldn't be here long, since it was only a way station for the young and upwardly mobile, a demographic which I had not been invited to join. I was called to yard work instead; some of the PVC pipe and pop-ups had never been replaced. Such home repair and maintenance were never high on my list of priorities, but there I was, dealing with a social call with my knees wet and the sun in my eyes.

His wife walked around the front end of the U-Haul.

"Henry," she said, "you have the keys. To the house." Her voice was challenging, and when she said house, she might as well have said "hovel" there was that much dismissal attached. There were lines from her nose to the corners of her mouth that made her seem not only stern but robotic, and I could tell that she was some years older than her husband. Light years more mature. Instead of moving out to Woodward Lakes with the rest of the administrative class, they had bought the McCrorys' house for a song, and I found out later that this was Liz all over. She was practical in the extreme. After Bill McCrory choked on a piece of steak while having a heart attack, his wife had sold the house, their only daughter's childhood home, for practically nothing, so intent was she on that elusive thing called closure.

"Elisabeth," Henry said. "Liz, this is our neighbor—?" He looked at me expectantly.

I told them my name and, gesturing toward the hole in the ground and the running garden hose, apologized for being sweaty and dirty and not fit for social interaction.

"Sure," she said and stalked off once he had thrown her his key ring.

"It was a long drive," Henry said to me, an explanation for her retreating back. "A long drive, and the AC quit in Blythe."

"Ah," I said.

"She doesn't deal with heat very well."

"This may not be the place for her then," I said.

"Well," he said, smiling in a way that seemed a bit idiotic. "It wasn't my idea. It was her job that brought us."

◉ ◉ ◉

"I didn't want to come here," Henry said.

"That's what we all say," I said, "except for the ones who were born here. The natives. Even if they leave, they come back, and then you can't get them away with dynamite."

We were sitting on lawn chairs on my back patio. The overhang was extra-wide and the shade was deep, and the misters were running full-tilt. I had taken a shower and put on some clean clothes while Henry carried their suitcases into the empty house. Liz had declined the invitation—she said she could feel the start of a migraine—so Henry and I were the life and membership of the party. Their belongings baked in the back of the U-Haul in their driveway while the rooftop air conditioner roared on the shakes next door.

"I don't understand," Henry said.

"It's a fact," I said. "Anyone who's born here comes back sooner or later. Anyone who comes here as an adult does so involuntarily and stays for reasons that can only be called mysterious."

Take me, for example. I had come to Fresno from Los Angeles. For a girl. She left. I stayed. And I was always running into those Fresno natives who got away but then came back, and they could never answer me why. Any more than I could answer why I stayed when she left. Why? Why? Why? The natives nodded their heads with their hands jammed into their jeans. They shrugged. They were embarrassed, I could tell, but it didn't change matters any. When someone asked me why I had stayed after the breakup, I pretended not to hear. I could have recited the facts. How Jeanine had gotten a finance job with one of the investment firms at the north end of town. She called it the job of her dreams and invited me to share in the bounty. We were friends from college who were occasionally more than friends until we either got bored with each other or got on each other's nerves. We liked each other well enough, but we had almost nothing in common except our respective needs of the social and sexual varieties. She was aggressive and ambitious and driven, and I worked temp jobs in order to write or tear up what I had written as the case might be. When, after five years, Jeanine said that her firm had offered her a promotion in their Houston office, she gave me the choice: come with her or stay in the cracker box starter home that she had paid for and was hanging onto as an investment. Did it matter where I ruined paper? I hate cockroaches and humidity, and our tolerance for each other was just about at an end, so I opted for the Bermuda grass and stucco and watched while the movers carted her stuff, which was everything but the Olivetti, away. When she left, I walked from room to room and listened to the different timbre of the echoes. Her name was the only one on the title of the house, but she didn't ask for much in the way of rent; I had told her that I would pay her for the taxes and the insurance, but there were some years when even that slipped. She didn't hound me, which told me how magnanimous she was and how irrelevant the house and I were to her. So my only real obligation was to make sure the house didn't fall down. I gave the shutters and trim a coat of paint now and then and swept the front porch. I took the garbage out on Monday evenings and waved to the neighbors, who seemingly changed every few years, and year after year went by as the neighborhood got older and newer neighbors brought younger and younger children. Since her departure, Jeanine had moved three more times to increasingly affluent markets, and the last time she called, she was in Boston and joking about either giving me the house or evicting me.

"You're too comfortable," she had said, "with the way things are. I ought to shake things up."

"You do you," I said. "It's your house."

I imagined her on a settee in her Beacon Hill rowhouse with a man-drink of some kind in hand and a boy-toy associate on a leash.

"Nah," she said, "I like knowing where you are."

"That's okay, too," I said, but then had one of those dawning realizations. You know, the kind of insight everyone else in the world has known but you were too dumb to see on your own. The fact was that as long as I had the house, I'd always be afraid to move because I didn't want to lose the little I had. The same fear that kept me from moving kept me from writing anything except the sort of thing that I knew was hopeless, those stories and novels that would either get thrown away or rejected over and over and over again.

I was stuck. In a rut of my own making.

I couldn't move; I could only move back.

I had become a native.

"You're a writer?" Henry said. It was a question, but he said it as though no one could have believed it. "And here I thought you were a gardener."

☉ ☉ ☉

What I didn't know at first was that Liz was a hospital administrator, and she'd been hired to put the organizational affairs of the downtown hospital in order. Henry's appointment, as it turned out, was merely a time-limited incentive to get her to come. I never could figure her out. She was probably my age, with a sharp nose and a pinched, foxlike face. In addition to the lines from nose to mouth, she had three lines that radiated from the bridge of her nose, as though she'd been squinting into a bright sun since birth. She left the house at six each morning, and her hair looked like a helmet, it was that stiff. But her role was clear; she'd been brought in by the hospital board to be the hatchet-man (or hatchet-person, rather), and middle managers of departments were falling right, left, and center, departments were consolidated and reorganized, and contracts were re-opened, re-negotiated, or canceled. She had a responsible position, so responsible that there were more than a few people on staff who hated her, doctors and nurses, cafeteria workers and clerks alike. She was prominently ranked in a *Fresno Bee* article of the most powerful (and, presumably, feared) business leaders in the county. What I couldn't understand was how she'd ended up with Henry, who seemed like a child's plush toy by comparison. A black-and-white penguin in a pink bowtie, for example, with a voice box that giggled at inopportune moments. She met him while she was working at the university hospital and he was in graduate school. Why would she have picked out Henry from among the available men in Tempe when she could have done so much better? She probably thought she could mold him into the perfect mate since he had no spine of his own.

For his part, Henry ran six miles each morning, taught his classes at the university in the afternoon, and used the rest of his time to insinuate himself among the powers-that-be, working the social ropes for a tenure track slot. His chances were limited, of course, since there were no slots available, and if there were, a white male in a blue blazer and sporting a newly minted doctorate from a merely okay school would not have put him anywhere near the top of the list. He was not to be dissuaded, however, and before Liz's return from her day of firings, he often walked across the lawn in the early evenings to tell me about his latest efforts at political ingratiation. I hesitated to blunt his enthusiasm, but I felt it my duty to warn him about what he should have already known.

"These jobs don't come around every day," I said. "You realize that, right? No matter how much you butter up the eggheads?"

"Oh, sure," he said. His voice was as bland and as smug as a tofu smoothie, as though he were among the Elect and knew an entry code he wasn't allowed to share. "I'll do my time. Something will turn up."

"Great," I said. "I hope it works out."

"Oh," he said with that smile that never failed to make me cringe, "something always does."

Truly, he was a ray of his own particular sunshine.

◎ ◎ ◎

I suppose here is as good a time as any to tell you about my own blind spot. Writing, be it fiction or nonfiction or poetry, is no more embarrassing than any other gaffe or bad habit committed over a lifetime, and yet I confess my own reluctance to confess. Call it my own source of personal embarrassment. Call it what you will. I wrote every day, but after twenty years, my publication record was this bare: three stories in literary magazines that no one ever read and an interview in the city magazine, an article for which I was paid but which never ran due to liability concerns. The subject of the interview, one of our august and no-more-crooked-than-normal city councilmembers, said something factually as well as politically incorrect about Armenians. He was unwilling to have the comment excised, he demanded that it be retained, and that ended that. I deposited the check and never thought more about it. I can only imagine that he was forced to read Saroyan when he was twelve and had suffered from the experience. Poor duck.

This wasn't what I'd bargained for in college where I took all the workshops that Armando Feliz had to offer. He was a stern taskmaster, that Armando, and he had us all convinced of our superiority, that ours was the noblest of callings: to plumb the mind and heart of the human animal through the vehicle of language. His schedule reflected his priorities; he woke at noon, drank beer in a booth at his favorite dive from one until five, taught his workshops at six, and then was back at the bar with his typewriter from ten until four in the morning. His routine did not vary, even on the weekends, and on the days when he had no classes to teach, he stayed at the bar and wrote. Since this was in the 1970s and 1980s, he conducted affairs with any number of the undergraduate and graduate-school women who were willing and even a few who weren't, but they all understood that for Armando, the daily word count would always come first. His art was pure. Did I ask any questions about why he had only a slender novel, *An Upside-Down Life in D Minor*, and an even slenderer collection of stories, *Holding My Nose and Other Expressions of Contempt*? I did not. None of us did, but we worshipped at the feet of the man who demanded honesty and authenticity and self-laceration. The man who sneered at the tastes of publishers and the public. We thought him a god, a model to emulate. The real deal. If publishers didn't recognize his mastery of the fictional form, then it was an indictment of publishing and, in a curious about-face of logic, it was also the validation of his genius. What we failed to suspect or acknowledge was that he might not have been very good.

Be that as it may, I wrote every day, even though I had next to nothing to show for it. I tried the literary game, but then, in spite of Armando's example, I moved on to the genres: I wrote a couple of police procedurals and a dystopian space opera. There was even one historical romance; I was so desperate for any kind of affirmation that I assumed even the village idiot ought to be able to produce a romance of the soapy, breathy variety. But no was no, regardless of type, and yet no matter how many noes I received I couldn't stop. Armando didn't stop. Stopping would be an admission of failure. The utter failure of a life. The only thing I stopped was telling anyone else what I did with my time. "Oh," I'd say when asked, "a little of this, a little of that. Here, there, and everywhere." Henry was the only one in recent memory who'd heard the truth, and that was only because he'd caught me off-guard in the mud and muck of a summer front yard. In the mean-time, when I needed some quick cash, I took calls from a temp agency since my typing was serviceable, given my years of prac-tice. I'd even learned a thing or two about word processing and data entry. When I needed cash quick-quick, I went to the blood center and sold plasma, hobnobbed with the bums and called it research for material.

My latest project was something of an *On the Road* riff with murders, inspired, no doubt, by Henry's brush with the unthink-ing cruelty of the world: nearly 200,000 words of the roads I *hadn't* taken, all of which led back to Fresno anyway, and the people I *hadn't* killed no matter how much I might have wanted to. In that respect it had the inertia of Beckett's waiting fools more than the forward propulsion of Kerouac's Sal or the gore of Har-ris's Hannibal Lecter. I knew, long before I began, that no one was likely to read it, much less want it, but I was unable to help my-self from returning to the story. Every morning, I sat down, and while that proverb about dogs and their vomit came to mind, I pushed caution and reason aside and started to type.

◎ ◎ ◎

Four years after they moved in, the "For Sale" sign went up in the yard next door. By this time, Henry had heard the stories about Dr. G. He'd taught and then tough-loved his life-sentence student Jason. He found the ironies of their murderousness delicious and their methods entertaining. He mentioned one or the other, if not both, with every visit. Ah, he was fond of saying, "The ennobling benefits, the wisdom of the humanities!" He was something of a friend, but he was also a turd of a human being. I knew that, even when we were sharing a bottle of wine. He laughed and laughed and pretended to self-deprecation. He enjoyed his own wit, and

I suppose I enjoyed the occasional company until I realized after a month or more that his visits had unaccountably stopped, and I couldn't remember when that had happened.

There were other ironies, of course, even closer to home. Liz had done her work at the hospital so well that the board was letting her go to find new opportunities. The euphemism for bringing in someone new, someone who hadn't alienated three-quarters of the remaining staff. Her reward for doing their bidding. As I say, I hadn't seen Henry for some time, and I assumed his absence was due to the fact that he saw his five-year window closing, that he'd finally realized there wasn't a job for him, there never would be a job for him, not here, not without articles or books to his name, and he was feeling a little embarrassed, a little humiliated, and wouldn't want to hear me say *I told you so*. I never would have done that, rubbed the salt in that particular wound, no matter how irritating he was, but the issue would have been lying at our feet nonetheless. The elephant in the room, to use the cliché. As it turned out, Liz was the one who came to the door one night in February just as I was putting out the lights.

"I'm sorry," she said. "It's late, I know."

The fog had rolled in, and it circled the street lamps and the stop signs, making haloes of the yellow sodium vapor lights.

Underneath the porch light, Liz's face looked like melted wax, but even after she stepped inside, her appearance did not noticeably improve: her hair had lost its usual shellac in the moist air of a long day, and her lips were trembling.

"Are you okay?" I said. "You look like you could use a drink."

"Sure. Whatever you have. Whatever's open."

I poured some unterrible red wine into a couple of half-pint jars and handed her one.

She drained half, then said: "Have you seen Henry?"

"Not recently," I said. "He used to be over here all the time, but he's been keeping himself to himself, I guess."

She drank the second half and held out the jar for a refill.

"He has a girlfriend," she said. "He *thinks* he has a girlfriend. And he *thinks* he's in the grip of romance, or something." She said this last with something like a sneer of amazement, that anyone could be so naïve. "She was one of his students, can you believe it? He's such a fucking moron. There, I've said it. Moron. Fucking moron."

Something finally made sense to me since I have my own streak of naïveté. I am nothing if not slow. She had been gone for a week, to one of those conferences where the hotel bar is absolutely necessary because it's where the real work gets done, and when she returned, she looked as though she'd suffered from a migraine or a hangover the entire time. While she was gone, I had noticed a different car parked in the next-door driveway. It was there several nights in a row, so I had assumed that Henry had needed a rental or loaner to replace his dying Rabbit; he was forbidden to drive the Mercedes that Liz bought the day after their Fresno arrival, and because he was such an oblivious and indifferent driver, she wouldn't even give him a key. On another day, I saw a young woman standing in front of Henry and Liz's front door. She had a bob of platinum-blonde hair and looked like a Marilyn impersonator who didn't have to try very hard. I had thought at the time that if she were selling candy bars for a good cause, Henry wouldn't have dental insurance enough to cover the damage, but somehow, I never put two and two together. It was Henry, after all, and she looked like she could ignite clothes just by wearing them.

Liz drank, and I drank but not as much since my job was to pour while she talked and vented her bitterness. They had come here to this awful town, she said, because her job also included a job for him. A little something to sweeten the pot from the hospital that was now in the process of firing her. And now her moron-mannequin of a husband was off playing the fool.

"Here's what he never tells anyone," Liz said. "When we were in Tempe, he diddled one of his little freshman comp girls. Or, rather, let me rephrase that: he *didn't* diddle her. He *wanted* to, but he was too *afraid*." Her bitterness managed to refer to both his desire for infidelity as well as the weakness of his nature. There were notes and gifts, phone calls in the middle of the night and letters. Nuzzling each other's necks. Kisses in the back row of a theater during a three o'clock show. But he had never crossed the line. Not entirely. "And now he's at it again. With this new one. What kind of college girl calls herself Hélène Jean-Marie de Vincennes, pretends to be French nobility and a prodigy in equine genetics?" She shuddered. "I don't believe it. She's a goddamn junior in college and a piece of work. When I caught him copying Neruda sonnets onto cardstock, he blushed, so I had him tailed. She waits tables at one of those leather banquette restaurants on Shaw and puts on her French airs to charm all the sixty-year-old farmers out of their tip money. Their tongues practically drag on the floor when she brings them water. Three years ago, her name was Carla Walker. She was the Raisin Queen in Selma, and she was riding on a float made out of toilet paper. That's as close to nobility as she'll ever get. She can have her horses. And ride them, too, for all I care."

"I don't know anything about anything," I said. "I didn't know about the girl, I swear. But you know Henry better than I do."

"There's nothing to know," she said. "And I ought to know because I know Henry: there's no there there. No depths to plumb except white teeth, a razor cut, and the clothes he bought with my paycheck."

Two hours later, she had passed out on my futon, and as far as I could tell there was no sign of Henry next door. This is the place in novels where she would hold her arms out to me, and I would have to make a moral and/or ethical decision, but since this is not a novel—not even a story—Liz only burped and rolled over with her face against the wall. I put the cover on the Olivetti, stacked the latest pages in my manuscript box–cum–trash can, then wrapped myself in a blanket and slept on the floor of one of the still-empty rooms.

◉ ◉ ◉

Look, I'm not one to judge. Didn't I say that there's no limit to what people will do? And how they'll surprise you? Chainsaw dismemberment. Acid baths and stun guns. Assumed identities. Here I was writing my peripatetic crime novel, a saga in which the road trip and all the murders were imagined, when all I had to do was look next door for the thirty-year-old who seemed to attract sketchy behavior and indifferent violence like secondhand flies.

One afternoon, a week or so after Liz's sleepover, Henry came to the door.

"I'm sorry," he said. "I'm sorry for the interruption. I know you're writing." He was apologetic, truly he was, even if he didn't think much of my avocation. Literature, for him, was written by dead people, and if nothing else, he was good about maintaining such boundaries. "I know I haven't been around very much lately, but I've got someone I'd like you to meet."

"Is this who I think it is?" I said. "You know that your wife came by, don't you? You know she's had her investigated?"

"Oh, Liz," he said. He spoke about her as though about someone recently deceased. "Of course. Of course she did. She would."

I walked with him across our shared lawn to another tract house of the same model. Inside, though, the house he shared with his wife couldn't have been more different from the one that Jeanine was letting me borrow. They had furniture that they had purchased deliberately, so it belonged together, and one wall of the family room boasted a stereo system that I would have envied if I were one of those audio geeks. But the true ornament of the room had sunk into the shadowed corner of the overstuffed couch.

"I'd like to introduce you to Hélène de Vincennes," Henry said.

One pale arm extended toward me. "*Enchanté*," she said. "Have we met?"

"Maybe," I said. "Let's say I caught a glimpse from my kitchen window, and I don't know how enchanting this might be for anyone, but have it your way."

She clicked her tongue against her teeth, a sound that went something like "Tst-tst-tst."

"Hélène was in my Modern American Poetry seminar last semester," Henry said. "She kept bringing me Baudelaire to read. A little—how shall we say?—needed French oxygen."

"You Americains have so little romance," she said. "All work, work, work. Sin and guilt."

"Oh," I said. "That is our weakness. We love sin and guilt. Guilt especially, sin is just a bonus."

She shifted slightly on the couch, and when she moved, it felt as though the room became charged with electricity. When she looked at me, I had to look away, especially as she began to recite: "Our soul, alas, is not bold enough!"

"Point well taken," I said, "even if I don't understand the reference."

"Come to the kitchen," Henry said to me. "Tell me what you want to drink."

I should have been at the card table and the Olivetti since I still had about a thousand words to go before I quit for the day, but I knew that no excuse beyond a death was likely to work.

"What do you think?" he whispered as he uncapped one of his overpriced and undrinkable beers.

"If that's what we're drinking, I'll have a glass of water," I said.

"No. Her," he nodded toward the family room. "She's amazing, isn't she?"

"Well," I said. "Well, yes. Amazing is one word I'd use to describe her."

He handed me the beer that I didn't want, and I knew that after I drank it, I'd have a headache and regrets and not just a little self-recrimination. I also knew that I'd drink it.

"Don't get me wrong. I love Liz. I honor her, I cherish her, but Hélène—"

He didn't need to finish his thought. He went back to the family room and the couch and the soft crook between her pale shoulder and neck. Did I hear her purr? He looked up at me for one moment. "What am I supposed to do?"

Poor Liz, I thought. We are such fools! I took a swallow and felt my headache bloom. Fools and idiots and shitheads! Men, especially. And doomed to follow the reins of our impulses.

◉ ◉ ◉

Since Jeanine left, no one has had any reason to come to this house, and those infrequent visitors who do come to the door are either selling, surveying, or lost. So when the doorbell rang a few nights later near midnight, I was surprised to find neither Henry or Liz or any of the new passel of neighbors whose names I couldn't remember. Instead Hélène or Carla or whatever her name was stood on the threadbare welcome mat.

She came inside and looked around at the family room, empty of any furniture other than the straight chair and the card table that held the Olivetti. I offered her the chair but she chose to sit on the floor with me.

"Okay," I said. "I suppose this had to happen."

"*Oui*."

"Oh, come off it, Carla," I said. "You're the Raisin Queen from Selma, not a member of the French aristocracy. Liz knows about you, and she knows who you are, and, by now, I'm sure she's told Henry."

After the night with Liz, I had gone to the library and used the microfilm readers, and there it was: the front-page picture of Carla/Hélène waving to parade spectators from the backseat of a Cadillac convertible. In black-and-white halftones, she had a sash and a tiara and a paper cone of roses. In living color, I watched her mouth harden then relax. "So what if I am? Henry doesn't mind. He understands that life needs a little spice here and there. No one's hurt."

"Liz would probably disagree."

"Pish," she said, and in that one non-word she made all damage to the marriage disappear. "I have made Henry that much more desirable to his wife."

Somehow, I doubted that, but there was no point in contradicting her. She seemed so certain of her blamelessness.

"Do you mind if I ask you something?"

Her expressive shoulders shrugged in the half-dark.

"What do you see in him?"

Her hand touched my knee, and I'll admit that the touch was almost more than I could bear.

"Henry is, how should I say, a little boy. He is eager, *non?*"

"He is eager, I'll give you that. And hard to stomach."

My hand closed around hers. Such a simple gesture but one which, in the moment, felt freighted by my own bravery if not stupidity. I was forty years old, but I wasn't sure. Maybe in the end, it's all the same.

"Why," I said through a choked and closed-off throat, "why are you here?"

"To tell you," she said, "that Henry and I are no more. I have broken with him. I can't be with a weak man, and as you might say, Henry is *l'asticot.* A little maggot. You can put your mind on easy. And—" here her eyes turned to mine "—we might proceed with each other. If it pleases." She squeezed my knee. "I have seen how you look," she said, "how you look at me."

"That's fine," I said, my voice still feeling strangled. "I confess looking and wanting, I don't know if there's a man who wouldn't, but first you have to tell me about the horses."

◉ ◉ ◉

The house next door sold in less than a month. They had bought cheap, they had put in a few well-chosen cosmetic improvements, and while they had camped out in modest quarters, the housing market had boomed, and Liz was guaranteed to double her money. With the quick sale and a shorter escrow, there was not much time between the "For Sale" sign and a fresh start. Liz had another hatchet contract, this time in Idaho, and she'd managed to broker yet another add-on appointment for her delinquent husband. They must have talked, and I can only imagine the ultimatum that Henry had been given. I thought that the day would come when the moving vans would arrive, and that would be that, and I would see them no more.

After that evening, I didn't see Hélène again, but Carla showed up every night after eleven, after her evening shift at Pepper Tree, when the lights of the neighborhood were off and the street was quiet. Her diction and syntax were still a little off-kilter, but I thought I could detect more and more of the Fresno County farm girl she had always been. Apparently, it is not so easy to doff a personality as it is to don it, and she acknowledged what Liz had told me: the tips were better while French. So what if she played a role while at work? Didn't we all? The role she played on the futon in my bedroom was all Carla, and that was more than enough. I couldn't believe my good fortune, and I didn't want to risk it by asking questions about the hours each day when she was somewhere and someone else. In the mornings, I often found her rummaging through my manuscript box, reading this scene or that. There were times when she laughed, a full, deep-throated laugh, and that was the first time I realized that in my imaginings of murder, mayhem, and travel, I was writing comedy after all. Helter-skelter, ha-ha. Who knew?

I deliberately stayed away from the house next door out of some sense of propriety and respect for their privacy. After all, I'm sure they saw Carla's car in my driveway each morning. I don't know what Henry might have made of his French princess abandoning him for his older, less attractive neighbor. But through the windows or over the fence, I did catch glimpses of him trailing Liz obediently as they did this or that task related to their move. Boxing up books, packing the plates and glassware, setting out used yard tools for a Saturday garage sale. As far as I could tell, Henry didn't seem particularly riven by either regret or guilt. Sadness, though, that was more than a possibility. While I hacked away at a hedge of stubborn rhaphiolepis, he waved once from his driveway. His wave was half-hearted, his expression hangdog, and he didn't come over to talk. I think we would have both been embarrassed. I think we would have found it difficult to know what to say.

The movers were scheduled for a Monday, but the Friday night before, the neighborhood lit up with the flashing red lights of an ambulance and fire truck.

The red lights went around and around while the two vehicles idled; the lights flashed among the Chinese elms and drew the attention of the neighbors, who stood—as if in respect—on the opposite side of the street. Children, normally on bicycles and skateboards, were still and quiet, their faces yellowed by the sodium vapor lamps. The lights went around and around while we waited with a collective intake of breath. We were waiting to see who had died.

◎ ◎ ◎

If I had been imagining this story, if I had been looking for some kind of unity of form and structure, Henry would have killed Liz and then disposed of her body in some particularly brutal and grotesque fashion. Remember the vat of acid, the electric chainsaw, or the pages and pages of my own endless project? He could have strangled her while she slept, buried her in the backyard, then poured cement over the top as a pad for a lovely fountain, a barbecue station, or a patio set with umbrella. And maybe autopsy results years later would show she had still been alive at the moment of her interment.

Henry could have used poison. Given the recent history of Russian politics, poison is au courant, after all, and the effects on the human body are particularly devastating and cruel. But we live in a Western society repulsed by poison, even as we are increasingly aware of food allergies and anaphylaxis. Peanuts, possibly. Shellfish. Liz and Henry were moving. Couldn't Henry have picked up take-out? Say, at Pepper Tree, where Carla worked? Maybe this was one last plea on his part for Carla to reconsider. The food could have been suitably doctored, a sign of Henry's desperation and endless love. Then again, think about this: Liz was a hospital administrator. Wouldn't she, knowing her own medical history, have an EpiPen or two at the ready? She would jab each thigh, call 911, and recognize that not only was her husband a fool, he was also a murderous one. Carted out of their house by EMTs on a gurney, she would look at her husband in full knowledge of what he was and say, "Remind me never to get in a rowboat with you." Think of it as *An American Tragedy Unfulfilled*. Let Dreiser roll over in a tomb of his own.

No, the truth was this: Henry lay down after a dinner of take-out pad thai, swallowed twenty Xanax with a pint of gas station vodka, and waited for his wife to find him. Which she did and, after deliberating a moment or two whether or not to call Emergency Services, finally, finally, finally picked up the phone. For, as it turned out, this was Henry's second try, the first having come near the end of their time in Tempe. Enough was enough, Liz thought, except when enough was forever. All it took was a new girl, a fresh face, for him to fall in love and adolescent infatuation. He was an idiot, Henry was, and he had no inner resources, but he was *her* idiot, she had inner resources aplenty, and she'd be damned if she'd let him go that easily. She would bring him back from the dead, and then she would make him pay at their next stop, their not-so-private Idaho. She'd give him a spine, if she could.

The truth was also this, and you are welcome to call it ironic, coincidental, or incredible, as you will: I never saw Carla again. You might know, if you follow those network shows that feature weird crimes and puzzling unsolved mysteries, what became of Carla or Hélène, since Hélène wasn't done after all, no matter how self-satisfied I might have been in my under-furnished bedroom. Little did I know I'd be a witness to, if not a character in, the events of network television. While the EMTs were reviving Henry against the background noise of Liz scolding her husband in strident and obscene terms, Hélène was making her next move, which was a doctor she'd met in the lounge at Pepper Tree. While I sat before the Olivetti, waiting to tell Carla about Henry, Hélène was working her charms on a dermatologist from Madera. He gave her a fifty-dollar tip at the end of the evening, and while the restaurant was being cleaned, she slid into his banquette and put a hand on the inside of his thigh. You should know that this dermatologist had a horse ranch in Parlier and a fondness for the Friesian, that breed of draught horse that belies its size and strength with an unexpected agility. I had seen the books that Carla carried in her student backpack—stolen, I can only imagine, from the library at the Ag School—and it seems clear in retrospect that she had had an eye on her mark for quite some time. Even Liz's private investigator had seen the direction of her research. Henry and I were merely dry runs, warm-ups, if you will, and we didn't present much of a challenge for her. French nobility, French poetry, contemporary fiction, the genetics of a nearly forgotten breed. She did her homework, and she became what she needed to be. In the end, she got her doctor, she got her horses, and she got her ranch; she became the unquestioned queen of the Friesian set, and all would have been well until she and her doctor found themselves land- and livestock-rich and cash-poor. So she pretended to die of leukemia with her dermatologist husband's signature on the death certificate, leaving behind an accident without a body, questions about her $3 million of life insurance, and about a dozen lawsuits.

I saw that episode, and I had chills.

In fact, I watched a rerun with Jeanine not so long ago. Yes, that Jeanine, who went off and made a fortune by beating the masters of the universe at their own game until she had enough and said she had all that she needed. She got out before the subprime wizards let it all go to hell, and she had nothing better to do than to come to Fresno for a vacation, which I figured meant my time in the cracker box neighborhood was about to end. She was finally ready to sell, and that meant I'd need to think about things. My future, such as it was, and the manuscript boxes that qualified me as a hoarder. After almost thirty years, I had begun to see myself as the immoveable object, but "Ozymandias" should have told me otherwise, not that I think of myself as either a statue or a ruler of nations. So the show came on, and I said, "Hey, you've got to see this. I knew this girl once upon a time. She really went off the deep end, you know?"

But Jeanine knew me, and she was smart enough to see things as they were instead of how they were presented to be, and she said, "Okay. Somewhere along the line, you got taken, too."

"Well," I said, "only a little bit. Not as bad as the moron next door."

So then I told her about Henry and Liz and Carla/Hélène, keeping my part in everything to a minimum. And she said, "Uh-huh. Uh-huh. And this story interests you why?"

"It's about two boxes worth on the east wall of the garage."

"Uh-huh."

Which was when Jeanine began to plow through my collected leavings, and if I'm honest, I have to count myself lucky that there have been two people, or maybe one and a half, who sacrificed their time on the altar of my self-preoccupation. I didn't see her for two weeks, except breakfast and dinner, and once, when I started to ask her what she thought, she told me to shut up until she was finished. It was still too early to say.

But there finally came a time when she was willing to talk to me about what she'd read.

"Look," she said, "I think it's time to face some facts, and you have some choices to make."

"Oh, no," I said, "this can't be good."

"First," she said, "I'm selling this place. After thirty years, it's more than time, and you'll need to find a new place to live, but we'll come back to that in a moment. Second, I've read the Collected Landfill, and here's my investment broker's verdict, unschooled though it may be. You don't know a thing about science fiction or cops and robbers. I won't even mention the romance, which is embarrassing on so many levels. As a writer of prose, you have a style made for television. Now wait," she said, before I could begin to object and defend myself, "there's a new Golden Age coming, so that was a compliment more than you know. I know some people, and they're always on the lookout for new material, and I think there might be an interest in your *Travels with the Grim Reaper* or whatever it is you're calling it. Maybe. But you'll have to learn how to get out of your own way."

"Okay," I said, "that's that. Like death, I knew this day would come. I guess I should pack. Although that won't take more than twenty minutes. Maybe I'll just cart the boxes to the backyard and light a match."

"Don't be so melodramatic," she said, and at that moment I felt to my shame that in some way I had been channeling Henry, the *asticot*.

"Listen," she said, "I told you I'm selling this place, but what I didn't tell you is this: I've already got another place on the coast, and this time you're an idiot if you don't come with me. I'm retired, but I need a project, and you're it. Here's what you're going to learn: in television, there are no dust jackets, there is no author photo, no bio, and no one except a few producers will know who you are. There's just money. Lots and lots of money. And more people in therapy than you can believe because they need it and can afford to go. We'll get you a therapist of whatever flavor you want when it's time."

"Good to know," I said.

"Now about this," she said tapping one of the most recent sections from the manuscript I was calling *My Fresno Book of Death and Disposal*. "These are awful stories, but you've written them like jokes, like the woodchipper in *Fargo*. What happened to your god Armando?"

I told her that truth came in many forms, and Armando, who was probably dead by now, would just have to take care of himself. As for the jokes, I said, she wasn't the first person to tell me that, but I didn't tell her who my first critic had been.

"They'll eat that up, those sick bastards," Jeanine said, by which I assumed her to mean the therapy-hogs of Hollywoodland. "Breakfast, lunch, and dinner," she said, "with liberal snacks besides."

◉ ◉ ◉

Jeanine was as good as her word. We moved to a sprawling hillside spot above Cambria, and she let me get on with my work-of-sorts while she negotiated my employment. Not to mention my clothes, haircut, and table manners. I might have objected except I'd never done such a hot job on my own. Within a year, *My Fresno Book of Death and Disposal* was in production with a streaming network I'd never heard of, which was not that surprising since I'd never paid for cable. So I was working for people I didn't know and a company whose name I could never remember, and the show was broadcast on a channel I didn't know how to access. Then again, no one knew who I was either. While the reviews were okay, the money—as Jeanine promised and predicted— was even better, and I almost had enough in my bank account to count for self-esteem. Who knew that happy endings were possible?

Still, I had my doubts. This business of making other people's physical calamities the source of comedy seemed like a bad bet to me and a sure way to jinx my own good fortune. I lay the blame at the feet of Flannery O'Connor, that Southern doyenne of the grotesque. In The Misfit's benediction of the Grandmother ("she would of been a good woman if it had been somebody there to shoot her every minute of her life"), O'Connor causes us to laugh at a tragedy and call it the comedic vehicle of grace. Maybe that was true once upon a time, but I worry about this present age, when all misfortune is mocked and traduced as a sign of inferiority and a mark of the less-than, rather than the divine putting a human being to rights.

I have learned to put my doubts aside, however, which was a good thing when one night the phone began to ring. Jeanine happened to be back in Boston for a reunion with some of her former coworkers, so I was alone, and my first frantic thought, since my imagination always bends toward the worst scenario, was that Jeanine had had an accident on the T.

But no. The voice I recognized instantly, even if I had a hard time putting the name together.

"Do you remember me?" she said. "Hélène Jean-Marie de Vincennes?"

"Yes," I said. "I remember. I remember quite clearly, Carla. Carla Walker. Although come to think of it, I thought you were supposed to be dead. Or maybe just dying somewhere."

"Oh, ha, that."

"Yes, that. Primetime viewing on network television can't be wrong, can it?"

So we chatted about this and that in a conversation of fits and starts. She asked about Henry, but there was nothing I could tell her past Idaho, and I asked how she had died and gotten away with it, but she said she was under advisement not to answer that particular question. And then I asked how she had gotten this phone number, since we had moved years before and from the beginning we had paid for the landline to be unlisted. Which was when she said something vague about research. Then she asked a question of her own: "Tell me, are you still having a mid-life crisis?"

"That depends," I said, "since I started another life entirely."

◉

Shop Tools

SHEILA AND GRAY HENDERSON WERE MARRIED BY A RETIRED Episcopalian minister in a small ceremony in a small church in Cleveland. The year was 1958, so all the pictures were black-and-white, even the ones taken with color film. After a year in a scrapbook, the prints faded; according to them, the bride and groom wore muted shades of an indeterminate hue. No one smiled. The late-morning sun was in their eyes, and they had things to do. If there were roses in their cheeks, they too were half-tones. For their honeymoon, they planned to drive cross country to California, where Gray had a job waiting with Lockheed. The first afternoon they stopped north of Cincinnati at a motel that had a pool, and Sheila thought her husband was trying to drown her when he dunked her for fun. She came up screaming and blowing water from her nose. First, they had undressed, and then he had pushed her head down on the pillows. He had split her from stem to stern in the name of love and a lifetime commitment, and now this? Suffocated, abused, drowned. He knew she couldn't swim. And she knew—because her mother had told her—that marriage entailed a host of unpleasant duties, but she hadn't been prepared. She hadn't understood how much like a burial marriage could be. The second night, they stopped at a hotel in St. Louis, and a porter unloaded their suitcases. As a joke, Gray's father, an industrial arts teacher at a high school in Lakewood, had put an anvil into the trunk because what newlywed couple didn't need an anvil? His rendition of tin cans tied to a bumper.

The porter pointed to the anvil wedged behind the wheel well and asked if that, too, needed to come up to the room. His eyes shifted from Sheila to Gray and back again. Sheila saw it and, in an instant, all was clear. Her husband was another Ed Gein, whose exploits and trial had become a string of stories in the *Plain Dealer*. She had only known Gray for a month before the wedding. She was seventeen. He was eight years older and had an air of experience. They had met in a stationery store when he had been shopping for protractors and she had been standing behind the register, imagining anywhere but Cleveland; she couldn't look away from his hands and the way he held the drafting tools he planned to buy. She had thought then, *He's dreamy. He could take me away.* She thought now, *He'll take me away, all right.* And, *I have made a horrible, horrible error.* She spent the second night of their marriage in the bathroom, hyperventilating and refusing to emerge.

"No, I'm fine." Even though she was gasping and short of breath, she had a Midwesterner's ironclad sense of courtesy and decency; however, she still had no desire to have the back of her head crushed while she slept and her body dismembered, her face turned into a mask, her torso a lampshade. Yesterday afternoon's activities had been plenty, thank you very much.

Because his mother died and he missed her, Ed Gein had murdered two women at random and robbed the graves of dozens more so that he could make fantastical creations from human flesh. He would later be immortalized in a novel and movie, both titled *Psycho* and both of which would be wildly successful in the near future. Sheila, though, had an imagination of her own, an affinity for amaretto as learned from a maiden aunt, and a tendency toward anxiety that seemed to have been with her from birth. Death was everywhere. She had no need of help from tawdry novelists or filmmakers.

Gray was an engineer who saw resistance only in terms of electricity; he had no idea what he'd become in his wife's mind. *You drive and you drive*, he thought, *headed toward the next forty years of employment, and you have a right to a moment of fun, a moment of pleasure, don't you?* But what did he know? He only knew that a draft beer in a hotel bar cost a buck and a half, as much as a six-pack, and yet here he was, drinking an overpriced Budweiser while waiting for his wife to calm down for reasons that were, as yet, unclear.

He learned, then, how to apologize, even if he didn't always know what he was apologizing for, and he learned to appreciate the missionary position, water safety, and a well-ordered garage with pegboard. Foundry tools, like an anvil, were relegated to a backyard shed. His wife was a delicate flower and delicate flowers needed tending. He consoled himself with the reminder that he hadn't married her for conversation.

Once they were established in Los Angeles, Sheila began to read the Bible for half an hour each morning after Gray left the house. She read for the miracles, but she had trouble remembering anything that she had read. She discovered a preference for Jeane Dixon and Edgar Cayce and stories of teleportation. She learned to keep chocolate in her bedside table and brandy in the cupboard underneath the bathroom sink, and she learned which would be the most efficacious in the twenty minutes before Gray's return from work. This and "Jesus wept" and the names of the other housewives on their street who wouldn't say no to a taste of brandy—that's what she would remember.

Over the years, Gray would work on government projects with top-secret clearances that, even at great distances, were responsible for the deaths of others, a kind of grave magic that he couldn't stop imagining. Sheila would wonder where the years had gone; she would search for them but find the brandy instead.

Now and again, she would be looking for something she used infrequently—the outdoor Christmas lights or the electric fryer or the patio folding chairs—and she would come across the anvil of their honeymoon, but as though it had a life of its own, it would never be in the same place twice. The outdoor shed, the garage, the front hall closet. On one occasion, the downstairs guest bathroom, behind the commode. They would not have children, but Sheila could not have said whether that was by accident or choice.

At the turn of the millennium, Gray retired. Once he was home more, he could see the deterioration in his wife, as though the effects of Y2K had been consolidated in her. She put her keys in the freezer, her purse in the oven. She spoke to the air. She turned on a burner and let a saucepan burn dry. She called him by a name other than his own. When he moved her into a board-and-care home, she claimed that what he was doing was one more betrayal in the progression: first rape, then drowning. Assault. Dismemberment.

"Darling," Gray said. "Don't be silly. Look at how nice this is." He pointed to the flowered couches and velour drapes. "You'll be fine here." There were three other women, arranged on one of the couches like apple-head dolls while the air conditioner cycled on and off. They stared at Gray and Sheila as though at nothing.

Gray sold their house a month after her move and put the proceeds into an annuity. He held yard sales and an estate sale, and what he couldn't sell, he donated to the veterans. He rented an apartment behind a gas station in a sketchy part of town, and he moved what was left. What didn't fit, he put into a storage unit in a storage park that had waterfalls in the front. He kept the anvil next to the television as a reminder of something he only dimly understood.

Every day at noon he drove to the board-and-care home and helped feed his wife, but even so, within two weeks, she was dressed in another woman's clothes, and she looked like the others.

On September 11, he found Sheila and the rest of the women sitting on the couches while the television was turned to the inescapable news and the replayed loop of one airplane crashing into the first tower and then another airplane crashing into the second. Neither Sheila nor the other women seemed to register what they were watching. Gray sat on the couch and held hands with his wife as though they were on a date in Cleveland, and Sheila said, "This isn't fun." Gray wondered if the pilots and hijackers could see the people in the offices that they were about to annihilate.

When he returned home to his apartment, he found the living room window broken and the front door ajar. The entertainment stand had been tipped over and books were scattered everywhere. His television, computer, and stereo were gone. He found the anvil a week later, under the bed as though in fear of recent intruders.

◉

Maybe . . .

. . . I'M NOT THE SMARTEST GUY IN THE WORLD. I never said I was, although there may have been times when I thought it, I was certain of it, and those, of course, were the times when my face got rubbed in the shit of my own making. Live and learn. Or not. Don't learn a thing: that seems to be the human way, and I am, after all, only human. Live and reap the consequences, sometimes more than once. That might be the better or more accurate way to phrase it.

Here's what happened: I came home from work. I opened the front door, picked up the mail from the floor, which was where George, my good-for-nothing, not even rent roommate, was in the habit of leaving it, and found that anything worth stealing was gone. There wasn't much that fit that description in the first place, so it didn't dawn on me right away. A six-year-old floor-model flat screen, a five-year-old laptop with a critical lack of memory, and the once-upon-a-time state-of-the-art stationary bike that I used more often as a coat rack. I could see the dust marks on the wall, table, and floor where they had once hung, sat, and stood, but other than that? Only the vacancy of the departed.

"What the hell," I said. "What the hell."

I might have said that I felt violated, but the likeliest explanation (other than George, who was too lazy) was also the least interesting and, I should also admit, the least likely to engender sympathy for me.

"Julia," I said when the most recent of my ex-girlfriends answered the phone, "am I to assume you paid the house a visit?"

"What do you think?" Julia was not that bright, but she could be snappy when she needed to be.

"I think I'm missing some things."

"Uh-huh."

"And I think you knew when I'd be gone."

"Like that's so hard to figure out. Just watch for the uncovered oil stain in the driveway." I could hear her moving to another room in the apartment she now shared with Destiny, the former third of our threesome. "You told me you'd pay me back two months ago."

"You know what I'm going through."

"So I got tired of waiting for you to get through it. Now we're done."

We were done. Finally and forever. Another lap nearer the finish line, as my now-dead mother was wont to say.

Then again, as my younger, still living coworkers say, Meh.

◎ ◎ ◎

If you came with me to work, you might have some idea of my sense of depression. Did you know that I'm an actor? Let me rephrase that: I *was* an actor, a real actor, with the Equity card to prove it. I played the Scottish Thane, the melancholic Dane, and back in the day I played Brick to Julia's Maggie the Cat. In my heyday, I had had a couple of overtures from Hollywood and New York, but I knew my limits. My gifts had their ceiling, and I was comfortable enough in southern Oregon at the Repertory, with no desire to chase the illusion of stardom on a larger stage. Life in rep was steady and consistent for ten months a year, and the other two months were manageable if one were willing to live with a certain level of frugality. I had a townhouse, and I drove a serviceable car, those big-ticket items that too many of the more ambitious members of my tribe couldn't say they possessed.

My undoing came, as they say, both gradually and suddenly. Ten or more years ago, roles were assigned in, how shall I put it, less traditional ways, and white straight males were no longer the center of the regional theater universe. Prospero was a woman. Portia was trans. Richard III was a deaf mute and signed his lines while the audience read supertitles. A revival of *The Music Man* in lily-white Iowa heralded a mixed-race cast and *Oklahoma!* was staged as gay farce with the cowboys in drag. Is this wrong? Not for me to say, although I doubted whether there was room for me in *Fences*. A statement was read before each performance thanking the local Native American tribes for allowing themselves to be raped, murdered, and removed, so we could tread the boards. What were the dead supposed to say, "You're welcome"? Not for me to say about this, either. I was not the only one of the longtime members left muttering in his or her respective latte, but by mentioning it, I guess I am saying it. Which was the problem. My saying something. Anything, for that matter. The casting. The earnest attempt to right each historical wrong. My last year with the company, I was assigned as ensemble for *Love's Labours Lost* and *Timon of Athens*, and I had two different walk-on parts for *A View from the Bridge* when I thought I'd be perfect for Alfieri. I wasn't asking for Eddie's role—let the young guys scramble for that one—but instead I had the walk-ons, and I didn't even require a costume change. I had more nap time possibilities than I had lines to say. I was also given five understudy roles in two other plays, and I remember looking at the notice board in the Green Room, running my finger down the list, and saying "Holy Mother Fucking Christ Almighty in Heaven, I have been cast down into Hell and beyond," which was just the moment that Jean Petrucchi, the artistic director, decided to stroll through and said, "No small roles, Frankie-boy." She told me the next day that I should consider this my year of grace and get my house in order. I was older, gaining weight and blowsy with drink, and I was delusional if I still had lead roles in mind. As for looks, I had never been standard fare in the first place, and it was high time that I look for work in theaters outside the area since my services locally had become so lightly regarded.

"It wasn't always this way," she said, not unkindly, "but now you know the score."

"Is it because of who I am?" I said. "Or any little criticism I might have offered?"

"Mmm," she said. "Don't go there."

"But I'm a homeowner," I said, feeling a little desperation creep into my voice, no matter my outrage. "And I have bills like anyone else."

"Repeat after me," Jean said, "VRBO. Or you could sell."

"Ha, ha," I said, but she wasn't laughing.

"I can give you some names of property management companies," she said, "if you're interested. And I can give your name to the artistic director in El Cajon. I hear they're staging *The Mousetrap* in February. Pulling out all the stops. Posh British accents, real tea and crumpets. Wool wardrobes. Right in your lane. You have the right instincts for Trotter."

"Thanks, but no thanks," I said, sure that something better would come along.

As it turned out, though, I didn't even last the year. *Bridge* closed in late June, and at the wrap, I was standing next to Julia, who wasn't at that moment either my girlfriend or ex-girlfriend, only a brief flirtation from some years earlier when we were in *Cat* together. In my memory she looked as though she'd gone full Maggie for the party, and by extension, so my thinking went, she'd gone full Maggie for me, but she assured me later that this was yet another way in which my perceptions were completely unreliable. "I was wearing jeans and a sweatshirt because I was striking the set half an hour before," she told me some months later. "I had no idea you'd bother to show up. Not that your presence would mean a change of clothes on my part. Or deodorant, for that matter. Don't flatter yourself otherwise."

That much was true enough: my attendance was far from guaranteed, and I knew that Julia was more interested in drinking with the girls on the college softball team, if you catch my drift; I had toyed with the idea of not going, given the small parts I'd been given to play and how punished and ostracized I felt. Why did I go? Fear of missing out? Fear of being thought too good for such things, as Jean had more than implied. But there we were, reunited in the rehearsal hall—Maggie and Brick from years and years earlier—and I felt myself expand with past glories and the favor that I had once enjoyed. Maybe that was enough for me to see her as we'd been on stage together, her a tall willow in a tight-fitting, champagne-colored sheathe, and me, a little less than tall, in pale blue pajamas and a cast, while the word "mendacity" echoed all around us.

"Don't do it," she whispered to me over the Two-Buck Chuck and the outlet store party trays. "I'm telling you. I'm begging you."

"What?" I said. "What am I going to do?"

"There's something in the air," she said. "Whatever it is, it's a bad idea."

I had no ideas, good, bad, or otherwise, until Julia-as-Maggie said something. I might have had a plastic cup or two or eight of that cheap-ass wine. You'll have to take my word for it. No ideas but grape until Jean came in, escorting Bobby Danforth, that little queen, the director of the production of *Bridge*, the two of them as thick as the thieves they were, since they'd stolen my part, I was so sure of myself in the narrator's role.

"Bobby Danforth," I called out while Julia drifted away from me. "Bobby Danforth, if it isn't my favorite turd in a jar.

You've taken my life and you've turned it into your own brand of syrup."

You're right. Not very creative on my part. Nor was my next gesture when I threw a full cup at Bobby and, despite my semi-inebriated state, hit him square in the chest of his favorite white linen shirt. No doubt the fabric had been woven by butterflies, but it now looked as though it were a medieval relic of sainthood.

"Oh, oh, oh," Bobby said, waving at himself as though he could turn back time. "Dear Jesus."

"Oh, fuck," Julia said, "do you see what you've done?" She looked over her shoulder at me while running to Bobby with a roll of paper towels and her sympathy but without any hope of cure.

"Mr. Delgado," Jean sighed, "come see me tomorrow morning at nine."

I was done. And I had only myself to blame.

◎ ◎ ◎

Things could have been worse. I could have had a terminal disease or been guilty of a felony when at most I had committed a misdemeanor, and the only thing terminal was my stupidity. Apologies were nominally offered and nominally accepted, I paid for new fairy-ware, but that didn't change the fact that I had lost the one job I was trained for, the one job I had wanted since the time I was sixteen and played Judas in a high school production of *Godspell*. I had some talent on stage, which was a revelation to me at the time, and it was the only place where I truly felt comfortable. I could inhabit a part, I could become someone else, and in doing so, I found something within myself that would have been otherwise unexplored.

Looking back at what I've written so far, I know I sound like the worst of the intolerant, sour-grape set. People lose jobs every day, often through no fault of their own, economic circumstances being as impersonal as they are. There was no question that I was responsible for my own demise in the end, but I couldn't help but feel that for years others had been taking away my life as well as my livelihood, for reasons that went well beyond my abilities or the job description. And you'd be well within your rights to say that now I knew how others have felt for decades or centuries. You wouldn't be wrong. But neither am I.

Salvation can come in many forms, often when least expected or looked for, and although loaded with all of its religious baggage, "salvation" is not too strong a word. After my meeting with Jean Petrucchi, I went home and sat on the couch in front of my television for the next three weeks while the carryout boxes and beer bottles stacked up around me.

What had I done?

I knew the answer to that only too well, I could tell others when asked, and yet I couldn't seem to understand that I wouldn't be going back onto an outdoor stage in front of twelve-hundred people. Never again.

In hindsight, I suppose I should have done what actors have always done: make contacts, send out head shots, reviews, and DVDs, work the audition schedule. Hit the circuit, up and down I-5. But I couldn't bring myself to do what needed to be done if I wanted to remain in theater, and I had long ago thrown away my chances for television or film. Instead, Julia was the one who came to my door and to my rescue once again.

"What?" I said. "Come to gloat?"

"No," she said, and then she wrinkled her nose as though in reaction to something rank, which was me. "And I didn't come to offer you maid service either, though God knows you need it, and it wouldn't hurt if you drove yourself into a car wash with the top down."

"Great. Anything else you'd like to tell me?"

"Vino Veritas," she said. "Think about it. I can get you an interview."

That's what told me I'd hit bottom, but that also told me there was nowhere to go but up, even if the view at present wasn't very promising.

◉ ◉ ◉

If wine was my undoing, then wine could be my rescue. That was how my thinking went, and if downfall and resurrection were sourced the same, I didn't mind the irony.

Vino Veritas was an ornate pile in the foothills five miles outside of town. Bankrolled by a group of doctors and lawyers, the winery specialized in various red blends with high tannin levels and whites that were too sweet by half. The owners had invested no small amount of money on food and kitchen employees as well as décor, and the winery had become a destination as much for the menu and the vistas as it was for the wine. The tourists from Napa came and licked their lips nervously, wondering if their terroir had moved north, climate change and wildfires being what they are.

Julia had worked at the winery off and on over the years. She had a facility with numbers, and since her parents had never believed she could make a life as an actor, she had a degree in accounting and a permanent, part-time gig as Vino's bookkeeper. If she ever gave up the theater, Dr. Winkler assured her, he'd bring her on full-time as controller with an office, salary and benefits, and a sixty-hour work week. Her parents didn't know how she could refuse, but then they'd never seen her as Maggie.

What made me less than enthusiastic about Julia's offer was the specter of my potential employment. I knew a few of the waitstaff and wine pourers, actors who, like me, had lost their places at the Rep and weren't able to hold onto a spot with any of the other local cabarets and dinner theaters. In other words, they had worked their way to the bottom of the performative food chain. They learned the language of the sommelier, talked knowledgably about varietals and mouth feel, bouquet and legs, and hustled plates of Caesar salad and pesto salmon and garlic truffle fries, charcuterie boards and bruschetta-and-cheese samplers to the overweight tourists at the tables while local musicians played covers of pale jazz and soft rock. Then, near the end of the evening, the waitstaff grouped together for the Pentatonix rendition of "Hallelujah," or at least as close to that as was possible given the voices that were available. This was what was to become of my future: to become a member of the has-beens, a collector of tips and a partaker of banter with the families of the West Coast vacation set, all of whom were identifiable by the shorts they wore and the plump knees that reflected the evening sunlight. Hallelujah, indeed.

◉ ◉ ◉

My interview with Dr. Winkler lasted all of ten minutes. I was Julia's friend, and I had her recommendation, so there was nothing more he needed to know. In his seventies and an anesthesiologist by trade, he was used to letting others do their work while he did his; he was a theater buff as well as a wine impresario, and his questions had more to do with my previous roles at the Rep rather than anything to do with food service or wine presentation. He was that much of a fan. I thought he was this close to asking for my autograph. After I was hired, Julia trained me for three days; she gave me a card with the tasting notes for the summer release, and I was told to memorize it. Hints of pear in the Chardonnay, aroma of black cherry in the Pinot, this one thing like that one thing, since the wine couldn't taste like itself, but some other fruit or grass or flower had to figure into its description. I didn't need to know anything about wine, she said, other than my lines. And if I wanted to know about my character's motivation, I needed only to look at the suggested tip percentages attached like a cue card at the bottom of each bill. I have had more autocratic directors and stage managers, but I knew enough not to cross her when she said ad-libbing was not recommended.

My first evenings at Vino went well enough. I managed the spiel about each wine, I poured and I paired, I bowed and I scraped, and I lost all shame at the end of each night when it came time to harmonize on "Hallelujah" and to collect what the credit card slips said was my due. The words, "No small roles, Frankie-boy," echoed in my head. For the first month, I played wine steward and waiter with all the hauteur of Mr. Darcy if Colin Firth had Morgellons until Julia pulled me aside one night and whispered, "You don't have to be an asshole all the time." And then she added, a bit more gently, "This is supposed to be fun, remember? For everybody."

So I adjusted my tune and began to wait my tables as Mark Darcy if Colin Firth had spent the previous hour smoking a joint, and wouldn't you know it, my tips improved along with my mood, and if I couldn't quite get behind "Hallelujah" I could stand near the back and lip synch while the rest hummed and crooned in their almost-on-key register. Which was when Julia-if-not-Maggie moved in because she was tired of chasing younger women and tired of living alone, and she said she was tired of preferences that had become more habit than passion. I had earned the pleasure of her company in a more full-time way, she said. I had been a good boy. So she said.

There had been others in my house over the years, other cast members and wardrobe techs, women from the costume shop and the scene shop, but since my mother died, Julia was the first who *lived* there with me, if you know what I mean. She rearranged the furniture and threw out the moldy jars of jam and suspect cheese that had languished in the refrigerator. She bought new sheets for the bed which was now a joint property, and she made me file my taxes on time.

"How do you live?" she said, as though she seriously expected me to answer.

"I live just fine," I said, "although I can't say I've taken good care of everything. I mean the average adult person has a list of Gotta Do's that's completely unmanageable."

"You're ridiculous," she said. "How old are you?" She meant what she said; she was holding a sheaf of parking tickets she'd found under the passenger seat in my car, and I wasn't about to argue; she was happy to believe me incapable of taking care of my obligations without her, and I was happy for her to be happy and happy enough to let her think what she wanted.

"Old enough," I said. "I'm old enough to know that not every little thing is necessary. No matter what the documents say."

"You're ridiculous," she said again, "and impossible."

I helped her remake the bed and move the couch, I held up pictures and frames, so she could mark their placement on the walls, and we left it at that.

Because I couldn't believe that my life could be at least partially righted so soon after the heartbreak of my dismissal. Really. As much as I grieved my loss of the outdoor stage, I tried to make up for it in my duties on the outdoor patio at the winery and in my performance on the new sheets. There were moments when we were a little mismatched, given Julia's proclivities for other females of her kind, and I wondered when the bubble would burst. But then, there were other moments when we came home of an evening, me in my black shirt, black pants, and black apron, Julia in her accountant/middle-management attire, when I pretended that we were any other middle-aged middle-class couple. We made choices about what to do with the rest of our evening and the rest of our lives based on what two people could reasonably afford. I could pretend that without really believing it. And then, maybe a year after we had been together, Julia came home from running some errands to tell me that Bobby Danforth had cast her as Blanche in *Streetcar* and our schedules, if not our lives, would be somewhat different once rehearsals and then performances got underway. She was excited, of that there was no doubt, but I could also tell that she was nervous about how I would react.

"I'm a big boy," I said. "That's exciting news, and I'm happy for you."

"Really?" she said. "You don't have a problem with this?"

"No, why should I? I know how to feed myself, and I know how to turn on the television when I'm lonely."

"If you're sure," she said.

"Sure, I'm sure," I said. "I'll be mouthing 'Hallelujah' with the rest of the misfit toys, but I'll be thinking of you the whole time, not without envy."

"You see?" she said and pressed her fingers to her eyes. "I knew it."

"That Bobby Danforth," I said. "No stranger, he, but kindness all the same. A little tit for tat, right? And tat for tit? Even a little queen like that can be persuaded, I suppose."

I went on and on in this vein in my most orotund of tones—I might have been drinking; I'm sure I was drinking—about the perfidy of the Repertory administration, their kowtowing to political correctness of the most extreme kind, and their lack of loyalty or care to those who had served them so long and so well, whereas Julia, for her part, had traded a roll of paper towels and a simulacrum of concern for the plumiest of plum roles. Meanwhile I watched as Julia-as-Blanche wilted in front of me.

Yes, I know: It wasn't my finest moment as a human being. But I would have made a hell of a Stanley if only someone had been willing to give me the part.

◎ ◎ ◎

My finest moment as an actor, though, came two decades earlier in a supporting role. I didn't have a single line. Let that mean what it will. This happened before Jean Petrucchi's ascendence as artistic director, years before *Hamlet* and *Cat*, when Jean was still a sometime guest director and I was maybe a year out of acting school and living in the townhouse with my mother, who was the rightful owner and already dying. One lap away from the finish line, as it turned out; that's where she was. We both knew it, but neither of us was willing to acknowledge the fact to the other. I was young and just that self-absorbed, and my mother was in pain and half-addled on various blends of oxycodone, and I suppose we believed that if we didn't say anything, nothing bad could happen. The Rep was auditioning for a black box production of *A Servant of Two Masters*, that old *commedia dell'arte* warhorse, and while Jean wasn't willing to give me one of the listed roles, she did ask me to dress as an usher—if an usher could be a vagrant—and wander the stage in a filthy red vest and headset made from tin cans and a cut-off piece of garden hose. I didn't get a haircut or shave for the duration of the run. My job, Jean demanded, was to make Truffaldino's life even more chaotic and less appetite-satisfying, especially during the banquet scene.

Like any good street-corner beggar, I held up a cardboard sign that read, "Desperate! Anything helps! God bless!" and the compliant, well-prepared audience threw their wrapped home-mades in my direction. Ham and cheese, egg salad, roast beef, now and again a turkey leg. I collected them all in a shopping cart with three wheels while the starving Truffaldino could only look on. I pulled down Pantalone's pantaloons while I washed his spectacles, and I pinched Beatrice's rear while I kneed Florindo in the groin whenever he approached. During rehearsals, Jean Petrucchi kept saying "More. More, Frankie-boy," much to the chagrin of the rest of the cast, who thought I was getting too much attention for a role that didn't exist in the script.

"Oh, come on! What am I supposed to do?" Andy Brantley, our Truffaldino, grew increasingly impatient as he saw his star turn slipping away. He nearly imploded as Jean gave me yet one more bit of business: I put on one of Clarice's dresses and collected yet more food in its capacious bodice. "Is there no end to this?" he said.

"No more than there's an end to homelessness or hunger, class or gender inequality," Jean said mildly. And in her defense, Andy *was* an asshole with a trust fund and a degree from Yale, and no one was sorry to see him cut down a peg or two by a social justice critique at his expense. "Sharing is caring, you know. Don't be greedy."

Matters became worse when the show opened, and the reviews from Portland and San Francisco came in. Both cited the unknown actor working in pantomime. The *Oregonian* critic called me "the second coming of Harpo, breaking through the fourth wall like a buffalo at a garden party," when, really, I was just giving full rein to the worst of my impulses as Jean egged me on. Little did I know that I had such behavior within me. In retrospect, it might have been better if such impulses had never been revealed.

What I should have known was this: my own time would eventually come, and the roles would not always go to yours truly. Nor would the rules within which we live stay the same. I was twenty-five years old at the time and the center of the universe; what did I know? I stayed in the warm, humid embrace of that center for the next ten years until my star began to fade, but I had never realized how fleeting such favor could be. I should have also realized that theater, like any other community endeavor, is meant to be a product of the whole and a redemption of the public weal, rather than for the benefit of one or another of its various practitioners. And that's a lesson I should have learned from the beginning.

◎ ◎ ◎

In the first months of my employment at the winery, my life found a bit of equilibrium, but you can probably guess some of the various ways I set about disturbing the waters. First, there was my lack of enthusiasm as well as audible sound in my nightly rendition of "Hallelujah," an exercise which continued to seem like pandering to the schmaltz in all of us. Not that I was against pandering, per se, but our provincial and amateurish treatment of such a song did seem like an offense against good taste. More than once Dr. Winkler called me into his office because the rest of the staff was complaining; and yet, he didn't do more than mention it before he was asking my opinion about the latest offerings at the Rep, so I couldn't believe my reticence was that grave an offense. More important were those afternoons and evenings after Julia began rehearsals when my evening shift was over at Vino Veritas, when I was alone and at loose ends. You can believe me or not: I *did* know how to turn on the television, and I *wasn't* unhappy to be alone, but I also wasn't unhappy to uncork a discounted bottle or two of VV's Pinot in those empty evening hours before starting in on the harder stuff. To my mind I was merely filling in the time the way that a four-year-old fills in the children's menu, although by the time Julia returned home at midnight one night in February, I had crossed any number of lines and was well on my way to blacking out. What started out as a commercial for my own well-being ended with me howling about the Rep and their crimes against me and the rightful plying of my trade. Mrs. Steinhauser, our timid common-wall neighbor to the west, called the police, finally, and in a decision of the rarest common sense, Julia waited until the next afternoon to bail me out and drag my sorry ass home.

"What is your problem?" she said. "I mean, really. You were pounding on Mrs. Steinhauser's door and peeking in her windows? Wearing your underwear?" Because she was a good person by nature, Julia's accusations came in the form of questions.

"I honestly don't remember," I said, trying to unknot my neck from the way I'd slept in the drunk tank, "but I think I was warm. I remember thinking I was a pirate. Arrr."

"It was thirty-six degrees, your underwear was on your head, and with the way you've been packing on the pounds, that's nothing that anyone wants to see. Trust me."

"It felt warmer than that to me. Now, if you don't mind," I said, shutting my eyes, "my head hurts, the light's bright, and your voice sounds like sandpaper."

"You're welcome," she said. "Let me turn the radio to death metal or NPR, whichever comes first and hurts more."

She wasn't above kicking me when I was down, but somehow, she kicked me with kindness, and she couldn't stop herself from laughing. I couldn't say I didn't deserve it—the kicking, that is—and deep down I knew she meant it for my own good; my drinking had become something of a problem of daily proportions whereas previously it had only been a sometime problem aggravated by the aggravations of unusual people or circumstance. Like Bobby Danforth or Jean Petrucchi or the social corrections that the Rep felt compelled to make. Or Julia-as-Blanche, who left to take her bows at three evening shows each week as well as two afternoon matinees once rehearsals were over. I attended a preview, and then I went again at her opening. I can't say I didn't like her performance. She was wonderful; I started crying convulsively at the preview, and my tears were so shattering that the woman two seats over handed me the ball of Kleenex she'd been saving for herself. Julia-as-Blanche was brittle, she was vulnerable, the embodiment of a life lived within her own delusions, and as tall and frantic as she managed to be as Maggie, she was that petite and despondent as Blanche. Maybe I saw a little something of myself in her performance. After opening night, I called her parents to berate them for turning their daughter into an accountant or for trying to. It makes no sense, I know, but I was angry at them because it wasn't me on stage with her.

"Don't you understand what a treasure she is?" I think I said.

"Who is this?" her father said. His voice was hoarse as well as phlegmy, what you might expect from a seventy-year-old rancher who'd lived his entire life on the eastern side of the Cascades amid all that dust.

"Who?" he said again, after I told him who I was. "Never heard of him."

"Not him," I said. "Me. Frank Delgado. I'm living with your daughter. You should know she has a gift, and you really ought to see her on stage. She owns it, man." Man. I called her father "man" because I was trying to channel my own rugged individualist in conversation with her cranky, conservative father.

"She's a lesbo," he said, "and you're drunk," which wasn't entirely true because I had only started the second bottle, but that didn't change the facts as they were: her parents were older generation killjoys who had dismissed their daughter when she tried to tell them, with her honesty intact, who she was. They were unwilling to believe that a person could have a multiplicity of desires, and they were equally unwilling to believe that a life in theater had anything to say that was superior to a life in cows; there was no arguing with them as Julia herself had once told me, and proof of that was her father hanging up on me. I was probably slurring my words since my diction has never been my strong suit. One more reason why my first role had been without lines.

As proud as I was of her, I was also as bitter as I had ever been, and every performance night at eleven o'clock, I couldn't stop myself from opening another bottle to celebrate as well as forget. Hence my encounter with Mrs. Steinhauser's anxieties, the police at midnight, and eighteen hours of civic confinement.

Oh, one last thing . . . In the middle of Julia's *Streetcar* run, while I was still doing penance for that last act of misbehavior, Destiny moved into the bedroom next door to our own.

◉ ◉ ◉

Destiny is difficult to explain, as a concept as well as the person I came to know. Let me start by saying that Destiny-as-roommate was not my idea. Here again, Julia must take a bow. And no, Destiny is neither pseudonym nor joke. Her parents, science fiction junkies and potheads, *were* having a laugh at their own expense when she was born in the year 2001, years after giving up their thoughts of raising a family. They might as well have called her Space or Final Frontier. They would have called her HAL, but no matter how out there they might have been, they were still constrained by their own gender biases. And then, 9/11 happened, and their baby seemed less a promise of renewal and optimism and more like an omen of the End of Days. The net result was that, as the years went by and our War on Terror seemed to be without end, they took less and less interest in her and more interest in the pot farm they were shepherding from underground economy to legitimate enterprise.

One evening, on a night when she didn't have to break down for two hours as Blanche, Julia finished with her second job cooking the books in the Vino Veritas office. I had mumbled my part of "Hallelujah," and then did my professional duty by rolling up silverware and polishing the glassware in order to get ready for the next day's stampede. At ten o'clock, I was waiting in the parking lot, listening to sports vomit on the radio in Julia's car, when I saw her coming down the stairs accompanied by the girl that I often saw running the dishwasher in the steam room behind the kitchen. This young woman (Destiny, of course) was wearing the uniform of her own generation: jeans with studiously manufactured holes, mismatched tennis shoes, and one of those T-shirts that is either purchased or pilfered from a concert. There were rings through her nose and ears and eyebrows because she was younger and angrier, and she was still damp from her labors, so much so that her hair, which was short and would have otherwise been spiky was, instead, lying flat against her skull, as though it had been pomaded.

I got out of the car and waited for an explanation.

"Look, Frank honey," Julia said. "I told her you wouldn't mind, okay?"

"Sure," I said, "I don't mind anything." Then I thought about the things I *do* mind, such as the smell of brussels sprouts and political ads on television, which was just the beginning of a very long list, and I had to shake myself to break the spell. "What don't I mind?"

"Destiny is going to stay with us for a few days," Julia said.

"Okay," I said. "And I know destiny since I am the master of my fate. Invictus and all that."

"Don't be dumb. She's got nowhere else to go."

"Okay," I said again. "I said okay."

"Look," Destiny said, and here she put her hands on her slim hips. "You don't have to do this. I told her there's no shortage of parks in this town."

She had one of those backpacks on a frame and what looked like the contents of a vagrant's shopping cart dangling from a carousel of straps.

"Not a problem unless it becomes one." I pointed at her pack. "You don't happen to have a baseball bat or a revolver in that thing, do you?"

"No," she said seriously, "but I do have a knife and some Mace. In case you're wondering. Or wandering."

"That's fine," I said. "I know to stay out of the way in my own house. We've seen one another in the hallways of the winery, but this is our first time to be introduced. Just so we're clear that those are only tools for defense."

"Don't jiggle the bathroom doorknob while I'm on the pot, and we'll be fine."

"Don't you worry," I said. "We have bushes and shrubs. I won't even use the bathroom. I'll shower at the Y."

"Frank," Julia said, "you can stop being stupid now."

So Destiny moved in, I steered a wide berth, and while it was only supposed to be for a day or two, the guest bedroom became hers before I knew what had happened. After a week I saw posters of Virginia Woolf and RBG going up, and the knick-knacks, left over from my mother's time, went into a box that was shoved into the closet, a little too summarily for my taste.

"I guess that's a lesson for us all," I said to Julia that night. She'd taken her bows to the standing ovation that had become so standard as to be meaningless; even so, she was still a little juiced with being adored, no matter how counterfeit that adoration might be.

"What?" she said. "What lesson?"

"How disposable we all are. This girl was only supposed to be here for a day or two, but she seems to have moved in, lock, stock, and barrel."

"You're bitter about your mother's Hummels and Lladrós being retired? Come on. You hated those things. It's not like you went in there to dust."

She had a point, but it did seem like a reminder of the harsh and bitter conclusion to which we all come in the end. It may sound coincidental, but my mother had died while Julia and I were playing *Cat*, and it was hard when I considered that my best year professionally had also been one of my worst personally. Night after night, Julia and I stood on stage holding hands, and then I went home to relieve the hospice nurse of her duties. I must have had some resilience then, but ten years later it was hard to remember. Money and self-esteem might have played a part, but if she had lingered past my salad days, I don't think I could have coped. As it was, her death might have had something to do with my version of Hamlet in the next season; in every scene with Gertrude, I nearly broke down, and while the reviews cited the tenderness, grief, and anger with which my prince approached his mother, they had no idea what those scenes cost me or where they came from.

Six weeks or so after Destiny took squatter's possession of the guest bedroom, I found myself more and more the third wheel of our wobbly tricycle of a relationship, and it seemed clear that Julia's former disposition was asserting itself. Is it any wonder why I snapped? Destiny and I would return from our respective duties at the winery, and both of us would then sit up waiting for Julia to come home from the theater, waiting to see who she'd choose. When I was losing out on her company two nights out of three, I had had enough.

"What the hell?" I said. "The figurines were one thing, but now she gets all the attention at playtime?"

"Jealousy doesn't become you," she said. "She's an eighteen-year-old girl who's had one bad break after another. Unlike some buffaloes who have been given everything."

She was speaking of the townhouse in which we were now ensconced. My mother had scrimped and saved and paid off the mortgage only to have both breasts removed without any observable benefit. Not to mention how the doctors poisoned her to save her. The best I could do was to keep the place insured and the taxes paid, neither of which was a small thing, given my recent reversals of income.

"I'll be the first to admit how lucky I've been," I said, "at least until recently. But Jesus, you might as well be sleeping with your ward. Doesn't that seem a little incestuous?"

"Oh, please," she said. "You make it sound so Victorian." But she had no response other than to close the guest bedroom door in my face.

That still doesn't excuse what I did in retaliation. The next evening, when Julia was off again playing the fragile Blanche, I took the winery key ring from her underwear drawer in the dresser, went to work at Vino Veritas, and stole about $4,000 out of the cash box in her office. As I said, I had the property tax and insurance to pay, and I was behind on any number of other bills that came through the mail like a constant stream of bad news. I was wrong, I admit that, but I justified my actions to myself by saying that (1) I wasn't getting any financial contribution from either Julia or Destiny, (2) neither Julia nor Destiny seemed to care one way or another how I might have been feeling about the changes taking place in my own house, and (3) I was only taking back an amount that, according to my calculations, I was owed. As it turned out, it didn't take Julia long to discover what I'd done, and it didn't take longer than the next moment for her to put two and two together.

"Look," she said, the next evening when she came to work on the books, "I'm not going to the police, and I'm not going to tell Dr. Winkler, but you have to make this right."

I feigned innocence as though recalling a role from the dark and distant past. "What are you talking about?"

"You know good and well," she said. In that moment, she was no Blanche and I was no Stanley, but we were thrown back again into Maggie and Brick, even if she was also picking up my Judas along the way. "I had some savings, and I've replaced what's missing, but I'll expect you to pay me back. That's only fair. Do you hear me? I never took you to be a thief, but now I'm sorry I ever trusted you. In the meantime, consider this my notice: Destiny and I are leaving."

I interpreted that to mean that because she was betraying me, we were even financially, but that's not how she saw it; she repeated her threat to report me to various authority figures if

I didn't make good with her on the theft. The betrayal, however, was still on.

"You know I don't have any money," I said. I was whining. You would be right to say so. "Half the time I get stiffed by the out-of-town fatsos."

"You've heard the saying about glass houses, haven't you?" she said. "Have you looked at yourself lately?"

◎ ◎ ◎

Maybe I'm not the smartest guy in the world. I said that already, but it bears repeating. Maybe it's what contributed to my undoing in the beginning and then the undoing of my undoing. I can be convinced of what's right, even if it takes me a little longer than the next guy, but by the time I acquire the conviction of certainty, the train has left the station, as the saying goes. The first Christmas after I moved back in with my mother, she looked at pictures that we had taken of ourselves while we ate dinner and unwrapped the presents we'd bought for ourselves. My mother scrolled through the JPEGs on the new digital camera and sighed, "Well, that's what we look like." What she meant by that was: we are who we are, no matter how industrious we might be to reframe our appearance in our own imaginations; in the end, we're the only ones to be fooled. At the time, my mother was wearing a turban and bathrobe that looked remarkably oversized, even when one considered all that had been taken away from her. She could not avoid the truth, in a way that I've never been denied for so many years.

Julia and Destiny left more quickly than I thought possible, and it took me longer than necessary to realize that plans had been in the works for some time. They had an apartment, they had movers, and—*for Christ's sake*—they had boxes. This is how oblivious I had been, and they were simply waiting for their moment to arrive, which I gave to them in spades as soon as I unlocked the door of Julia's office.

Some months later I got the news from Dr. Winkler that, regrettably, my services at Vino Veritas were no longer needed. This, too, I should have foreseen. Julia had been remarkably reticent regarding my actions, but when I couldn't pay her back for the money she had replaced and when she realized that all of my castoff electronics wouldn't make a dent in what I owed, she finally broke the news to her boss in a way that made only me look bad. If she was a good actor, she was an equally good accountant, one who knew how to talk her way around the spreadsheets of a thriving business.

"I hate to do this, you know." The good doctor looked me up and down. "I know this hasn't been an easy time—you're an actor, not a wine pourer, after all—but we can't function like this." He looked at me again, as though for the first time. "Have you put on weight?"

So I was fat and I was a thief, albeit uncharged, and I was without employment, but that didn't mean I was without dependents. After Julia and Destiny left, I embarked on a program of self-improvement. I locked up the liquor and put the key in a place I hoped I'd forget, and I started walking, mile after mile, figuring that, even if the exercise was not robust, the time it took was time spent away from the refrigerator and any longing I might have for the liquor cabinet. I was in the habit of walking down East Main and through downtown and into the park, on the trail that straddles the creek. Which is where I met George, who was maybe forty years old—although to all appearances, with his gray beard and the lines crosshatching his face, he could have been Medicare eligible and beyond. He was sitting on top of one of the picnic tables and holding his panhandler's sign, a collection bucket at his feet and a tallboy of vodka in the inside pocket of his trench coat. His sign read, "Free Freedom! Punished for self-characterization!" which meant nothing to me, except that it caught my attention. I had a dollar so I dropped it in his bucket.

"What could that possibly mean?" I said, gesturing to his sign.

"Sit down," he said, "and let Freedom tell you all about it."

Which he then proceeded to do, a wild tale that involved any number of time-tested bugaboos: aliens and the CIA and the Trilateral Commission, you name it. He was clearly crazy, and my only role was to smile and nod and mutter syllables that could be mistaken for encouragement. He went on and on while I inhaled the cedar-scented air, and none of it could have been true until he finally admitted that at one time, he had been a duly elected member of the town council, a position he held for three or four years until one of his claims came under scrutiny. Part of his campaign literature mentioned his service during the Iraq invasion, an experience that had left him sympathetic and understanding of those who were veterans suffering from stress-related disorders. As it turned out, however, the closest he had come to military service was his position as a security guard for the Macy's in Eugene. He had once chased a shoplifter into the mall parking lot, where the shoplifter was hit by a car, resulting in a lawsuit for the department store from both the shoplifter and the driver of the car that hit him. After years of whitewash and smokescreen, Freedom had been brought low by one of those military-imposter shaming groups that you see periodically on the news. Without admitting anything, he resigned after the story broke, not willing to risk the humiliation of a defeat in the next election.

"I *felt* as though I had been in Iraq," he said. "You know? If you can feel it, you can be it. I mean I read everything about the invasion. Even the poetry. 'Here, Bullet.' Etcetera, etcetera."

"I know you," I said. "George, isn't it? George 'Freedom' Manwaring. You were in the newspaper every day for a month."

"Okay," he said. "You got me." On the glum side, he was, with his cover blown. "And you're Frank Delgado. You were Hamlet back in the day."

"True," I said, "but like you, I don't advertise."

Now that Julia and her little doxie were gone, it seemed fitting that I do my bit of penance. This vagrant who was Freedom would find a home in Destiny's old room, but as with Destiny, a temporary good deed became something of a permanent cross to bear. He brought out my mother's tchotchkes, which I thought sweet, but then it became clear that he only wanted them as garment hooks from which to air out the second skin of his trench coat. More than once I walked down the hallway and heard the horrifying sound of delicate kitsch hitting the hardwood floor, and over time, no matter how many times I showed him the bathroom and shower, the odor that began to permeate the upstairs became more than I could bear. The mail was tossed hither and yon on the floor and dirty dishes grew like mountains in the sink, Julia stole all my out-of-date electronics and that smell from the guest bedroom evolved from body odor to rotting leftovers. And then I didn't see him at all.

What was I supposed to do?

I could have called Julia because I felt helpless or the police because it was appropriate. Instead, I pounded on the door and yelled, "George, I know you're in there." I pounded and pounded but got no response. I shook the doorknob, but it was locked, and I was too rattled to find the key, so I broke down the hollow-core door. I was expecting to find George in his oily and dirty clothes, his eyes rolled back and his mouth a rictus of surprise, victim of heart attack or stroke. But instead what I found in the middle of the unmade bed was a week's worth of dirty dishes and half-a-dozen piles of shit on the floor. The shit had been artfully arranged, but there was no George. So much for my one brief bout of intended altruism.

That's when I did call Julia because I needed to tell the story to someone who would listen even if she wouldn't care.

"He's probably back in the park," she said. "He's sick in the head, and there's nothing you can do about that."

"I guess."

"Speaking of which, the other one's gone, in case you hadn't heard."

After accusing Julia of trying to micromanage her life, Destiny had gone back to live with her feckless, pot-obsessed parents, who—against all the odds of their own life-mismanagement—had made good on their cannabis investment and were now Republicans and small-business owners. She returned to a home that was cleaned weekly by a team of Oaxacans who worked only for cash, used clothing, and canned goods. When Destiny took off her manifold rings and studs to let her face heal, they bought her a cashmere sweater set and paid her way back into an online GED program. Humans. Is there no end to our talent for surprise?

"That's not the worst of it, if you can believe it," Julia said. "You might look the part, but I was all set to be Falstaff."

"I'll believe anything," I said, and it was the truth.

"Comedy," she said. "I was finally going to do comic relief. I was looking forward to getting a laugh."

The Rep had planned to do an adaptation of *Henry IV, Part I* with an all-female cast when the pandemic hit. Julia had been preparing to play in a fat suit so large that she could bounce herself onstage, but then the lockdown orders came. The theaters closed, and the winery closed the kitchen and tasting room, and even if she still had bookkeeping work to do, Dr. Winkler had to cut everyone back to minimum hours. She was nearly out of luck, almost as much as I. Did I feel vindicated in some way, that I was not the only one whose life was suddenly in free fall? Surprisingly not. Only sorry for the everything that everyone was losing. It turned out I didn't wish ill upon Jean Petrucchi and Bobby Danforth and the identity politics of theater. Not really. Not in my heart of hearts, not in the deepest part of myself. If I once did, that was my mistake; we are all that desperate to be seen and heard, and I ask the universe for forgiveness.

"We've both been abandoned," I said, "but things could be worse. I know it's not ideal, and I'm not your cup of tea, but you're welcome to give up the apartment and come back. The guest bedroom will need to be steam cleaned, but taxes and insurance won't be due for another six months, and we can figure things out as we go."

"Maybe," she said, "but you should know that the last pay period, Dr. Winkler paid us in cases of Pinot. So I'm not a light move. We'll need a truck and a strong back, but your alcoholic needs will be met and your weaknesses exploited."

"Get thee behind me, Satan," I said, "but I've been known to hoist a glass or a bottle. Much to my own regret."

"Okay," she said. "We'll sell cases as we need the cash. And that will be my job: to keep you in check. God knows it's a part I've played before."

"You're not unhappy, coming back here to live?"

"Why should I be?" she said. "I know you about as well as anybody. I know where all the fault lines lie. Why shouldn't we be happy?"

"Wouldn't it be funny," I said, "if that was true?"

◉

The Stories of an Only Child

I. Theologians, 1959

Before I could be enrolled in kindergarten, the Episcopalian school affiliated with my parents' church required my parents to teach me the Lord's Prayer. So one late summer's evening, my mother called me inside, and I sat between her and my father on the sofa in the den. I had been playing with my best friend, Carla Benson, who was a year older, and we had been arguing about which hand went at the bottom of the bat, the right or the left. We had just discovered that she was left-handed and I was right, and we were hitting each other over the head with our plastic bats.

"I killed you," Carla said.

"Killed you first," I said.

"No, you didn't."

When my mother picked me up by the arms, I complained because we were having a good time, and because the long California evening still had light left in it, the sky streaked in bands of red and orange, and to the east only the lightest shade of the purple night. Despite my protests, she brought me inside, much to Carla's disgust.

"Weanie head," Carla said.

"Snot brains," I said.

"That's quite enough," my mother said, "both of you. That's revolting."

In the den, my father was watching television with a high-ball glass in his hand and a prayer book in his lap. My mother switched off the set, and the black-and-white picture shrank to a pinprick of light which remained for a minute or more, unwilling to give up the ghost.

"There's something important your mother wants to discuss," my father said. Looking above the rim of his glass at my mother, he took one final swallow. "Me, too, I guess."

"It's time, kiddo," my mother said, "that you learn how to pray."

Actually, I already knew how to pray. Every evening at bedside, my parents knelt with me while I said the child's evening prayer:

Now I lay me down to sleep,
I pray the Lord my soul to keep.
If I should die before I wake,
I pray the Lord my soul will take.

When the last two lines scared me too much, my mother recited for me an alternative ending that went "Guide me through the starry night / and wake me when the sun shines bright." So far, I hadn't died, but then we said the alternative ending quite a few times as well, making our plea for waking as well as soul preservation. I had worried about dying ever since I fell into a koi pond when I was three. By the time my father pulled me out, my eyes were bulging in their sockets like a carp's, and I've gone by the name Fish ever since, a reminder of my near miss. In spite of my fears, my father, a lapsed Catholic, didn't believe prayers should be changed. He knelt with us but refused to recite the corrupted version.

"This is a special prayer," my mother explained. "One that God Himself gave us to say."

"Himself," my father muttered, "that's what the H. stands for. Jesus H."

"Alan," my mother said.

"It goes like this," my father said. He recited Matthew's version from memory with his hands folded on the prayer book, his eyes closed, his forehead furrowed in concentration, like the good acolyte he had once been. My mother and I watched while he mumbled the last lines—the Protestant addition—unwillingly.

"Aren't you supposed to kneel?"

"Yes, absolutely," my father said. "Hell, we ought to be genuflecting. Haven't had a good genuflect in years." He would have gotten out of his chair if it weren't for my mother's fingers on his shoulder.

"You can say it kneeling, sitting, standing, or even when you're in bed at night," my mother said. "It's all-purpose. The only thing you have to make sure of is that you mean what you say."

Taking turns, my mother and father helped me through the prayer, line by line, until I could say it by heart. Then they asked if I understood. I said yes, but in my bed that night, as I said the prayer over again for myself, I wondered about the art God did in heaven and if hallowed was the same as hollow, His name echoing dully like a pipe, a box without a present inside.

In my bedroom, there was a nightlight which my parents turned off when they went to bed, a lamp with an inner shade that turned, propelled by the heat of the bulb. On the outer shade was the picture of a passenger train rolling through forests and mountains. When the inner shade was turning, the train appeared to move. Now, while I had been saying the prayer to myself, the movement of the nightlight's reflections seemed ominous and foreboding. Dark shapes loomed at the foot of my bed, then leaped to the ceiling and raced across the walls. Once, to stop me from playing with the electrical cords of floor lamps and the television set, my father had told me a story about the troll who lived in the outlets: he burned the skin off the bones of little boys, making their hair sizzle and pop.

"Our Father," I began. "Our Father." My mother had said that the Lord's Prayer was a source of comfort and consolation, but try as I might, in the face of certain trolls, I could not remember what came after.

☉ ☉ ☉

The minister of St. James was a dedicated Anglophile named Chadwick. Father Chadwick was unmarried and did not much care for children, so he had appointed a retired minister, Father Millerton, to the post of school chaplain, a volunteer position with one singular benefit: the parsonage at the corner of the church parking lot, a ramshackle adobe house, that Father Chadwick neither wanted nor cared for. Father Millerton had outlived his family—war had claimed his two sons, disease his wife and daughter—and he lived alone in the three-room adobe. At noon, when kindergarten was officially over, the entire class of fifteen five-year-olds was led to his living room, where he served cookies and punch, and he taught us songs, and we prayed for our families, our pets, and the missionaries in the Belgian Congo. He also told us stories from the Bible, how Jesus turned water into wine, the night Daniel spent with the lions, and the day the sun stood still; he likewise told us about the missionaries in the remotest parts of the world—how they forded raging streams in Indonesia on the backs of crocodiles, how thousands of pygmies and cannibals who wore no clothes had responded to the word of God but only after they had killed the messengers of the Gospel. Father Millerton had once served as a missionary in Dutch Guiana before ill health had forced him to resign, and his stories usually consisted of one faithful servant of God whose death hastened the conversions of thousands of natives. The songs he taught us were ones like "Onward, Christian Soldiers" and a children's hymn about the saints of God, whose various occupations included doctor and queen, soldier and shepherdess. When we sang the line about the saint who was slain by a fierce wild beast, I felt a furrow of claws and teeth running the length of my spine.

I loved Father Millerton, but not everyone shared the same opinion. During his stories there was as much whispering and covered laughter as there was attention. He was a big man who wore thick-soled shoes, and his black clerical shirt and trousers were always dusted with the snow of his dandruff and the scattering ashes of his cigars, a habit he said he'd picked up in the Guianas to ward off insects. His thick white hair fell in disordered hunks over his forehead. His flat red nose sat in the middle of a remarkably square face, and now, when I study photographs, I think he must have borne some resemblance to Charles Laughton as Quasimodo. There was no mistaking his resemblance to the drawing of the pigs in our classroom's blue set of Bible stories.

My mother was not entirely certain that she approved of Father Millerton either. She had qualms about fierce wild beasts, and she felt that "missionary" was far from the wisest career objective, whereas my mind was filled with pictures of fabulously decorated men and women, unconverted heathens ready to drop to their knees, a picture no doubt influenced by *National Geographic*.

One day, after the class had been led to Father Millerton's living room, after our cookies and punch and stories and songs and prayers, and after the last of the other students had departed with their mothers, my mother still had not come and I was left with Father Millerton. Dean Patterson, the fattest boy of our class, was the last to leave before me. As his mother pulled him to his feet, his belly stuck out between his trousers and his T-shirt, and he whispered to me, "Crazy, crazy Millie," while sticking his fingers in his nose and grunting.

"He is not," I whispered back, afraid that an adult might hear.

When Father Millerton returned from his kitchen with a fresh package of cookies, Dean and his mother were leaving. Dean's face wore the look of the penitent.

Father Millerton set the cookies on the floor in front of me. "Well," he said, "so it's just the two of us." He sat down on the floor, crossing his legs Indian-style. With a sigh of relief, he removed the white clerical collar. He winked at me. "I told Father Chadwick I'd wear it," he said, "but you don't mind, hey?"

"No."

"Good boy."

He tore open the bag of cookies and motioned that I should help myself. "Now we can get to know one another," he said. "I'd like to get to know each of you children. Jesus loved little children. Did you know that?"

"He is the shepherd, and I am His lamb," I said, repeating a lesson learned that very day.

"Yes! Absolutely!" Father Millerton beamed. He slapped his knees, and the cigar ash rose in a cloud then resettled on his not-so-black pants. "We are all Jesus' lambs. Did you know that? Yes? I ask you now, do I look like a lamb, hey?"

"No," I said, slapping my knees as well. At this moment Father Millerton looked even more like the demon-possessed swine than I had remembered.

"Of course, I don't," he said. "I never looked like a lamb in my life." He tugged at one ear. "A pig, maybe." When I didn't say anything, eating a cookie instead, he ate one also, and then I ate another one.

We talked for a while of baseball, of Father Millerton's favorite team, the Dodgers, two years in town, ripped from the womb of Brooklyn. They had lately won the National League pennant, and Father Millerton was full of praise for his champions, the pitchers Don Drysdale and Johnny Podres, outfielders Duke Snider and Wally Moon. This last player Father Millerton talked about the most, his inside-out swing sending high pop flies—Moon shots—just over the short outfield fence of Memorial Coliseum.

"He has used all of his God-given abilities," he said, "and he is an example to us all."

While Father Millerton talked baseball, I ate cookies. We were sitting in the middle of the living room floor. Mementos hung all around us. Religious scenes took up one wall near the door—Jesus in the garden of Gethsemane, Joseph sold by his brothers to the Egyptians. On another wall commemorative plates, each one marking the opening of a World's Fair or the date of another Christmas, sat in rows on specially built shelves. On the far wall above a television set with a round picture tube hung the pictures of Father Millerton's dead children and wife. The sons were dressed in their uniforms and refusing to smile. The daughter, much younger than the sons, looked pinched and uncomfortable, as if the disease that would claim her was already at its deadly work. The wife, on the other hand, was white-haired and hearty, and I was sorry that she was no longer alive.

"I see you're looking at my family," Father Millerton said.

"No," I said, "not really." Speaking of dead people always made me nervous, a nervousness that had its origins in my own near-death experience but was exacerbated by the funeral of my mother's uncle. He had been dressed in a dark suit and white shirt that I had never seen him wear, and his sharp chin protruded above the rim of the opened casket.

"They were the best family that a man could have," Father Millerton was saying, "and they were so good, God took them away from me early so He could enjoy them all the more."

"Mrs. Winter says that dead people get to see Jesus," I said. Our teacher, Mrs. Winter, had taught this particular lesson on the occasion of the death of the class frog. "They get to see Jesus and watch what we're doing."

"You're something of a scholar, I can see that already." Father Millerton stood, moving in front of his pictures. "They're watching us this very minute; I have to believe that."

A chill went up and down my back, and my body shook so hard that I had to turn my head away from the family photographs. I ate more cookies and counted the drops of blood on Jesus' brow.

Suddenly, Father Millerton bellowed, "Do you believe, son? I mean do you really believe in what you say?" He said this in a great, booming voice, and it was not just in my imagination that I heard the plates rattling on the walls. Now, I think that it was the voice he used in the Guianas, his own natural PA system used for preaching good news to the natives and savages, his words not to be lost in the buzz of the cooking fire or in the drone of insects. But then, in his living room, his voice startled me, and I edged backwards along the floor. Father Millerton grabbed me by the wrist.

"I ask you," he said, his voice now a whisper, "do you believe?"

"Yes," I breathed.

"In what?" Still the hush of seriousness. One ham-like hand brushed my cheek. "In what? Tell me, son."

"Jesus," I croaked.

He exhaled as if he had been holding his breath. "Good," he said, "good boy." He scooped me up and carried me outside. The sun was bright and we both blinked. "The angels are rejoicing, Fish. Did you know that? They're having a party with cake and ice cream and cookies because of you." He held me in his left arm and tweaked me on the cheek with his free hand. I giggled and we were better friends than we were before.

"There is joy in knowing Jesus. And you—with a name like yours—you must be one of His favorites. You know he fed multitudes with the meat of a few fish? You should feel blessed."

I was happy, it was true. I was very happy and light as air, buoyed up as I was in the arms of Father Millerton. I was very, very happy. But then, I was usually happy, though it was not to be a feeling I would always have.

"When I see the faith of children," Father Millerton was saying, "I believe all the more."

He had walked to the rear of the house, and now we were facing the baseball diamond. To the left were the classrooms and on the other side of the diamond, the church. The buzzer signaling two o'clock recess sounded in the classrooms, and children, all older than myself, poured from the flung-open doorways, choosing up sides for quick fifteen-minute games of kickball and freeze tag and jump rope. Two girls and a boy ran to Father Millerton. They grabbed his legs and the boy held onto his belt loops. There were others who made pig noises and pushed up their noses, but Father Millerton walked past them, paying them no heed.

"Do you know," he said, sitting us down on one of the lunch tables, "do you know that Jesus said that if you have faith the size of a mustard seed you can tell the mountains to move and they'll move? Or those palm trees over there—tell them to hop into the sea and they'll do as they're told? How much faith do you need, what do you think? Tell me that."

One of the girls answered: "A mustard seed is very, very small."

"And yet I haven't moved a tree in years," Father Millerton said. "But then, maybe God hasn't desired that to happen either." He began to speak more to himself than to the four of us sitting clustered about him. "God's wishes," he said, "His wishes come first."

I was watching the palm trees which surrounded the baseball diamond. They were waving in unison, timed by the breeze, swaying back and forth in the motion we used with our hula hoops, their shaved trunks bending, the ragged fringe underneath the new fronds catching the air like fingers. With all this movement I could well believe their roots might lift from the ground in some spectacle of animation, then march the hour's drive to the beach and the ocean. Anything was possible, for Father Millerton had said that it could be so.

"I once saw a Saramaccan native throw a rock at another man. The rock struck the man in the temple. He fell down with a groan and died. While some of the natives detained the man who had thrown the rock and others attempted to revive the victim, I heard—as if in words—God speak to me. 'Help the man up,' He said. 'No, Lord,' I said, 'for I saw the breath go out of him, he's dead as a doorknob, he's dead as my daughter back in Illinois.' 'Raise him up,' I heard. There were no audible words, I'm sure, but I knew. I knew in my heart what God's direction was to be. Yet like Jonah, I tarried, a victim of doubt. *Raise him up,* He said, and this time I knew that I must perish ere I avoided the Lord's command. I walked to the little group huddled around the corpse. His mother was wailing and striking herself on her breasts and shoulders. I touched her and said, 'Everything is all right.' She didn't understand me, of course, because I spoke in English, but she stood up. I grabbed her son's cold and lifeless hand, my own heart filled with a heavy doubt, but obeying God nonetheless. 'Jesus, Jesus, Jesus,' I said, and I felt the blood rush back into this young man's limbs, hot and vital. He scrambled to his feet, a dazed look on his face—as if to say, 'Where have I been? I've gone and come back again'—and by nightfall the entire village had come to know the Lord Jesus."

We all gasped and the other boy said, "Wow."

"You children have the power of pure belief, neither shaken by doubts nor disfigured by uncertainty. You are the next generation of saints and you must work to preserve your youth."

The buzzer was sounding, marking the end of recess and the beginning of the last period of classes. The other boy and the two girls began to move away reluctantly. Each one of them said, "Goodbye, Father Millerton." They touched him, and one of the girls even did a little curtsey.

I was sitting on his spacious lap, my head resting against the black of his shirt, seeing once again the dead native who popped back into a new life. This made me think of the dead, white-haired wife trapped behind the glass of the picture frame.

"Maybe Mrs. Millerton could come back," I said.

He smiled. "I think about it at night," he said. "But no. Even Wally Moon must have his talent joined with God's wish before he can hit a home run."

"Maybe you could go to her," I said.

"Yes," he said, though the smile was disappearing. "That's the more likely story, isn't it?"

Across the baseball diamond, Father Chadwick, wearing his black suit coat even in the afternoon heat, walked toward us, the last milling children giving him wide berth. When he had reached the lunch tables, he stopped in front of us, refusing Father Millerton's invitation to "a seat and a discussion."

"Father," Chadwick said, "what have you been telling these children?"

"The truth, Father," Father Millerton said.

"I'll have you know that I just now overheard two of your young disciples telling the other children that they could make the mountains disappear."

"Overheard out of context, I'm sure."

"Telling war stories again, hmm?"

"They are not war stories," Father Millerton said quietly. "They are the exact record of my ministry in the jungle." I thought his voice had never sounded so subdued.

Father Chadwick ignored his older colleague, and turning to me, he said, "Fish, your mother called. She's had difficulties with her car, and I'll be taking you home." He began to pry me away from Father Millerton's shoulder. "And you," he said, addressing the older man, "I would ask you to remember that you are the chaplain of this school and not a proselytizer for your own brand of mysticism."

"God is inside you, and His Power is at your discretion," Father Millerton whispered in my ear as my fingers were persuaded to let go.

Father Chadwick led me across the baseball field to the rear of the church and the parking lot. Once, as we walked, I turned to see that Father Millerton had remained seated on the lunch bench, carefully unwrapping the cellophane from a cigar. His black shirt was open and collarless, and his white hair was blowing in the wind. Father Chadwick pulled me along, helping me into the backseat of his car. Then I was warned not to stand with my arms hooked over the back of the front seat. Nor was I allowed to put my shoes on the seat's upholstery. But I was to tell Father Chadwick everything.

"Don't take him too seriously," he said when I had finished my very dramatic retelling of the native and the rock. "Old people don't always mean what they say. You have to listen politely, but you don't have to believe them."

"I believe him," I said.

"But you don't have to," my mother said later that afternoon. "You can't always believe every story you hear. Sometimes stories are meant to be enjoyed, but no one believes that they're true."

I did not say anything to her then, but I spent the evening with Carla Benson, telling her of the palm trees which could walk if God were to will it so.

◎ ◎ ◎

The next year I was in first grade and at school all day, but Father Millerton was not. He had been relieved of all duties and placed in the diocesan retirement facility. A short time later he died, and my parents did not tell me until I had begun to ask for his address so I could write. I thought of him often. The church had suffered financial difficulties and Father Chadwick, in addition to his regular church duties, was forced to live in the parsonage and serve as school chaplain. We learned no more songs and we were told no more stories except for very forgettable ones involving talking bunnies and moralistic cows.

This was an election year, and my parents—who held very definite views—watched each of the televised debates. They bemoaned Nixon's waxy looks as opposed to Kennedy's youth and obvious vitality.

"It's not a fair fight," my father said, "putting this stuff on television. Next thing you'll know we'll be electing actors instead of lawyers. Where will be then?"

Ever the businessman, my father opposed the creeping tide of socialism at home and abroad; Nixon was the man to put a stop to that sort of nonsense. My mother was suspicious of Kennedy's Vatican connection. As my father said, it would be bad enough to turn the country over to immigrant bootlegging Irish. It could only get worse by handing it on to a bunch of ritual-burdened Italians. He'd had enough of it to know.

The morning after the election, my mother woke me with her tears, and I immediately prayed that the right man had been chosen. That my mother would cry about the outcome of a presidential election may be surprising now—it was not then, our nuclear then, when a political choice could alter the fate of the world. My mother was sitting in the den, sniffling into a wad of Kleenex, watching the latest election news coverage. When the results became increasingly clear, my mother sniffled all the more.

I told her that she should not worry, I had prayed to God and God would grant our requests.

I put my head in her lap. My mother combed my hair with her fingers, and I felt the wetness of her damp Kleenex on my neck. "When you pray," she sighed, "you need to pray when it'll do some good. You should have been praying a long time ago, when people were making up their minds."

The thought occurred to me then that God might not work with time in quite the way we do, but I remained silent on the subject. Instead, I said, "Don't worry, someone will shoot him."

The words jumped out of my mouth, stillborn in the air. I had no idea where they had come from, though I knew they were true, and I was afraid of what consequences they might bring once voiced.

"You don't mean that," my mother said. "I don't much care for his politics, but I don't wish for that."

Neither did I. But three years later I felt that my hands had held the gun even if they hadn't pulled the trigger, my initiation into a world where faith and guilt, knowledge and power are equal. And constantly at war.

II. Monopoly

Summer and a troubled time.

An hour before my mother was to leave for a visit with a sick friend, the German shepherd from across the street bit me on the hip and leg. On the other hand, my mother's friend was dying of lung cancer, and she was leaving a husband and two sons. During the Depression, Walter, the husband, had lived with my father's family until both he and my father went into the service during the war. Now, our two families spent every New Year's Eve together, and while their sons, Greg and Jerry, were not my sort—

with little interest in either books or sports, they cared more for things that exploded—we had grown accustomed to staying up past midnight on that one night a year.

But then, my mother had just finished snapping her hose into her garter when the neighbors from across the street carried me screaming to our door, apologizing, but swearing on their honor that Rudolf had been fully inoculated against any and all doggie diseases. I had come to their door, hoping someone could play catch, hide-and-seek, or war, when Rudolf, a trained police dog, broke away from the cleaning woman's hold and pinned me to the cement of the front porch. His teeth tore holes in my jeans and left four perfect punctures in the meat of one thigh. He had bitten me only to let me know he meant business. Most of my screaming was due to his snarling and his drool.

My mother thanked them for bringing me home, then called the hospital to tell the husband that she wouldn't be coming for her visit. "Tell Mavie how sorry I am," I heard her say into the phone. "Please, Walter, I'd be there if I could."

She hung up the phone, then cleaned my superficial wounds, babying me with a vacant, preoccupied look in her eyes. I lay on the couch in the den underneath my grandmother's quilt. *I Love Lucy* was on, and the Ricardos were arguing across the couch in their black-and-white apartment. An hour later, the doorbell rang, and my mother went to see who it was.

Walter stood on the porch. At the time, my mother thought that she had never seen anyone look quite so gray. Already at the age of thirty-five, his hair had become a natural silver, but with the strain of his wife's sickness, his face had turned the color of refrigerated fish. The circles underneath his eyes were swollen into full-fledged bags, the capillaries in his cheeks exploding like popcorn. My mother invited him inside, asking if he would like a drink. It was ten o'clock in the morning. He took straight bourbon.

"How's Mavie?" my mother asked.

Walter shrugged. A policeman who worked the night shift in the downtown detention center, he was still wearing his uniform including the gun belt.

"They called at four this morning, while I'm booking hookers from Beverly Hills," he said. "One of the nurses said it was touch and go, and I better get down to see her before she went, but then she didn't, so I stayed anyway and watched her breathe. The hookers took up a collection. See this?" He spread a fan of fives, tens, and twenties, like a card shark. "Do I have to give it back if she's not dead yet?"

They were in the kitchen, and I had wrapped the quilt around myself and lay in the hallway between the kitchen and the den.

"She looked better two days ago, I thought," my mother said.

"No, she didn't," Walter said. "You don't have to kid me. She looks worse all the time. I watch her and she gets worse right in front of my eyes. Maybe two weeks at the outside, the doctors say. She lasts that long, I'll be surprised as hell."

"Walter," my mother said, "I'm sorry."

"Yeah?" he said. "Me, too."

My mother poured more bourbon into his glass.

"If you want to bring the kids over, I'll be glad to keep them," she said.

"Thanks."

"Maybe the three of you ought to come for dinner tonight. I bet none of you has eaten in a week."

"Hamburgers," Walter said. "We've had hamburgers and pizza. Maybe a little beer."

"Come about six," my mother said. "Where are the kids?"

"The neighbors', I guess."

I took the quilt with me into the kitchen. "They have a dog?" I said. "Reason I ask, I got bit."

"You got bit, huh?" Walter stared at me with his puffy, almost-closed eyes while my mother told him the story.

"Any dog bites me," he said, putting one hand on the pistol at his hip, "I'd kill the son of a bitch."

My mother hustled me back to the couch. She refused to listen to my claim that I was not sick. She told me to lie there without making a sound. "Watch the television," she said.

When I complained that soap operas were the only programs on after *I Love Lucy*, she told me to close my eyes and count stars.

"Use your imagination," she said before returning to the kitchen. "Make up a story. Entertain yourself, please."

Walter was saying that what he really wanted to do was go to the beach and bury himself up to his neck in the sand. He asked my mother if she wouldn't like to go for old time's sake.

"I couldn't," she said. "The kid's not feeling so good, and I have lots to do around here."

"When I lived with Alan and his folks, they always went to the lake. They were the only family I ever had, they even took me with them on their vacations, and they were the best vacations I ever had."

"Better than your trip to Las Vegas?" my mother said. "You said you had a good time last summer, I remember."

"Sure. A great time. Mavie won twelve dollars on a nickel machine, then lost it all back. That was the highlight. We spent the night in one of those parking lots they call a campground with the wind blowing about eighty miles an hour. Dust blowing straight through the tent. We had to keep all the flaps up, and it must've been a hundred that night, at least. Hotter than hell. Mavie kept saying, 'Isn't this fun? Isn't this an adventure?' I said it was shit. On the way out of town, I stopped at a drug store for some aspirin, and I lost five more bucks in a quarter machine they had on the counter. She thought that was fun too, even though she'd been coughing all morning long. I thought it was dust. Then she was coughing in Yosemite, and she coughed straight through to New Year's."

I heard a chair scrape backwards on the kitchen floor, and Walter stumbled through the den and into the spare bathroom. On his way back, he stopped at the couch and sat next to my feet.

"You're feeling kinda shot up," he said.

"A little." I didn't feel that bad, and I moved away from his breath as well as his evident distress.

"If that dog ever looks at you again, you just take your Monopoly board and go home."

"What?"

"Your daddy and I used to play Monopoly together when we were about your age, and your daddy had a strategy he always used. No matter what, come hell or high water, he was going to buy Boardwalk and Park Place, didn't matter if he never landed there, if he could buy it from someone else, he'd get it and build, even if that's the only property he had. One time I got both of them, and I told him I'd never sell. He said, 'Walter, this is my game, and in my game, I get Boardwalk and Park Place, and if I don't get 'em, I'm gonna take my Monopoly board and go home.' That was that. He closed the board, and all the tokens and the money and the property titles went sliding into the box. That was the last time we played. He said it wasn't any fun for him if he didn't know beforehand that he was going to get Boardwalk and Park Place. You see, that's what I'm doing now, taking my Monopoly board and going home. It's not that I don't love her, you understand, or that I don't have the greatest respect for your daddy." *What was he talking about?* I didn't have a clue. "But what the hell am I supposed to do? I go to see her every day, and I take the kids, we do the happy talk, but we all know she's going to die. I'm human. I don't have to apologize for that, do I?"

My mother opened the door to the patio. She said that Walter should go outside if he wanted to talk things out.

"Little pitchers have big ears, don't you know?" she said. "And they spill everything."

She helped him up from the couch, and he staggered out to the patio in my mother's embrace while she shot me an evil look that crossed her eyes.

That last New Year's Eve, I managed to stay up past midnight, and over my mother's protests, my father had given me a small glass of champagne with which to celebrate. Greg and Jerry waited until I had taken a sip and then they began to laugh so I couldn't swallow for trying not to laugh myself. They kept it up for so long that finally the bubbles in the wine fizzed out my nose with a burning stinging hurt. But I outlasted them. They each fell asleep on the floor sometime after one in the morning while I wedged my eyelids open, watching as our parents played cards. The game they played was called Hell's Bridge, a form of rummy. My father said that it had gotten that name because you always wanted to say Oh Hell, and that was about as wild as my parents ever got as far as I knew. I remembered the four of them: my mother playing with her usual mixture of naivete and luck, asking if she couldn't please pick up that particular discard; my father calling my mother Crudbucket because that was the very card he wanted but she was sitting on his right and there wasn't a thing he could do about it; Walter, hunched over in his chair, running his free hand through his straight silver hair, concentrating on his cards as if the competition meant something; Mavie, tapping the dining room table with her lacquered fingernails while sending a stream of cigarette smoke into the air above the game. The winner that night as I remembered it was my mother, who beat Mavie by two points after Walter recalculated the scores.

Now, Walter was shouting, his words indistinct and slurred. I heard glass breaking. Then my mother opened the door to the den.

"Come here," she said. "I need you to give me a hand."

"I'm injured."

"Now."

On the patio lay the scattered pieces of the bourbon bottle. There had not been much left. Beyond the patio, Walter lay face down in the dichondra, a thin red line of blood streaking the back of his silver hair. It was very peaceful. The automatic pool sweep was tracing patterns across the surface of the water. The breeze rocked the palms against the blue background of summer sky. In the yard of the house behind our own, a dog was barking and whining and jumping against the chain link fence.

"We need to turn him over," my mother was saying. Her hair was mussed, and her voice seemed strained somehow, out of breath. "Then I'll get him underneath his arms if you can get his feet."

We rolled Walter onto his back. Dirt and grass stuck to his face and uniform. His silver hair had gone wild. Fortunately, he was not a heavy man, and we did not have far to go. We put him on the chaise lounge, and my mother covered him with a beach towel advertising Coppertone.

"He stinks," I said.

"I'm going to wake him in about three hours," she said, "and tonight when they're here to eat, you won't mention a word of this, not even to your father."

"No, ma'am."

"He's had a very hard time. His wife is dying, and his kids are going out of control, and he doesn't know what he's doing half the time. He says things he doesn't mean. I'd hate to make things any worse for him."

Then she noticed that I was standing on only one leg, and she remembered that there had been more than one difficulty this day. She shooed me into the house with a Poor boy, poor boy, and she tucked me in on the couch once again.

"That was a mean old dog," she said. "I'll bet you were scared."

"Naw, I wasn't."

"No?"

"Maybe a little."

"*I* would have been terrified. He would have gobbled me right up."

"I kicked him," I said, inventing. "He got me down on the ground, and I thought he was going to take my whole leg off, then I kicked him right in the balls."

"The what?"

"He let go of me and crawled underneath a bush."

Her attention was drifting. To the patio, I could tell.

"I'm gonna take my Monopoly board and go home," I said.

"Hmm?"

"He's drunk," I said.

"We said you weren't going to talk about that, remember?"

"Rudolf nearly ate my whole leg," I said, closing my eyes.

"You must have been very brave."

"Can I talk about that?" I said. "Tonight at dinner, can I tell everybody how Rudolf bit me, and then I had to kill him. He was dragging me on the ground, and no one knew what to do until I started hitting him, and then I shot him with a pistol until he was dead."

"You don't want to kill anything."

"It's just a story," I said.

"Not even," she said, "in a story."

III. Lost

Unlike many of my older relatives who seem to recall the color and textures of every significant moment—birthdays, anniversaries, christenings, etc.—from thirty, forty, and fifty years ago, I have found that, the older I become, the more my memories have receded into increasingly remote corners. Do I remember the first girl friend of my childhood, not *girlfriend*, of course, but one who spoke to me nonetheless of the mysteries of gender, that beautiful

Other that remains forever alien? No. My best efforts of remembering are overwhelmed by invention rather than reconstruction. Do I remember the birth of my first child in the welter of early-morning and sleep-deprived imagery? Only if I consult the photographs that I don't remember taking. My memories near and far in time seem to suffer the same short-changed fate; the experience is half-lived and then boxed in tissue like a Christmas present purchased in July, placed in the back of a closet, and then forgotten when the big day comes. My mother died of Alzheimer's disease, and while she endured that nightmare limbo of knowing-without-understanding what was happening to her, she struggled to reclaim her past, any past—even to the point of changing my father's name, talking to me as though I was her brother, and speaking to my wife as though she was a rival for a past teacher's attentions. She fought. She fought the inevitable erosion, her growing paranoia, her only ally. She fought against her body and her brain, those traitors, whereas I seem to live each day as though it occupies nothing particularly special or sacramental or noteworthy, time slipping from one moment, one hour, one day, to the next, a drowsy, somnolent present scarcely inhabited, let alone experienced or understood, celebrated or mourned.

Here, though, is one memory of nearly fifty years ago that remains fixed and, to the best of my knowledge, is a matter of fact rather than the construction of an airy and unreliable imagination:

I am alone in the vestry of St. Bartholomew's Episcopal Church, where my parents and I are members. Since my confirmation at the age of twelve, I have served as the single acolyte at the 8:00 a.m. service, a service attended by no more than twenty early-rising parishioners, a service without music or high church folderol—no incense, bells, or whistles, as my father liked to say. No baloney. An engineer working for the military in electronic defense, he is big on reducing baloney. My mother, on the other hand . . . she wouldn't mind a few whistles or a little baloney, but then, isn't that just one of the differences, one of the many differences, that must be negotiated in marriage?

The highlight of the service is, without fail, the celebration of Holy Communion, the Eucharist: the wine and wafers, the body and blood of our savior in the magic and majesty and mystery of faith. For the past three years, I have been the sole assistant at these services, the only one willing to arrive early and then carry out the details of the Eucharist alone with Father Alban. I carry the processional cross, I distribute the offering plates to the ushers, I help Father Alban with the preparation of the wine and wafers for the great feast. I am, according to Father Alban, indispensable.

Father Alban is, at this time, in his mid-sixties, nearing what most expect to be his retirement age, but since the minister, a former Catholic priest, married late and had his children even later, he is hoping to hold on until the age of seventy at least. This is what he has confided in me, his weekly assistant and teenaged confessor. Father Alban has a thatch of gray hair, a florid face, and hanging jowls, and except when he is officiating at service, he smokes cigars that permeate the vestry closet and all that is contained therein: his black robes and stoles as well as the red cassocks and white surplices that I wear. No incense, maybe, but we have our holy smoke nonetheless. Over his black clerical shirt, Father Alban habitually adopts a green cardigan that I can imagine him wearing on the golf course where he is usually to be found on Monday afternoons after his labors of the week are through.

In my possession is a bulky gray cable-knit pullover, a hand-me-down from Father Alban's son, who is four years older than I. Ironically, Father Alban's son does not attend services at St. Bartholomew's. As a sign of his independence, he declared himself an atheist and turned his back upon his father for insisting upon a tired and worn-out mythology. He will insist upon this for his first two years of college before, in a spasm of religious fervor, he will declare himself to be born again, a true Christian, and turn his back yet again upon his father, this time for his adherence to an old, out-of-date, and sterile religious sensibility. Like everything that has been anywhere near Father Alban, my sweater refuses to give up the odor of his cigars, and despite dry cleaning and airing it on the clothesline for three days in harsh winter sunshine, my mother is forced to admit defeat. She says that whenever I wear it, she doesn't need to see me for the smell; disoriented, she can't help but think that she has hatched a union boss or a gambler for a son.

On this drizzly January morning I have exchanged said sweater for my cassock and surplice, and I am sitting in the side chair in the gray, aqueous light of the vestry, waiting for Father Alban's arrival. It is a time of dreamy timelessness, due no doubt to the fact that an hour before I was still in bed. In such a state, I can imagine that I am part of a divine mystery. This much remains of my confirmation classes and the expectations I have of faith. "Listen for that still, small voice," Father Alban is fond of saying. Something might happen . . .

And then, as though in fulfillment of my fondest hopes, I hear a light tap on the vestry door. However, when I open it, I find Mrs. Alban rather than the messenger of God; Elizabeth Alban, who is my age, stands behind and to the side of her mother. Mrs. Alban is one of those women whose bearing is regal, her hair a platinum helmet, her face a mask of perfect make-up. There is talk among the adults of the congregation that Mrs. Alban bullies and browbeats her much older husband, which means that the true leader of this flock is a harpy in designer clothes.

"Oh, David," Mrs. Alban says, "I'm so glad it's you."

"Yes, ma'am."

"Father Alban isn't here just yet."

"No, ma'am."

"But he will be shortly, if you would be so good as to make sure everything is ready."

The women from the vestry committee have already set out Father Alban's black cassock and surplice and the stole that matches the liturgical season, so there is nothing for me to do, not really, but I agree anyway.

Elizabeth rolls her eyes in a face as defended as a wall. Enlisted as I am in her parents' cause, I know that she doesn't think much of me, but that doesn't stop me from admiring the tight cashmere sweater that stretches across her chest or the single short strand of beads that emphasizes the valley between her breasts. Somehow, nothing that she and her mother wear smells of anything but the perfume of themselves.

At church, she may be molded in cashmere, but at school Elizabeth wears headbands and caftans, jeans with patches, and leather jackets with fringe; she occupies the center of a small coterie of girls who are more physically precocious than any boy within our class. They have been linked to seniors and in some cases to young men already in college. Rumors of sexual activity and aborted pregnancies are their emotional currency while, like an outdoor cat whose every effort to dart through a door is met with a foot, I have only circled the outside of their knowledge and experience.

"Thank you, David," Mrs. Alban says again. "He will be here in just a moment."

She turns with Elizabeth in her wake.

But it is not just a moment. In fact, Father Alban does not open the vestry door until ten minutes after the service is due to start. Every minute after eight o'clock, I have peeked through the side curtain to eye the congregants, my parents among them, who sit patiently, perusing the order of service with its announcements and calls for petition and intercession. I can only assume that Mrs. Alban has informed them of the delay.

When Father Alban does come through the door, his face is even redder than normal, and there is a pronounced scratch along the right side of his jaw. In his wake there is the inevitable cloud of cigar smell in his usual, familiar cardigan but something else as well, something indefinably antiseptic, as though he has just come back from a long-dreaded and extended visit to the dentist.

"Late," he says, tottering a little bit as he leans against the high garment table where his vestments have been laid out and arranged. He breathes deeply, slowly. "Well. You can't unring the bell."

Despite his seeming infirmity, he removes the cardigan and smoothly slips into the various pieces of his costume, transforming himself from the frail golf-course-worthy cleric to the conductor of a mysterious rite. Each new vestment envelopes him in another layer of authority.

"Right," he says. He clears his throat once, twice, and then a third time. "Let's go."

We have done this service together now for three years, and our movements are automatic, as tightly choreographed and intimate as a one-act play. Twenty-six silent paces down the center aisle—there is no music, *remember?*—turn and lock the processional cross into its holder to the right of the altar.

"Almighty God," Father Alban begins, "unto whom all hearts are open, all desires known, and from whom no secrets are hid: Cleanse the thoughts of our hearts by the inspiration of thy Holy Spirit, that we may perfectly love thee, and worthily magnify thy holy Name; through Christ our Lord."

"Amen," we say in response. *Amen, indeed.* And away we go.

We recite the *Kyrie*, we respond to the collect, we listen to the lessons. Stand, kneel, sit, like the orderly drill team that we are.

This morning, not surprisingly, Father Alban chooses not to deliver a prepared homily. Instead, he faces the congregants, all of us standing, and then turns to look out the windows that line the north side of the sanctuary and frame a picture of ferns and vegetation not native to our part of California.

"It's a beautiful day," he says to a window that frames a gray sky, overcast and dank. "Too beautiful by half."

"Be that as it may," he continues, "fair or foul, we are enjoined by the Holy Spirit to speak the truth in all times and in all places lest we suffer corruption masked by the appearance of virtue."

His wife and daughter, in their accustomed seats at the end of the first row, sit impassively.

"'Confess yourself to heaven,'" he recites, his eyes closed. "'Repent what's past; avoid what is to come; / And do not spread the compost on the weeds, / To make them ranker.' Amen."

A few puzzled amens rise from the congregation while Father Alban signals for us to be seated. We are Episcopalians; we say "Ah-men" in rhythm and rhyme with those ubiquitous cups of Japanese noodles. We would never think to say A-men with the long Baptist "A"; that is not our style. Neither is it our style to ask questions in public, for the secret to serenity, so we aver, is obliviousness, and our remedy to all uncertainty comes in the recitation of the Nicene Creed and our corporate acknowledgement that—without mention or embarrassment of specifics or details—all have sinned and fallen short of the glory of God. Without mercy, in general and in other words, we are fucked.

We stand, we sit, we kneel. All is as well as can be in this best of all possible worlds.

I retrieve the offering plates and hand them off to the ushers, one of whom is my unsmiling father, wearing as always his suit and an unfashionably narrow tie. The other usher, Don McCaskill, who teases me and calls me a putz when given the opportunity, winks at me; his attire, a brown-and-yellow plaid sport coat and a wide green tie of the type we called a belly-warmer, is an assault to the eye. My father is sober and industrious, vetted yearly by the FBI and possessor of a national security clearance—he's serious—while it is well known that Don McCaskill is often to be found in the bars along Devonshire Boulevard, chatting up his buddies from the car dealerships in Reseda and telling off-color jokes to the waitresses; why then do I find his garish colors, clashing patterns, and sarcasm the provision of more comfort?

While my father and Mr. McCaskill pass the plates among those few occupants of the pews, I help Father Alban with the cleansing of his hands and the preparation of the elements. Father Alban breathes heavily as I pour water over his fingers, his breath a bloom, a cloud above me. He counts out the wafers, he pours out the wine from cruet to chalice with an unsteady hand. Then I receive the plates again, now dotted with a sparse scatter of change, folded singles, and a few dog-eared offertory envelopes.

Afterwards, Father Alban leads us through the Great Thanksgiving and the battery of prayers preceding the offering of the great meal. It is at this point in the service that my mind invariably wanders, no matter how pure my intentions. I would like to say that I commune with our Lord and Savior as I have been taught, murmuring Seabury's words, a meditation within the soul deeper and more intuitive than words alone. However, this is not the case. While I begin reasonably enough ("It is very meet, right, and our bounden duty, that we should at all times, and in all places, give thanks unto thee, O Lord, holy Father, almighty, everlasting God . . ."), I find myself thinking instead and only of Elizabeth's and her friends' reputations and of her soft cashmere chest that is another mystery among mysteries. If the touch of God seems remote and other-worldly, a woman's breasts seem even less likely and more fantastic. And as we turn the corner and head for home ("And here we offer and present unto thee, O Lord, our selves, our souls and bodies, to be a reasonable, holy, and living sacrifice unto thee . . ."), I have completely lost sight of my purpose for being, for being here, except as the site of daydream and reverie. If I have any conscience whatsoever, I should refuse the body and blood, but like all cowards before and since, I choose to forget what is past, accept only the present, and ignore the nuance of moral consideration: I eat and drink. Yes, I eat and drink. Even as I partake of such holy food, I am so lost in considerations of Elizabeth's otherliness—the rise of her breasts, of course, but also the plunge of her back, the curve of her legs—that it takes me a beat or two before I remember to help Father Alban dispose of those elements—the wafers, the too-much wine in the cup—leftover from the service.

While he drinks the dregs from the chalice—he has maybe overestimated how much was required, perhaps?—the slack skin of his throat moves as he swallows. I see only Elizabeth, however, in various compromising poses.

I am lost in thought, if not in deed.

◉ ◉ ◉

Mrs. Alban is at the vestry door waiting for her husband before we can finish recessing down the aisle.

"David, give us a minute, please," she says, "so Philip and I might have a word."

"Sure," I say, although my father will be waiting in the station wagon with my mother, his left elbow resting on the ledge of his opened window, the radio tuned to the news, the fingers of his right hand drumming the wheel while my mother sits quietly, closed in upon herself.

"We won't be but a minute."

And with that she closes the door in my face.

"She gets what she wants," Elizabeth says. "She always has."

I shrug. The behavior of adults is not something I understand, not entirely, except that it does seem advisable to be invisible as well as unheard.

◎ ◎ ◎

Fifteen minutes, twenty minutes pass, and the door remains closed. Elizabeth stands still—*as a statue, perhaps? the cliché might mean something, after all*—while I shift from foot to foot, conscious of what, in any other circumstances, might be regarded as feminine garb: my red robe, white surplice, dress and blouse. There is a murmur just beyond the door, higher and strident and with the urgency of a knife one moment, sonorous and more placating the next.

I pull the surplice over my head, undo the buttons of my cassock. "Look," I say to Elizabeth, "do you mind hanging these up when your parents are through? My dad's gonna have a cow as it is."

She looks at me with more than a hint of a sneer. It's the sort of thing a ten-year-old might say, but it's the truth and the best I can do. But then the hard planes of her face undergo a curious revision.

"Lucky you," she says. "Making your escape. It sounds like she's ripping the old guy a new one."

"I'm sorry," I say. "I like your dad."

She shrugs. "He's okay. Clueless in the concrete, but okay in the abstract."

"I like him," I say again, defending her father for reasons I don't understand or question.

"Don't worry," she laughs. "Me, too." She scuffs the toe of one pump against the worn carpet of the hallway, studies her shoe. "Like he says," she nods toward the vestry door, "'you can choose your god and your friends, you can choose your spouse for better or worse, but you don't get to choose your family, your neighbors, or your fellow believers. They are who they are.'" She shrugs, looking at my acolyte's attire now draped in her arms. "His words."

Outside, in the parking lot, I walk quickly through what has turned into a steady rain and jump into the back seat of my father's station wagon.

"Sorry," I say. "The vestry was locked."

"Uh-huh," my father says. "Phil Alban had a load on. Don Mc-Caskill told me before the service. And Don McCaskill would know."

"Robert," my mother says. "Please."

"No mystery," my father says. "It was coming out of his pores. He could have lit a blowtorch."

My father starts the car, and we splash through the parking lot.

Halfway home, we pass through the intersection at Rinaldi and Encino, where flares dot the perimeter of an accident: a Corvair and a Renault, a comic-book version of Ralph Nader's nightmare. Steam rises into the falling rain from the rear of the Corvair, the front end of the Renault lies buckled, the owners waving their arms at one another, their words silent behind our windows.

"They were having a fight," I say. "The Albans. In the vestry. They were yelling at each other. She was yelling at him."

"Sometimes people fight," my mother says fiercely, looking straight ahead through the rain-spattered windshield. "And sometimes they have good reasons."

◎ ◎ ◎

Years will pass, and I will come to know certain things. In hindsight, it will become obvious that, although it will take thirty more years, the seeds of my mother's dementia were already germinating, terrorizing her for decades before her fate was given a diagnosis and a name. Father Alban will take retirement without prior announcement six months later, move to Arizona, and die even more quietly and with less notice two months after that. One paragraph in the church newsletter will be all that will mark his passing, a postscript noting that his wife would return to the Los Angeles area following his interment. No mention of Elizabeth or Philip Jr. My father will die as well many, many years later, but not before telling me that in addition to creating some of the big-boy toys in use by military intelligence and even the CIA, he had also served as a kind of dress rehearsal spy, beta-testing the products in Japan and Germany and the Arabian Peninsula, a Cold War techie for hire, his "business trips" the source and spark of my mother's growing terror while her mind began its long unraveling. He will take satisfaction in telling me how secrets are unlocked, but he will spend ten years atoning to my mother, whose deterioration will kill them both. And it will be up to Don McCaskill, that alcoholic gossip, to tell me more about the Albans.

I have come back to Los Angeles for a forty-year high school reunion. Since high school, I have tried, like so many of my generation, my full share of -isms: from Episcopalianism, there has come a laundry list of convictions: fundamentalism, transcendentalism, agrarianism, communalism, capitalism and social work. These days, I've settled on literature and narrative, but I'm not ruling anything out. In the hotel ballroom, classmates mingle and mix beneath crepe paper, balloons, and grainy enlargements of yearbook photos, bad hair, dreadful clothes, and worse skin. Some look the same, while the rest of us wear the scars of what life and our own poor choices have done to us. There's enough shame to go around that no one need feel embarrassed. Elizabeth does not attend, but I hear someone say that she has moved to Nevada, she's remarried, and is mother to six children in a blend of three families. She goes to a dozen school activities a week and shows real estate on the side. Her brother died three years earlier while on a missionary trip to Ghana from a cut that went septic. As Vonnegut might say, *So it goes* . . .

Later in the hotel bar, a man in his eighties and lime-green pants palms the side of my face and says, "Jesus, it's Bob and Marty's dumb little kid. I wondered if this might be your year."

"Don," I say, "Mr. McCaskill. Still haunting the bars. Who knew you were still alive?"

"Don't be a wise-ass."

"Sorry," I say. "Although look out there." I point to the ballroom at the graying heads and the limping couples on the dance floor, "half of my class could keel over at any minute."

"I'm sorry about your parents," he says. "I couldn't tell you at their funerals because I don't go to funerals as a matter of principle. I don't plan on attending my own."

"You could change your mind," I say, pointing to my wristwatch, "but I wouldn't waste any time."

"Jesus, you've become a bitter kid. Like you believed all the hocus-pocus and now you don't."

"I seem to recall seeing you in a pew on a Sunday morning."

"And I remember you hanging onto Phil Alban's every word."

"I liked him," I say. "He was a decent guy."

"Yeah, a decent guy, but that wife of his—what a piece of work. She had him coming and going."

"I thought he had some things to say, Father Alban. I thought I might learn something."

"She was the one," he says. "Of things to say, she had no shortage. She tells him that she's been having an affair with some pharmaceutical salesman in Northridge. He goes out, gets hammered, and then three hours later, she has to pull him out of his car so he can serve Communion at St. Bartholomew's. She tells him she doesn't want a divorce, doesn't want to alter appearances or perceptions. She doesn't want to ruin his career when he's so close to the end, anyway. She wants to work things out, but she has to be honest. So they patch things up, and then he gets a cancer diagnosis. Colon, stomach, somewhere in the guts. She packs him up and takes him to Arizona, so they can get across the border for Laetrile. Didn't matter. He was a goner anyway."

Sometimes, people fight. Sometimes people behave badly. They fail one another and then surprise everyone with the depths of their sacrifice.

"And you know all this how?"

"Trust me," he says.

"What were you doing—hiding in their bedroom closet?"

"Jesus," he says. "I know how to listen to what other people say, even when they're not saying anything. Man, you are one bitter little putz."

IV. The Soul of the Gorilla

The scrimmage of appetite everywhere.

—DELMORE SCHWARTZ,
"The Heavy Bear Who Goes With Me"

I was a fat boy and shy. Problems one and two of my childhood.

My belly separated my T-shirts from my shorts, I wheezed when I walked. Rolls of fat circled my wrists until I was twelve. My mother never shopped for jeans in any place but the shelf marked "Husky." Although the name on my birth certificate was Calvin, I answered to Butterball or Porker with greater regularity.

To make matters worse, my shyness, rather than shielding me from others' attentions, only served as an incentive for those who wished me to become gregarious, make friends, be precocious. Get the fat boy out of his shell. Aunts introduced me to cousins. Friends of the family introduced me to daughters and sons. A well-meaning adult's questions, intended to draw me out, were met with my vigorous silence.

Performers seemed especially challenged. When I was two, my parents took me with them on a trip to Ensenada. In a cantina, a rotund Mexican clown singled me out as his Other, the only person not laughing at his tricks and pratfalls. My parents were drinking margaritas and laughing along with the other *turistas*. The clown fell face forward, his nose went flat, and I cried in my mother's lap. When he held his breath, his nose popped back into its original red bulb, and I cried again. I cried when he shook his orange hair in my face. He squeezed my hand, and a horn beeped; I howled. He sat on my father's lap and cried along with me, and I wailed until my father asked the poor man to leave.

A year later, I dove underneath a table in a Hollywood dinner theater when the wife of Spike Jones serenaded me with a song. My parents had placed me in the seat closest to the stage. With the aid of a booster chair, I was tall enough to cock my elbows onto the stage itself, and I watched at close range the dancers and musicians. The colors and the lights whirled about me. I was entranced by the balls and bowling pins of the juggler; I marveled at the man who could make the doll talk. Then suddenly, spotlights were focused on the stage, and one was focused on me, and Helen Grayco announced a special Moulin Rouge dedication for a special member of the audience. For an instant I froze in the light like any good possum. Then, howling once again, I swam through the legs and feet of the adults at our table. My father hooked me by a belt loop and held me while she sang and I squirmed. I remember that she was terribly offended. She refused my parents' apologies, and it was very nearly the last time that they took me anywhere. My father in particular seemed ready to give up on me.

That same year, at a party for my father's boss, I fell into a koi pond while running away from Mr. Flaherty's teenage daughter.

By the time my father pulled me out, my eyes were bulging in their sockets like a carp's, and I've gone by the name Fish ever since, which, although preferable to Butterball or Porker, was one more invitation to questions and unwanted attention. Problem number three.

◉ ◉ ◉

Oh, what am I to make of myself now? Maturity has been kinder than youth. My weight hovers around the national average for those of my height, and I speak when spoken to in terms socially appropriate. Yet all it takes is some intimation of the past, some trigger of humiliation, and I become Fish once more. Several nights ago, I met my cousin for dinner. Eight years older than I, Francis knows all of my selves—Calvin, Fish, Butterball, Cyrano— and there can be no disguises. Without my knowledge, she invited a friend of hers to join us at the restaurant. Was she playing Cupid? Ellen was lively and blonde, a tennis player and owner of a boutique for women's athletic apparel. She and Francis imme- diately began to reminisce about their time together at boarding school. Which led to questions about my childhood and snickers from Francis. "How about the pork loin," Francis said, pointing to the menu, "or maybe the turkey breast."

Ellen was puzzled.

"Private joke," Francis said. "Fish understands."

"Fish?"

And for the remainder of the evening, I languished at the table in a state of silent torpor, paralyzed by the animal anxieties of childhood. Anxieties about which my father knew nothing. His environment was the party; he drank, he sang, he told long, com- plicated stories with no point other than the narrative detours they provided. Rumors of his affairs were legion, and when he took a walk during his lunch hour, he was often stopped by women who needed to ask directions or the time but whose needs were otherwise. It was no small frustration to my father that I failed to act as a successful prop in these encounters.

Once, while my mother attended an evening service at St. Stephens, my father whispered that he had something to show me. He had met a celebrity. In his job as a loan officer at a bank in Beverly Hills, he often met second-string actors and entertainers, those who were clawing their way up as well as those scrambling to cushion their inevitable descent. He opened a drawer in his desk where he kept his stack of *Playboys* and turned one issue to the centerfold of Miss September. Wearing only a utility belt, hard hat, and linesman's boots, she was bent over slightly, peering into a junction box, a pair of needle-nose pliers clutched between her teeth. Gravity pulled at her breasts. The blonde thatch of her pubic hair glowed between her legs.

"Now that's workmanship," my father said, "but nothing you need to mention to your mother."

I was twelve. And now fast-forward to high school and problem number four. Girls. Of course. What else could it be?

Still fat, still shy, still the Fish of my four-year-old self, but now stricken with the torment of hormones. Girls seemed to like athletes, so I went out for the football team. As a fat boy, I became an offensive lineman; as a clumsy oaf, I was relegated to the junior varsity's third string. The only dates I had were with ninth grade girls with braces or bad complexions, daughters of my mother's church friends. The girl's mother always drove, we sat in the half-dark of a Walt Disney feature, then waited at the curb for a station wagon to arrive. Good-night was signaled by a kiss on the cheek in full parental view.

How was I to square this experience with that of Miss September? Or the rest of the months of the year, for that matter, whose histories I had perused from the stash in my father's desk drawer?

◉ ◉ ◉

Late that fall I went to a basketball game, alone as usual. I was perched on the top row of the bleachers in a far corner. Players rushed back and forth on the court. The team benches and the scorer's table were positioned on the far side. Behind that was the crowd from the other school. Cheerleaders on both sides exhorted the crowds. On our side six girls danced, synchronizing their steps to the music of the pep band. On the other side, four girls and four muscular young men performed gymnastic routines—lifts, pyramids, backflips. The four young men wore white sweatpants and yellow polo shirts. Their arm muscles bulged underneath the ribbing of the sleeves. Each of them lifted a girl with one hand, supporting them underneath their bottoms. The girls went up, then came down, cradled in the flexed arms of the yellow polo shirts. *Oh, to slip on those arms, those hands! To touch what they had touched and have no one be the wiser.* The other school's crowd cheered, the girls hugged their partners, and then I knew. I climbed down from the bleachers and went home, long before the end of the game.

◉ ◉ ◉

I bought the gorilla suit in a Hollywood costume shop, and if it had a flaw, it was that the suit was all of a piece. No pockets, no fly. The gorilla's body was a tight-fitting set of arms and legs with a long zipper running from neck to waist, reminding me of the sleepers I'd worn as a child. In the beam of a flashlight, I changed my clothes in the restroom of an abandoned gas station. I pulled the gorilla's head over my own, then practiced a knuckle-dragging walk in front of the fly-specked mirror. With the head removed, I ate the first of six bananas. I hooted, snarled, grunted, clicked. I sat underneath the sink in my costume and waited until the first quarter of the varsity game was well under way. Then, slope-shouldered and stump-legged, with money for admission in the hard gorilla palm, I ambled down the dark sidewalk to school and the lighted gymnasium.

At the door, I grunted at the counselor who was taking money and paid for a ticket. I dropped the exact amount into the startled man's hand with my clumsy big ones. The sounds from the stands were muffled and echoing inside the gorilla's head. A time-out had been called. The players were huddled around their respective coaches, and the cheerleaders were dancing to "Marrakesh Express." I paused a moment at the door to check that the long zipper was still anchored at my neck. Then, secure behind my wall of hair, I made a knuckle-swinging, lurching advance upon the dancing cheerleaders. Delia Frampton was closest. One arm was extended in my direction, and the gorilla grabbed it. He spun her around, and before she knew what was happening, she was doing a sprightly polka with a downsize gorilla.

The crowd on both sides roared. The pep band faltered; the other cheerleaders stopped their routines one by one. We danced like crazy, and the band caught up with us. Before the time-out was over, Janie Rodriguez had cut in on Delia, and together we did a wicked little tango, her breasts flattened against the gorilla's chest. With Elaine Crowell, the gorilla bopped to a fifties sock hop beat. I could not dance a lick, but the gorilla was doing fine, and my suspicions were confirmed: while playing a role, one can get away with things one wouldn't dream of doing otherwise. The ventriloquist can insult his audience through his dummy. The short runt of an actor can win the beautiful star as Napoleon. The gymnast can don white trousers and a yellow shirt and handle girls in ways their mothers would not approve otherwise. I did not have the muscles or the yellow shirt, but I was dancing as I'd never danced before because the gorilla was a terrific dancer. He was filled with bravado and daring; he possessed a social confidence that I had never known.

When the time-out was over, the gorilla pinched Elaine Crowell's butt. She jumped, but she didn't get mad, and she patted the gorilla's shoulder. I also noticed that Janie Rodriguez, though apparently not watching me, was walking ever closer, her hips swinging back and forth underneath her short skirt, waiting for the gorilla's hand. He pinched her, too—brazen, accommodating creature that he was—and she said *Thank you* besides.

Next he charged into the stands, pointing his huffing, banana-breathing face into the faces of tiny screaming children. He made fun of the football players who looked uncomfortably like the gorilla themselves. He mimicked them until they pushed him down the steps. On his way down, he kissed the hands of other pretty girls. Then he circled the court, grunting and huffing. He bounced the basketball a few times, made one free throw out of two, pointed to the referee's chest, then flicked him in the nose when the official looked down at the thick, black finger. The skinny center from the opposing school tried to push the gorilla away from the court so the game could resume. The enraged animal pounded his chest. He pulled the skinny kid's shorts down to his knees, then escaped through a rear exit before he could be cornered underneath the bleachers.

I didn't take the head off until I hit the men's room of the gas station. And then I didn't take it off until I'd beat my chest with both hands and watched the gorilla in the mirror once again. The head came off back to front. Sweat streamed down my own face, and the cool night air chilled. I dressed in my own clothes, ate a last banana, and walked home with the gorilla underneath my arm.

⊚ ⊚ ⊚

The next home game was two weeks later. During the interval there was much talk as to the identity of the gorilla. The school newspaper ran a picture of him as he danced with Delia Frampton, a large question mark for a caption. In the locker room, one of our defensive tackles loudly announced that the next time that cocky sonuvabitch gorilla pinched his girlfriend Elaine, he'd tear the hairy cocksucker's heart out. I made a mental note of that, and I was sure the gorilla would see the wisdom in staying away from Elaine in the future. The center from Chaminade—the one whose shorts the gorilla had dropped, revealing his less than pretentious jock strap and his pinched red cheeks—also sent a message to the gorilla through the PE department. He'd be more than happy, he said, to duke it out with the overgrown chimp. Any day, any time.

I heard other things as well.

Janie Rodriguez let it be known that she wouldn't mind finding herself alone with the gorilla for an hour or two. "It would be different," she said before the start of a geometry class. One grade ahead of me and two years older, she took many of the same classes as I did; she was struggling to pass this last required math class and so graduate.

"What do you mean, different?" another girl said.

"Oh," she said, rolling her eyes. She crossed her legs and pulled on the hem of her skirt which was coming apart. "You know. Different."

"If you want different," I said, "you might as well go out with me."

She giggled.

"It's not so funny."

She giggled again, her arms crossed underneath her breasts, a gesture I remembered from her sixth-grade year when she had blossomed volcanically, straining the tight cotton blouses of her childhood.

"What would we do?" she said.

"We could go to a movie," I said. "Or dinner."

She shrugged. "Guys take me to movies and dinner all the time. And their mothers don't have to drive."

"Yeah," the other girl said, "guys are always taking her to dinner. Older guys."

"I could go for a gorilla," Janie said.

"It's just a costume," I said. "What's the big deal? Some guy is wearing the costume. Sooner or later, he's got to climb out."

She shrugged again, hugging herself all the tighter.

"It's *different*," the other girl said aggressively, "that's all."

"I never had a gorilla," Janie said.

Later in the day, the word was traveling: Janie Rodriguez would be on her back for the gorilla at the conclusion of the next home game. I dreamed of the event: Janie, naked, reclining on a couch that was vaguely red, vaguely plush, her breasts ripe, bobbing fruits, one hand brushing the tuft of hair between her legs, and saying, "Hurry," as feverishly I tore off my second head and unzipped my second skin.

◉ ◉ ◉

The sound of cheering carried the two blocks to the gas station as the clatter of a distant train. When the crowd began to stomp their feet on the metal bleachers, the train was destroyed by explosions.

I was very nervous and excited, and though I wore no clothes underneath the costume, my sweat was rank and fierce. In the bathroom, I checked my watch every five minutes, then unzipped the outfit so I could spray myself with deodorant once again.

The rubber lining of the suit was dripping with my impatience.

I waited until half-time before making my appearance. The teacher at the door warned me against any monkey business, then laughed at his own joke. The two teams were walking off the court to the locker rooms and the band had begun to play. Legs kicking in unison, the cheerleaders did a can-can. At the far end, Janie Rodriguez was kicking a little higher than the rest, I thought. I watched for the flash of her gold panties underneath the purple of her skirt.

The gorilla grunted, smelling reward, but Elaine Crowell was the first to spot him.

"It's him!" she squealed.

I'm not sure what I expected. Grunt a few times, maybe. Play tricks on the referee, or de-pants another skinny basketball player. Possibly. Anything that led quickly to throwing Janie Rodriguez over the gorilla's shoulder and carrying her off to the privacy of the forest.

Instead, Elaine broke away from the other girls, leaving them to kick and fall on their own. I reminded the gorilla of certain dangers, but animal that he was, he was not receptive to words of caution: Elaine hopped into the gorilla's arms without so much as Please. Then with her legs at the gorilla's hips, she executed the female part of a dip-and-swing while, over her shoulder, I watched the defensive tackle making his way to the bottom of the bleachers.

"Let go," I said. I tried to pry the girl's fingers from behind my gorilla neck.

Frightened now, the gorilla was not so kind. He dropped her on the downswing before the big lineman could pulverize him into monkey paste. He circled the court, braying in front of the visiting crowd. The tackle was after him, and so too—from another section of the stands—the center from Chaminade. Elaine held onto her boyfriend's arm, pleading with him not to kill the gorilla. The boyfriend slapped her, and she sat down at center court blubbing. Several teachers had by now reached the floor. The gorilla retreated further to the rear, turning his head every which way, waiting for his next attackers. The rear exit was unlocked, and I hustled the gorilla outside before anything else could go wrong. We ran across the parking lot, and a pair of head-lights caught us in the eyes. A car door opened.

"Get in," said a voice.

We did as we were told. I slumped into the Volkswagen, in-side my sack of gorilla skin. The gorilla's head tipped against the car window.

"They treat animals so shitty," Janie said. She was shifting from second to third gear, and her bare legs caught the flash of light from the street lamps overhead. A gold bracelet hung from the wrist that worked the floor shift. She patted the gorilla's knee.

"Argh," the gorilla said.

"You were just having a little fun, that's all."

"Harg, hoo."

"I know." She drove without saying what it was that she knew, and the gorilla didn't ask for clarification.

She was heading the small car toward a section of new con-struction in the foothills, on a street notorious as a lover's lane. The Volkswagen whined as it took the hills. The skeletons of new homes dotted the tops of the ridges. Cars, bumper to bumper, lined the sides of the road, an arm, a leg occasionally appearing in the windows. The gorilla sat up straight in his seat, watching the girl's breasts rise and fall beneath the wool sweater.

At the top of the hill, the girl made a U-turn and parallel parked between a jacked-up Z/28 and a blue Dodge van.

"Well," she said, "here we are."

She leaned back against her door; she pulled at the gorilla's hand, putting his paw upon her thigh. In front of them, the San Fernando Valley was spread out, the grid of city streets regular and ablaze with light.

"I think we could have some fun," she said.

She lifted the wool sweater up and over her head. She shook her dark hair out, inviting the gorilla to her. His clumsy fingers worked on the back of her bra, bending the strap this way and that, desperate to untangle the mystery of the hooks. Then the heavy breasts were free, and the girl slid the straps down her arms.

"Oooh," the gorilla said.

"Mmm," the girl replied.

Games are fine, but they are still games. The gorilla was holding a beautiful girl in his arms, but his arms weren't my arms. His hands were touching her breasts, her thighs, but my hands couldn't feel a thing except for the rubber lining in the hands of the monkey suit. When her eyes closed, I pulled the head off and kissed her before she realized what was happening. Her mouth opened and my tongue explored the regions beyond her teeth.

"Let's get in back," I gasped when we had stopped a moment for breath.

She opened her eyes. "Fish," she said. Her voice registered the disappointment. One hand fluttered in front of herself.

"Who were you expecting?" I said.

"I wasn't expecting anyone."

We kissed again, but the contrast between the first time and the successive one was stark indeed. When the knob of the gear shift jabbed my stomach, I was reminded of who I was; I thought maybe I'd be better off to walk home. I pulled the head back over my own, prepared to go. Then Janie took my gorilla hand, jamming it between her legs.

"Be rough," she said, sliding down in her seat.

"Huh," the gorilla said, now at work on the hooks which fastened the short skirt.

"I'm a little animal," she said.

The gorilla peeled back the skirt. The gold panties disappeared, revealing the rounded hips, the firm tummy, and the jungle at the juncture of her thighs.

I had the gorilla's head removed in a second and was working on the front zipper, but her hands held my arms as they were—encased in the costume.

"Not like that," she said.

"But I'm not feeling a thing," I said stupidly.

"You're ruining it," she sobbed.

So back went the head, up went the zipper, and once again the gorilla's two hands caressed and stroked and massaged in place of my own. When her eyes closed, off came the head and down went the zipper again. Then came her protests and back went the head. *Hooo, hooo, argh,* repeatedly.

If I had known then what I know now, I would not have been so anguished. Now, I understand the expectations of disguise, and I have been at various times a corporate lawyer, a professional athlete, and a gemstone salesman from San Francisco. Never Fish. Last night I posed as a conventioneering test pilot, and Shelly, the girl I met at the Holiday Inn, giggled when I told her that together we could fly. "Oh, sure," she said, even though we both knew we were headed for one of the rooms above our heads.

Now, I know that the value of disguise is directly attributable to the ease with which we project our fantasies, no matter whether we play the deceiver or the deceived. And never—a magician hoarding his secret—do I reveal the actual nature of my business, a teacher of tenth-grade literature who, even while teaching *Gatsby* to the next generation of gorillas, pretends to himself that he's an imposter, a substitute filling in for the real teacher, who has gone without official leave.

As far as it goes: as she turned back the synthetic covers of the hotel bed, Shelly informed me that she was not a devotee of the Pill (fear of future, deformed offspring), nor the diaphragm (bladder infections). And since these are such troubled times . . . She smiled sweetly. So before we made love, I walked downstairs to the lobby, then outside and across the street to the gas station on the corner. I had been there before. The station was closed for the hour was late, but the men's room had been left unlocked as I knew it would be. There I had my choice of French ticklers,

Rainbow Rods, and the ever-present Trojans. I had four dollars of quarters jingling in my pockets, and I bought three of the brown Trojans, feeling neither exotic nor perverse. Then, in a room on the sixth floor, we flew: skin to rubber to skin, for old times' sake, disguised to the very end.

With Janie, my only mistake had been the selection of my costume, too distinct from my own sense of self—too much hair, too little zipper, no quick crossover from the person that I was, to the person I had projected myself to be, no slippery ambiguity of personality with which we are all possessed. In fascination, Janie wrestled with a mature gorilla, but resisted with indifference a boy two years younger than herself. An hour of Push-Me-Pull-Me. And my own swollen member, having threatened to flood the rubber suit half a hundred times, now throbbed against such abuse.

"Okay," I said finally in the heat and steam of the Volkswagen. "Enough."

"Don't be mad," she said.

"I hurt."

"I don't know what's wrong with me," she said.

She collected her clothes in a pile on her lap. The windows dripped with condensation.

"It's not that I don't like you," she said, "but I like him better."

She buried her face in the clothes.

"Marilla go home now," I said.

I was out the door of the Volkswagen, the gorilla's head over my own, walking between the parallel lines of cars and lovers and the characters that lovers conceive.

"Maybe another time," Janie called.

The gorilla waved. I walked. The Volkswagen chugged past me, Janie driving with one hand; with the other she wiped the inside of the windshield with the gold panties.

Ahead the valley lights shimmered in the darkness while I walked downhill. I heard the grunting and huffing from the parked cars. I removed the gorilla's head. Then, in the manner of *homo erectus* who straightened his back and stood, I ditched the suit in a storm drain and walked back to the gas station, not caring who saw me along the way.

V. The Secret Life of Engineers

My father was well into his eighties and dying before he told me certain things.

My mother, he told me, had had a nervous breakdown sometime in 1966, about the time I was due to start junior high. One day she was fine, and the next day she woke up crying and cutting the bed sheets to ribbons with a pair of kitchen shears. The crying he could ignore, my father said, but the shears . . . Well, you never knew what those shears might be aimed at next. Let the Freudians among you think what you will. Have a field day.

"You never knew, did you?" my father said.

"No," I said. I couldn't have been more glum. To be unaware when one's own mother heads off to the loony bin? "Where was I?"

"Camp," he said. My confusion made him happy, of that I could tell. "Three weeks in the beautiful Mojave Desert."

The brochure had promised archaeology, geology, and desert survival skills, but the reality was tube tents, a desert wind that froze us each night, and high school and college-age counselors who lectured us about Marx and Lenin and Mao, then gave us hits off their joints. They turned a blind eye when we got into their stash of Boone's Farm and Ripple. We learned slogans, "Hell, no. We won't go," being among our favorites. I came home with tonsillitis, a hangover, and a revolutionary attitude.

"I came home from Japan," my father said, "when the neighbors started to complain. She was wandering the block in her nightgown. There were the bed sheets. The shears. She had pulled the stuffing out of the mattress. Your mother dropped you off at the YMCA parking lot, and then she went crackers. She didn't like to be alone."

My mother's dislike of solitude was directly related to my father's absences. Absences that to my mind were not that frequent or that long in duration, but seemed to my mother to be interminable. "I didn't get married," I remember her saying, "so your father would have a ride to the airport." While my father was gone, my mother bitterly counted the hours. When I was younger, we often spent the nights at my grandparents' house; she didn't sleep well since, without him in our wood-frame house, every creak and groan was evidence of burglars and rapists, murderers and thieves. "One of these days," my mother often said, "he's going to come home to the sight of our bloody, dismembered corpses, and won't he feel bad then?" Frankly, I didn't think my father, who was guilty of terminal cheerfulness, was capable of feeling bad about *anything*, including the deaths of his family, either real or imaginary, whereas my mother was able to feel terrible about *everything*, including those events confined entirely to her own imagination, a psychic space that was diminished—if only slightly—when she was no longer alone.

My father, on the other hand, never minded being by himself. On several occasions during the three years that my mother was dying, we offered him our spare bedroom, but he declined each time. "Don't think I don't appreciate it," he told Ellen, "but the last thing you kids need is an old fart hanging around, clogging up the sofa and stinking up the bathrooms."

Ellen and I looked at each other across the kitchen table, connected by our guilt, since that was more or less the assessment we had each come to, the offer being made out of assumed obligation more than any true desire. Ellen felt that obligation more keenly, but she was also the more greatly relieved by my father's refusal. She loved my father, she insisted, but he was stubborn and insensitive and a pain in the ass, and if he were to live with us, she'd probably want to kill him about fourteen times a day.

"Don't worry about me," my father said. "I've got ten good years yet, twenty if I follow that dumb doctor's orders, and I don't intend to become a burden."

"All right, then," Ellen said. "I'm going to hold you to it. The moment you need help in the bathroom is the moment I hand you the Jonestown Kool-Aid."

My father, whose cancer would kill him in six more months, said: "And don't think I won't be grateful."

◎ ◎ ◎

My father was fond of Ellen, and he wasn't shy about telling me I was damn lucky such a fine woman thought me worthy, but he told me about my mother on a night when Ellen was gone, visiting her sister and her sister's gun-toting family. I had invited my father to dinner, and it was just the two of us. We were sitting outside, drinking a beer, while I burned a tri-tip on the grill. I wondered whose evening would be stranger, Ellen's or mine.

"What I don't understand," I said, "is why your business trips made Mom so nervous."

He shrugged. "Why don't you have kids? What makes you so nervous about giving me grandchildren?"

"When did you ever want grandchildren?" The smoke from the barbecue changed directions, and my eyes began to smart. "I mean really want them."

"A man gets to be my age, he expects to be surrounded by ankle-biters. Maybe you should switch to boxers."

"Dad," I said, massaging my temples, for it had been a long day, and there were stacks of exams on my desk inside waiting to be graded, "my choice of underwear has nothing to do with our not having children. I'm forty-nine years old, Ellen is forty-one, we have our jobs. We're too old to have children. We've told you for twenty years that kids were not in the picture."

"It's never too late to change your mind. Not these days. I was thirty-two when you were born. Your mother was thirty-six. For our time, we were freaks of nature. Ancient."

"I know how old you were, but that's not the point."

"And what is the point, Mr. Smarty-Pants? People in their sixties are having kids."

"The point is why Mom got so upset every time you had a business trip."

That shrug again. "She didn't like what I was up to."

"Are you telling me you had women in Dayton and Washington, DC?"

My father was an electrical engineer whose company held contracts with the Air Force and the Defense Department; his travels were most often circumscribed by the Pentagon and Wright-Patterson, places I didn't associate with extramarital dalliances. At least once a year, men wearing white shirts and skinny ties came to our cul-de-sac, knocked on our neighbors' doors, and asked what they knew of my father's personal habits. Vetting his security clearance. If he'd had affairs—or indulged in any other manner of vice, for that matter—it was unlikely that he'd kept them a secret.

My father sighed. "I never cheated on your mother," he said. "Not that it's any of your damn business. Not really." He sighed once again. "She didn't like the *work* I was doing."

"You built stuff for the military. I know that. Mom knew that. What was the problem?"

As a lifelong Republican from Ohio, with a Midwesterner's staunch regard for the government, my mother would not have minded the idea of my father sitting across the table from some blue-suited colonel, negotiating a contract for radio-intercept equipment. My father was one of the heroes of the Cold War, if only a soldier of its lower echelons.

"I didn't just build it," my father said, and now he was the one who turned glum. "I didn't just build it; I used it, I tried it out. A few times."

"What are you saying?" I said. "Are you saying what I think you're saying? Are you saying you were a spy? My father was a spy? I mean, Jesus. Building equipment is one thing."

"What?" my father said as evenly as he could. "You think we built it to sit in a box?"

◉ ◉ ◉

My father rarely appeared to be anything but cheerful or optimistic, a speaker of platitudes and clichés, a pose that often was the source of tension between us when I was a teenager and in the throes of adolescent pessimism and cynicism. "What's the matter with you, Merry Sunshine?" he asked each morning of the year I turned sixteen. Hair askew, fogged with sleep, staring at the Formica of the breakfast table, I could have killed him. He, on the other hand, had been up for hours, using the early morning to be productive. He showered, he shaved, he doused himself liberally with the cologne that, according to my mother, smelled like the underside of a recently employed saddle. And then he was at the desk in his study by five-thirty, putting in a couple of hours of uninterrupted work before the office and the telephone and the questions of the sixteen junior engineers who were assigned to his different projects and problems. At six-thirty, he took a break to wake me up by turning on the overhead light in my room and doing his best Ed McMahon: "He-e-e-ere's Johnny!" I left the house by seven-thirty, and I counted it a good morning if I could make my escape without encountering him after the breakfast table. That my father, who favored the plaid sports coats of used car salesmen and who laughed as loudly as any Rotarian, might be a spy made no sense. Spies wore black trench coats, they kept their own counsel. They didn't tell Polack jokes or stories about the farmer's daughter. They didn't recite bon mots about the duration of Rome's construction. They didn't have families and a three-bed, two-bath in the San Fernando Valley.

◉ ◉ ◉

They had gone to Tokyo for a project funded by the CIA, he and another engineer, Ed Huckaby, one of his best friends at work. "It was just an idea I had," my father said, "and it should have worked. There's no reason why you should have to place a microphone inside a room in order to hear what's going on. You have a diaphragm in every window. You bounce infrared off the glass, you get a portrait of the audio inside the room. Ed and I rented an office across the street from the Soviet embassy, and we were just about set up when the call came about your mother."

"So let me get this straight," I said. "You were in Japan eavesdropping, I was in the Mojave getting stoned, and Mom was going nuts."

"Your mother got over it, but that pretty much sums it up."

"Jesus." I turned the meat on the grill.

"Wait a minute," my father said, "who said anything about you getting stoned?"

"I guess," I said, "we all have our little secrets."

My father harrumphed.

"We had a saying in the intelligence-gathering business: 'Secrets don't make friends.'"

"I heard that when I was five," I said, "from my kindergarten teacher."

"Same thing," my father sighed. "Same thing."

◉ ◉ ◉

In her last years, while her mind lost entire decades of experience, my mother's one enduring memory consisted of abandonment. Her father had died when she was ten, her mother had been distant and bad-tempered ever after, and her older brother and sister had been only too happy to leave an unhappy house. She had come to expect that those she loved were in a constant state of withdrawal, and her marriage had confirmed what she had always suspected—that the more one loved, the more one risked being left behind. When he was fifty-five, after thirty years of business trips, my father's firm reorganized, departments and personnel were shuffled, and my father no longer was required to travel. My mother, however, seemed incapable of believing that the arrangement would last, and even when my father retired five years later, she worried that a call would come, and her husband would be gone. That fear became her overarching concern and then—when my father was no longer able to care for her—was realized: he moved her into the Memory Care Unit of the Willow Springs Retirement Center, and following the dinner hour of that first day, he left her in the company of those similarly afflicted. A few weeks later, although she could no longer remember his name, calling him Mel or Tom, Richard or Henry, my mother still fretted over his absence: "Where has he gone to now?"

"Mom," I might say (though she did not know me at all by that time), "he'll be back tomorrow. He visits you every day."

"Oh. He does?"

"Yes. Yes, he does."

Those last years before he moved her into Willow Springs were tough on my father; my mother had become a habitual night walker, and she had been quick to open a door and beat a hasty exit in all kinds of weather. She was looking for my father, who was asleep beside her in their queen-sized bed. But he never saw the irony: her great fear of abandonment had given wings to her feet, thus leading to the separation that she feared most of all.

But long before that time came, she grieved my father's absences. Not long before I left home for college, I woke in the middle of the night. A light was on in the kitchen, and despite the fact that the dishwasher had run earlier that evening, I heard my mother hand washing the dishes.

Steam rose from the twin sinks, and although she was sniffling and I heard a hiccup or two, her movements were abrupt and economical.

"I didn't mean to wake you," she said when she had become aware of my presence behind her. "I couldn't sleep, and the dishes didn't come clean."

"That's okay," I said.

"You think it's silly, don't you?" she said. "Not being able to sleep?"

"No."

"Of course you do. No one your age has trouble sleeping. You might have a hard time waking up, but you never have trouble sleeping."

"There are nights," I said. "I don't always get to sleep right away."

"But you get to sleep."

"Sure."

"Then that's a different thing." She rinsed one of our drinking glasses and held it up to the overhead light. "You know, the glasses are clean, but they always look dirty. Soap residue. Minerals. We have hard water. Even when things are clean, they're dirty. Your father says we should get a water softener, but then the tap water will taste like salt. I don't know," she sighed. "It's always something."

"Mom," I said. "The dishes look fine to me."

"You're good company, but you're going to leave home soon. Your father loves me, but he's never here. This is what my life has become: taking your father to the airport and washing dishes that ought to be clean."

I went back to bed, only to be awakened a few hours later when I found myself on the floor as though my bed had spit me out. The house was rocking, and there was a roar like a freight train. My mother met me in the doorway to her bedroom.

"It's an earthquake," she said, and like the true pessimist she was, whose vision of life was confirmed by the absence of her husband and other natural disasters, she added, "only an earthquake." We hugged each other while the house pitched up and down. We could hear the sound of a bookshelf toppling in the living room. Dishes, glassware, and canned goods crashed to the floor in the kitchen. Seconds became a minute or more.

When the house stopped shaking, I thought I knew what Dorothy must have felt when her house finally settled to earth.

"That's it," I said. "Finally."

"You think so," my mother said, and sure enough, a few moments later we felt the first of the after-shocks that would startle us, waking or sleeping, for the next week. "Nothing ever ends quite when you think it should."

"Boy, oh boy," my mother said when we had made our way to the front of the house. "Would you look at this mess?" Nearly every cupboard in the kitchen was empty, spilled out onto the linoleum in a pile of shards and splinters. A pipe in the guest bathroom had broken, and water was running across the hallway. "Your father has a knack, doesn't he," my mother said, "for missing all the good stuff. It's a talent."

She kicked the handle of a coffee mug that was missing its mug. "You better get the shovel."

◎ ◎ ◎

As a family, we eat our beef rare, medium rare at most, but that night I left the tri-tip on the grill. "Look," my father said, "your mother had a point. I was gone a lot, and she didn't like to be left alone. She didn't like to imagine what I was doing. I knew that, but what was I supposed to do? Quit my job? She complained about my being gone, but she was tougher than she let on. She could rise to the occasion. She could think positive. Before and after her little hospital stay. She was strong, your mother. Don't kid yourself. She was no shrinking violet. Remember the Christmas tree fire?"

One New Year's Eve—as he did every year—my father had cut up the Christmas tree and put it in the fireplace, lit a match, and watched the dry pine needles go up like a blow torch. Only to discover this year that the flue was closed. Flames curled outside the brick work and began to eat at the wood of the mantel. While my father wrestled with the garden hose and I tore through the garage, looking for a bucket to dip water from the pool, my mother doused the fire with the drinking water we kept in the refrigerator. She stood in front of our mini-inferno with the old plastic orange juice container and threw water at the flames.

"Okay," I said. "How about the earthquake?"

"How about it?" my father said. "My point exactly. She was a trooper, that mother of yours, until she didn't have to be." He cast a critical eye toward the barbecue, where smoke continued to billow. "Maybe I'll take another beer," he said, "since you seem determined to burn the meat."

◉ ◉ ◉

My father was in the air when the earthquake hit. An early-morning flight from San Jose. From the sky, my father said, there was nothing to see that was any different from any other morning. Maybe the freeways weren't as congested as he might have expected. Moments before they landed in Burbank, the pilot made a brief announcement. A 6.5-magnitude quake. The walls of the Van Norman reservoir cracked. Evacuation was planned for a wide swath of the San Fernando Valley. My father picked up his station wagon in the Park-and-Fly lot, then drove home along streets strangely absent of traffic. Signal lights were inoperative for most of the way, and the feeling was apocalyptic. In the meantime, my mother and I had shut off the water and shoveled out the kitchen. She consolidated the perishables in the darkened and warming refrigerator. We listened to a transistor radio and heard the reports that, depending on the damage to the reservoir two miles away, we might need to leave, an announcement which made my mother mutter that this too would be just like my father. While we worked, we saw the strange flashes of blue light as power transformers blew in the neighborhoods around us. We wandered outside to watch the man-made lightning arc across the sky. In the backyard, all of the cinder block walls were leaning or on the ground, and our neighbor's Labrador was cowering under an oleander. The pool deck was wet where water had sloshed out in waves.

"You will remember this for the rest of your life," my mother said. "I will, too. I just won't have to remember it as long."

We listened to the radio and kept to our work. An hour after the evacuation plans had been modified, and our house was no longer considered threatened, my father barged through the door and immediately took inventory.

"All right," he said, "so I see you have things under control."

"Nobody's hurt if that's what you mean," my mother said. "And it's nice to see you too."

"I got home as soon as I could."

"Isn't that fine," she said and handed him a bucket. "Here. Make yourself useful. Fill the toilet tanks, would you? Thank god for the pool. We may not have running water, but I will not be reduced to going in the bushes."

My father did as he was told. He dipped buckets of water to leave in each bathroom. He set up the camp stove and made us fried egg sandwiches for lunch and root beer floats for dessert. Together we stacked cinder blocks in the back yard.

Around five o'clock that first day, my mother announced that she had a headache; she was going to lie down and take a nap.

"It's been a long day," she said, "and I've had it."

"That's fine," my father said. "That's a good idea. The kid and I will handle things."

"If I feel the ground shake one more time, I'm going to throw up."

"We'll keep things quiet," he said. He handed me a chisel. "Here," he said, "it's time we start learning the fine art of cinder block rehabilitation."

We chipped mortar for a week, and then we rebuilt the walls. My mother stayed in bed.

◉ ◉ ◉

"She was fine until I got home, and then she fell apart. Which was better than the time I went to Japan." My father shifted uncomfortably in his lawn chair. "Then she fell apart the moment we were both gone."

And that was when the phone began to ring. Ellen, calling from Portland and the chaos of her sister's house.

"Have you killed him yet?" she said in lieu of a more conventional greeting.

"Not yet." Through the kitchen window I watched as my father lifted the barbecue cover, speared the tri-tip with a fork, and dropped it on a plate. His face betrayed nothing, but I suspected judgment of my abilities behind the neutral mask.

"Did you know the old man was a spy? Sort of a spy. He worked for the CIA once upon a time. Can you believe that?"

"That explains a lot."

"I'm serious."

"So am I."

"All these years, I thought he was a boring engineer, and then it turns out he was wearing a trench coat all along."

"Jesus," she said. "Did he show you his decoder ring, too?" In the background, I could hear Ellen's sister yelling at her kids. She threatened murder and mayhem, blood and body parts. I could imagine a stampede of nieces and nephews and my enraged sister-in-law chasing them with a pool cue. Ellen breathed into the mouthpiece, and I had the sense that she had pressed herself against a wall until the violence passed. The noise on the other end ballooned and then subsided. "I am visiting the world's greatest incentive for sterilization," she said.

"And get this," I said. "My mother went nuts before she lost her mind."

"Wouldn't you, married to him?"

"Oh, come on," I said. "He's my dad."

"Just because all the skeletons are coming out it doesn't mean you have to defend him."

"I'm not defending anyone. He deserves a little respect, that's all."

"Okay. Be the good son." Her voice softened. "Talk to you tomorrow?"

"Sure," I said. "I love you." And then—aware that we had nearly overstepped with one another—we both hung up.

Outside, my father was shooing the flies away from the meat, which he had covered with a piece of aluminum foil.

"Don't worry," he said, waving his hand at the plate. "I saved it. But it was a close call."

◉ ◉ ◉

My father's funeral, like my mother's, was sparsely attended. But my father's memorial was the more curious affair. Whereas my mother's service attracted the women of her church who still remembered her from before Alzheimer's took her away, my father's memorial service was attended by old men in mismatched coats and ties and hair in their ears, the last of his work associates, Cold Warriors of the electronic frontier.

After the service, Ed Huckaby stood near the back, one hundred pounds overweight and sweating in the stuffy reception hall, his face the color of veal. One of the last to make his way through the line to pay his respects, he clapped one meaty hand on my shoulder and guided me toward the coffee urn and the pastries.

"Your father," he said when he had settled his bulk in the plastic folding chair, "was a pain in the ass. But I suppose you know that."

"Yes," I nodded. "I know that only too well."

"Still," he said, "he was your father, right? And there's nothing to be done about that."

"That's true," I said. "Nothing at all. And it's a little late now in any case."

"Your father," he said, "had a lot of ideas. That's what he was good at. Ideas about this and that. That and talking. My god, he could talk all day about nothing, so long as he was excited about it."

"And optimistic," I said.

"You bet. He never believed that things wouldn't get better. Even with your mother. When she got sick, he never believed otherwise. He took her to doctors, he took her to quacks. He kept waiting for her to get better."

"She was terminal," I said, "but he was terminal with optimism."

"And half-baked ideas," Ed Huckaby said. "Don't get me wrong. Your father was a good engineer, but he was a better visionary than he was a mechanic. He tended to break things when we worked on prototypes; his designs were not always in touch with reality. He said goofy things, but every fourth or fifth idea bordered on brilliance."

"Mr. Huckaby," I said, "since we're talking. Can you explain something to me? That summer that my mother went into the hospital, and my father had to come home from Japan."

"What?" he said, genuinely alarmed. "What was this about your mother?"

"My dad told me that he had to come home early from Japan because my mother had something of a nervous breakdown. I was away at camp, and Dad was in Japan with you, and she snapped."

"No! That's what he told you? That your mother was sick?"

"He didn't tell me *anything* until a few months ago."

Ed Huckaby shook his head. "Shit," he said. "That figures. Pardon my French."

He continued to shake his head, and I thought, Okay, here it comes, this is the part of the story where he tells me that my mother was a cocaine addict or having an affair, that everything I ever knew about my mother and her relationship with my father—but most especially my mother—is completely turned upside down. But nothing is ever completely itself or its opposite.

"Your mother wasn't sick-sick," he said. "She was sick of the situation, sick of being alone. Look at all of these old farts. See the camel-hair blazer next to the pastor? That's Guy Beebe—two divorces. Or talking to your wife—Lars Cunningham, no divorces but his wife committed suicide in 1976, on the Fourth of July, no less. She called it her own patriotic sacrifice in honor of the Bicentennial. His daughter has been in and out of rehab so many times, they've reserved a room for her. My wife and I haven't lived together in fifteen years. We do better as guests in each other's houses. You might not think so to look at us, but we were once a pretty dashing lot back in the day. Eavesdropping by day, drinking by night. That Tokyo trip, now that was a trip. We spent an entire week testing the equipment, then we'd go down to the Ginza and drink vodka with the same Soviet fuckers we were trying to hear. What a racket. When I wasn't drunk, I was hung over, and when I wasn't hung over, I was drunk. I'd have stayed a month if anyone would have let me.

"Your father was the exception. Your mother called the embassy in Japan, she tracked him down, then started talking divorce since—in her words—they'd been separated for the past ten years. So he hopped the first flight home. He missed it. He missed that Tokyo trip because he was sitting on a plane. He barely left the airport."

But first he sent my mother a telegram. DON'T DO ANYTHING. The first available plane was a milk run, and I could imagine him fidgeting, pacing the aisle between the seat backs, cracking his knuckles and his neck, driving the stewardesses and the other passengers wild. He flew twenty hours from Tokyo to Guam to Honolulu to LAX, then drove straight from the airport to the florist and laid on his own peculiar version of charm and roses, chocolate and persuasion. *Engineer amore.*

"Your father was embarrassed by the idea that your mother wasn't happy. That she wasn't happy even though *he* was. He hated the idea that he couldn't *fix* whatever was wrong. That's what engineers do: they fix things. We might not have anything like an interior life, but we fix the things that we see. Or we try to. He wanted to fix whatever was wrong with her. Or you."

"Me."

"Sure. He talked about you all the time. He was proud of you, but you were moody and unresponsive. Christ, what else would you be? A teenaged boy. Who ever heard of a teenaged boy who wasn't moody and unresponsive? You drove him nuts."

Ed Huckaby stirred his coffee. "He couldn't fix your mother, he couldn't fix you, and then it turned out he couldn't fix that damn window idea of his either."

"It didn't work?"

"It didn't work. Hell, we picked up more street noise than anything else. We should have seen it coming, don't you think? If a window can be a diaphragm for the interior to the exterior, why shouldn't it go the other way? For that matter, every time the air conditioning went on the walls vibrated so much that it overwhelmed whatever readings we picked up from the window. But that was your father. He sold his share of terrible ideas because he believed every one of them."

Carrying a plastic tub full of unwashed plates and cups and saucers, Gloria Valdivia, the daughter of one of my mother's oldest friends, passed by our table, and Ed Huckaby looked like a man whose sensibilities were being severely tested. One meaty hand rose from the table and fluttered as though to brush a waitress's backside, then came to rest next to his cup and saucer. "Look, I'm not trying to diminish your father in any way," he said. "We did a lot of good work together, and he loved you and your mother. That's all I'm saying."

"And that's good enough," I said.

"It'll have to be," he said. "Won't it?"

◎ ◎ ◎

The night of our barbecue, my father and I ate in silence. We tried to talk, considering the conversation we'd had on the patio, but topic after topic died between us. We ate our tri-tip, chewing quietly as though we were both deep in thought instead of what we were: two men who had no ideas and no clue what to say to one another.

"You know," my father said at last, cutting the last of the meat on his plate, "medium may be better after all."

"Who knew?" I said.

"Not me," my father said. "After all these years."

"Well," I said, "better late than never."

"And knowledge," my father said, pointing his knife at me, "is power. No matter when it comes."

"But ignorance," I said, "is bliss."

"And that," my father said, "is par for the course."

◉ ◉ ◉

Although my father hated baseball—too slow, too boring, too *passive*—I once managed to coerce him outside for a short game of catch after his return from work. Don't get me wrong; we had played catch before, but I remember this evening as being different in some way. Still wearing his dress shirt and slacks, he uneasily donned a glove and chased my errant offerings. I pretended to be my idol, Sandy Koufax, despite the fact that he was left-handed and Jewish and talented, and I was not and not and not. I threw wide, I threw high, I threw balls into the dirt at my father's feet. I was twelve years old and afraid of the ball, so I knew I'd never be much of a batter. But I believed myself promising nevertheless; no one expected pitchers to do anything but cower at the plate.

"You'd do better," my father said, "if you didn't turn your body so much. You stick your leg out to the side like that, and it gets your arm all confused."

"But that's the way the major leaguers do it," I said. "That's the way Sandy Koufax does it. Whitey Ford, Warren Spahn."

My father was unmoved. "You think they know everything? I want to see your left leg come straight toward home plate. It's straight-forward engineering. Forget about kicking it out to the side like that. You look like a son of a can-can dancer."

"But *all* the big-league pitchers do it," I whined. "Don Drysdale and Johnny Podres."

"I want to see the bottom of your left foot coming straight for me," my father said.

"Fine." I sulked, then retreated to the line of my imagined pitching rubber and threw the ball in the dirt where it bounced and hit my father in the shin. My second pitch, I threw over his head and into our neighbor's yard. The one with the tangled ocean of ivy and the testy German Shepherd who patrolled the fence line day and night.

"You see?" my father said. "You see that? Now we're getting somewhere. Too high and too low, but at least you're good side-to-side. You only have to work on the up-and-down. Once you find your ball."

"Yes, sir," I said, even though I was already imagining the ball sacrificed for my greater good and my glove stored in the back of the hall closet.

"That's something to work on," my father said, "because Rome wasn't built in a day."

"And patience is a virtue."

"You said it, kid." He handed me his glove to be put away, as glad to be done with our catch as I was.

Don't get me wrong. My father didn't stifle an all-star talent with his uninformed expertise. And I haven't carried around forty years of lingering resentment as a result. What I have carried is a skepticism of unbridled optimism, people with big ideas, and introspection better left for greeting cards and bumper stickers. I have also learned to mistrust such easy skepticism. The night of our barbecue, my father finished his plate, then signaled his readiness to go home.

"I'm bushed," he said, "all done in. I ate and now I'm ready for bed. I won't even offer to help you wash up."

"No problem," I said. "The dishes can wait. I'll grab my keys."

I retrieved his jacket and he shrugged it on, even though the temperature had not yet dipped below eighty. Outside, the stars were bright in a gassy, inflated sky.

My father settled himself into his seat, fiddled with the seat belt, and adjusted the seat back while I drove him the three miles home. "Did I ever tell you what I did the night before I moved your mother?"

"Nope, you never did. More secrets from the former spy." We were stopped outside the door of his condominium. "What did you do the night before you moved her?"

"Wise guy. Maybe this should wait another day."

"No, Pop, I'm sorry. Tell me now."

"You know I never wanted to put her in that place. It was nice enough, but you know what it was like. No matter how clean a place like that is. Shells of human beings. Babblers and dribblers. We watched the news then went to bed about eleven-thirty, and all I can think about is how I'm taking her to hell in the morning. I lay in bed next to her for three hours. I can't sleep. I can't stop thinking. I can't even close my eyes. But I must have fallen asleep after all because the next thing I know is I'm hearing the door chime on the burglar alarm. I wake up and your mother's not in bed with me. I get up, put on my robe and slippers. The front door is wide open. For over a year, your mother hadn't been able to work the shower or the faucets in the sink, but somehow she's managed to undo the lock and the deadbolt and open the door. By the time I get outside, she's half a block away. In her nightgown, of course, with her arms across her chest, practically running down the sidewalk in her bare feet. I'm jogging just to stay behind her. What a pair, we are, in our bed clothes! It's like something out of a dream. Your mother manages the half-mile to the convenience store on the corner. She makes her way around the gas pumps and then goes in the door. I don't have the heart to go in, so I watch her through the windows. It's three in the morning, and the world is asleep or committing crimes, but your mother, whose brain is half gone, is making conversation with the Pakistani behind the counter. Even outside in the parking lot,

I can tell she's asking him questions that make absolutely no sense. Where is the birthday cake? Whose car are we taking to the beach? I can read that off the glass. Once her brain started to go, she was always asking these kinds of things. No connection. No context. Completely out of the blue. The poor Paki is looking at your mother, puzzled, as though he's seriously considering an answer.

"When I open the door, he takes one look at my robe and slippers and steps back. I know what he's thinking: it's a slumber party for the nearly dead. Don't worry, I tell him. She's a champion sleepwalker. I'm sorry if we've bothered you. Honey, I say to your mother, it's late and time we were heading home. She starts turning in circles as though she's just now waking up. And then she looks at me. Who are you? she says. Who are you?"

"But you got her home," I said.

"Eventually," my father said. "And then four hours later, I was driving her to Willow Springs. She never forgave me. I know that."

"There at the end, she didn't know she had anything to forgive."

"It's easy enough to rationalize," my father said. He opened his door. "'Who are you?' your mother asked me, and the problem was I didn't know what to tell her."

◉

Domestic Arrangements:
Orwell Had It Right

WOULD I DO IT OVER AGAIN? Would I make the same choices? You might well ask, at this stage of events.

If one's life is analogous to a Choose Your Own Adventure, then how did I end up here? I taught school, I wrote stories, but there's no reason in the world I can see why I should have landed on either one. Teaching middle school English was a paycheck with an order of fiction writing on the side, an obsession more than hobby even if it was consigned to hours no one else wanted. But I have to confess: I was neither talented nor particularly driven, just stubborn. When I was younger, I spaced out in classes, and my reading consisted of sports biographies and the collected Sherlock Holmes. Elementary. And dumb. Boy, was I dumb. A budding intellectual or artist I was not, and I wasn't very good in anything that I chose to do, either in front of a classroom or the construction of a narrative. Daydreaming, on the other hand . . . I was the Pavarotti of daydreaming.

All of which is to say: if America is the land of opportunity, it is also the land of many myths, political as well as social. Take your pick. My preferred delusion is this: as a red-blooded American, you can be anything you want to be, so long as you put your mind to it along with your time. Well, I put in my 10,000 hours and then some. But all I had to show for it was a file cabinet filled with rejections and a hard drive littered with stories and novels and the bits and pieces of the same in stillbirth. Five years after the fact not even I wanted to claim them.

Writing began as a hobby of sorts. Idle entertainment. In high school and college, I thought it might attract girls. Fat chance. They gravitated toward the drummers and the pool sharks, quarterbacks and others who promised them hard times and worse. That was freshman year of high school. Scribblers didn't rate a single rung on the ladder, not even for those who wrote off-color parody lyrics. The storywriters might as well have not existed. Or worse, got lumped in with the *Star Wars* fanfiction nerds. Help me, Obi-Wan.

Although let's be candid, shall we? I wrote my share of crime stories and the hard-boiled, and I dabbled in speculative worlds as well, so maybe I can't throw stones without hitting myself in the eye. But in college I became convinced that narrative was the place for exploring the human condition, and if one or more of the characters didn't end up dead or in an asylum, I was disappointed with myself. Because that's the lesson of literature, isn't it? If it ain't depressing, it ain't art. Who wants—or needs—that? Apparently I did, in story after story, with nary a laugh to be found. And that's a hard lesson to unlearn.

Would I do it over again? I don't know. I can't even phone a friend. A teacher's retirement sometimes feels like a deal with the devil, and a writer's calling nothing but a siren's song. That's my answer. My most truthful answer. My final answer, my dearly departed dead-as-a-doornail Regis. My newfound friend. I don't know.

◉ ◉ ◉

When I retired from teaching, I told Janie that I didn't want to have any kind of party. Back in the day, this was, before lockdowns and quarantines and face masks, and long before vaccinations.

"Let's get a pizza," I said. "Extra cheese, let's go wild."

"Alan," she said, "don't be ridiculous. This is a milestone in your life. It needs to be marked and recorded and celebrated."

"Or French fries and onion rings," I said. "Cholesterol be damned. We could get drunk on Moscow mules and whiskey sours, and then vomit at two o'clock in the morning. Wouldn't that be nice?"

We went back and forth in that vein, Janie insisting that major events demanded commemoration, while I responded that the only thing worth celebrating was my freedom from the prison house of Garfield Middle, thank you very much. I could celebrate just fine through self-destructive behavior in the privacy of my own home. Freedom from listening to the PA system and the daily garble of announcements. Freedom from fellow teachers and administrators, most of whom I could do without. The papers and paperwork. The note-passing and inattention. Parent-teacher conferences and back-to-school nights that are a foretaste of death. Done. And maybe I could get back to having a coherent thought, one that might actually make its way to paper.

"We could go to dinner," she said. "Some place nice."

"Fine."

I agreed reluctantly, with a single caveat: we could go to dinner, and I could still drink more than necessary, but only if I wanted to and needed to and only if she agreed to drive home.

"I could call the boys," she said. She was nervous, that much was clear, and she thought that if the boys were present, angrier impulses might not prevail. I could see it written in her eyes and forehead.

But as it turned out, Cole and Josh had lives and obligations, and their schedules didn't match, and I know Janie was disappointed that we couldn't have a whole-family *pachunga* with all of its attendant safety rails as well as its dangers. But that gets harder and harder, doesn't it? And maybe the worst family gatherings are the ones that we force upon ourselves. Not to mention the self-imposed cheerfulness, borne not from the way we truly feel but from the way we think we ought to feel given the situation. Maybe you won't believe me, but I love my wife and our boys with a fanaticism that surprises and frightens me in those moments when the emotion strikes from out of the blue. I sense the shadow of the word "love," and it's automatic, the worst kind of heartburn. Around manufactured events, however—birthdays and anniversaries, weddings and graduations—my emotional system goes haywire and disconnects. Shuts down. And then I just feel bad by default since I can't seem to summon up the Hallmark font that the event requires.

So that last Friday of my last semester of my last school year, I turned in my grades, and then we went to Finley's, just the two of us, and we sat at a cloth-covered table and ordered a bottle of red at twice the price of the local Stop & Shop.

"Isn't this nice?" she said. She twirled her wine in her glass as though the action meant something.

"Nice to be done," I said, "if that's what you mean. Done and done."

"Is there anything you'll miss? Anything you'll regret?"

Janie sometimes has a tough time turning off her minister persona and that gift she has of making meaningful small talk, turning everything into a question that encourages other people to tell stories about themselves. I've watched her work room after room over the course of two decades, so my response might have been a little overly severe.

"Five years turned into thirty in the blink of an eye, and I miss the person I was. You know, being able to get out of bed in the morning without having to assemble myself first. I miss the writing that I might have done instead of the papers that I graded."

"I meant school," she said. "Is there anything about teaching you'll miss?"

"No," I said, as flatly as I could manage it. "Not students, not parents. Not colleagues, nor administrators. Nothing and no one."

Just then, the door swung open and, as if on cue, in came four other teachers from Garfield, each one at least twenty-five years younger than I was and with at least that many more years left to serve of their sentence. One of them was Hilda Upton, who taught the eighth-grade honors group and played the poet as well as any hammy actor. She dressed the way she thought poets dressed—various combinations of black—and she had a starchy, condescending air that she somehow managed to pass along to thirteen-year-olds, children who don't need adult help enhancing their affectations, their social awkwardness already more than well-established.

I saw Hilda, I saw Janie recognize Hilda from Christmas parties past, and I saw Janie begin to raise her hand to wave her over. Janie, by virtue of her work at the Church of the Open Door, recognizes that no one gets to pick the members of one's tribe. You are either related, or you are lumped together; the luck of the draw prevails, and no autonomy or choosing is involved. All are welcome, no matter how irritating. She is either a better human than I or better at hiding her own annoyance.

"That's really not necessary," I whispered. Maybe I was hissing more than whispering. "Leave them be."

After all, they were celebrating, too. In their case, the start of their summer, their temporary foretaste of freedom, and the only thing I would do was remind them of what permanent freedom would look like: a little older and more broken down than they wanted to believe possible. Not a look into their futures. They also would have felt compelled to come by, shake my hand, and politely express congratulations on retirement. They would have done that, and I would have known how perfunctory their well-wishes had been. I also knew how much Hilda and I disliked each other, how we each thought the other a poseur, how much we would be glad not to see one another on a daily basis.

It hadn't always been this way. When Hilda was first hired, she was eager to talk with those colleagues she knew who were trying to write. She showed me a set of her poems, which I didn't understand, since I'm a fiction writer and poems often seem as though they're written in order to make fiction writers, not to mention the average reader, feel stupid. I do know that in one poem, titled "Curdle," the speaker was angry for reasons that were never identified—I think the assumption was that the reader should already know—and I told her as much, but I also told her I'd be interested in finding out more. Let's talk, I said. Maybe I was a little in love with her youth and her affectations, not to mention her naked ambition. Schmuck that I was and am. In return I gave her a story about a man who receives threatening, anonymous notes at work, undermining his confidence in all things, personal as well as professional; she took it, said thank you, but about it she said nothing. Nothing. Not then, not ever. Not a word of either criticism or praise, which may be the most damning review of all. She never told me why her poem was angry, and we never had that writer-to-writer chat.

At the end of her first year at Garfield, *American Poetry Review* published "Curdle," and she was the talk among the faculty for a week or more. Forever after, when visitors came to campus, she was introduced by our rotating cadre of principals and guidance counselors as the creative writer on staff. Posters with her picture and an excerpt were printed and distributed to all the English classrooms in celebration, and Hilda's image glared at me from the bulletin board on the south wall above the words "You expect it to be something / it's not . . ." I left it up for years, long after everyone else had taken theirs down, and even after the corners ripped away, I kept moving the thumbtacks closer and closer to the accusation of her face. It served as both punishment and goad since I had violated the writer's prime directive: "Do your work, don't talk about it, don't look for community, sympathy, or applause."

One day in the faculty lunchroom, I came in and heard Hilda end a sentence with ". . . dead white men." At which moment, she pointed a finger at me and laughed, saying, "Like him."

"In your book," I said, and I felt the humiliation in the burning of my ears, "I guess two out of three is enough for a conviction. If you wait long enough, you'll be three-for-three, and that's what we call a tough out."

After that, we did not talk much beyond the basic courtesies, and although to my knowledge, Hilda never wrote or published another line—maybe it was her gift that had curdled—I never told Janie what had transpired. Could I explore or explain the nuances of my envy in any way that didn't look bad or reveal the embarrassment of middle-age infatuation? I wasn't sure I could.

In any case, before Janie could draw Hilda's attention, she and the rest had turned away, headed toward the bar, and throughout our dinner, we heard the barks and shrieks of their periodic, Friday-before-summer-vacation laughter. When we left our seats, their thirty-year-old voices were still echoing from the bar, and I could tell that Janie, in that moment, would have preferred their company to mine. I can't say I blamed her. I wouldn't have been my first choice either.

That, in itself, might be the best reason for a dog.

◉ ◉ ◉

Unlike the popular mythology, dogs are notoriously bad judges of character. Hitler had Blondi, the German Shepherd given to him by Göring, and to all reports, she loved him. Distrusting the cyanide capsules given to him by Himmler, Hitler ordered one to be tested on his favorite bitch as the Soviets closed in. That's gratitude, isn't it, after a lifetime of unquestioning devotion? Hitler was distraught, and other observers reported that Blondi's death affected them more than Eva Braun's. All of which is neither here nor there, I suppose, but let's not give dogs the ability to discriminate moral character.

Which brings me to our pair: Bastard and Dorothy, the first a "gift" from Janie and the second, my returned best wishes. Yes, you could say that they were both an impulse borne of unacknowledged anger. As Janie's story goes, Bastard's presence in our lives was simply a good deed gone horribly wrong; he was just an abandoned dog for which Janie felt responsible. I don't buy it. Somewhere, in the back of her mind, she wanted me tethered. That's what I think. The boys were a little terrified of Bastard's energy and random behavior, so it was up to me; every afternoon after school, I'd have to deal with an agitated Jack Russell when what I wanted to do was write three sentences and delete two. If one afternoon I'd had enough and "accidently" left the side gate ajar, would you blame me? I didn't mean to, but I might have, since resentment will have its way. I felt bad enough after the fact, I can tell you that. I picked up that damn dog from the asphalt, and I carried his body to the backyard. I made the boys dig the hole because those are the responsibilities we have when someone else makes a choice without asking what anyone else thinks. I should have made Janie recite "The Lord is my shepherd" and deliver a eulogy since Bastard was her big idea, but her face was enough for me to see, a mixture of sorrow and relief since she was no more fond of that dog than the rest of us.

So why did I get Dorothy a month after I retired? Maybe I was afraid of being at home all day with no more excuses about time and the writing I wanted to do. On the other hand, some part of me knew even then that my motives were payback and impure. I think I was hoping to see Janie on the other end of a leash, being towed by ninety pounds of ill behavior.

When I told Cole about Dorothy, I could hear him shaking his head on the other end of the phone.

"Uh-huh," he said. "Bastard wasn't enough? Why are you doing this? What does Mom think about it?"

Our younger son is a computer geek whose idea of pets is whatever can be built. He would make a wife if he could. His older brother, on the other hand, keeps ferrets, the smell of which brings tears to my eyes.

"I don't know," I said. "Really. It's a mystery. Any relationship is."

"Oh, Mr. B," Cole sighed, "you really don't know anything, do you?"

◉ ◉ ◉

In their early years, our boys often called us Mr. and Mrs. B, even though our last name is Peterson. They still do now and again, long after they left the house for their own lives and their own choice of adventures.

They gave us our pseudonyms for two reasons. The first was a reference to the married pair of beavers in *The Lion, the Witch and the Wardrobe* who are constantly sniping at each other. Their frantic back-and-forths are generally caused by Mrs. Beaver's insistence that the house should be clean and that they have absolutely everything they're going to need before they leave. No matter that their world is falling apart and the wolves will soon be at their door, she will make sure—in their winter without Christmas—that she has the good stewpot with them for the journey. Much to Mr. Beaver's dismay, her foresight is usually validated by events.

The second is similar: that old comic strip known as *The Lockhorns*, back when newspapers with their funny pages still landed in our driveway; somehow, our boys conflated that tooth-and-nail couple with the characters from that older-than-old radio sketch, *The Bickersons*. Do you see a pattern? Yes, anger, clear as could be. Even if we refused to see it. Josh and Cole claimed that their earliest memories were of the two of us fighting, insulting, debating, arguing. I have no similar memories, odd as that may seem, and neither does Janie; we thought we were having a conversation. Exchanging friendly banter. Discussing options. We didn't see our interactions as argument, at the end of which there would be a winner and a loser.

Here's another oddity: if we seemed to be fighting, they never asked if we were getting a divorce, even though so many of their friends' parents had gone down that road. I guess they assumed that they were trapped in a guerrilla war from which there was no escape, or they knew, deep down, it wasn't so dire as it might have seemed otherwise. Then again, Josh may have unconsciously known something when he said, "You guys sound exactly alike, no matter what you say."

Of the two, Cole might have been the younger, but he was the bigger twerp.

"And how are Mr. and Mrs. B. this fine evening," he said more than once when he was ten. And generally, he inquired after our health on those nights when we were trying to make sense of the bills. Adult orthodontia for Janie, car repair for my ancient Escort, the roof that was falling apart above us all. Our voices might have been raised. Mine surely would have been if Janie had paid for youth group T-shirts rather than billing the church or the children's respective families.

"A little personal responsibility wouldn't be out of order," Josh said, and somehow, he caught my cadences, right down to what Janie called my Pompous Basso Profundo.

"The more we give," Cole said, using all of Janie's earnestness, "the more we get. When are you going to figure it out?"

On and on they went, our own tweener vaudeville team, a reminder that parody may be the greatest mirror, no matter how hard it is to be both subject and audience.

We thought their perceptions of us as adversaries were hilarious, but they never understood how indifferent to each other we had once been. Her brother had been my best friend in high school, and even after Gary and I got an apartment during college, Janie never made much of an impression. Plain Jane. Little did I know she should have been named Calamity for the disturbance she would cause in my life. She wore secondhand clothes and was six years younger, and her teeth were so bad, she kept a hand in front of her face. Whenever someone asked a question and forced her to speak for herself, up went the hand, and you would have thought you were witnessing an episode of *The (Wo)Man in the Mask*. And then I heard the stories of their mother and her series of trailer park romances. Tattoos and cigarettes, whiskey and amore. Her brother told me his worries about the sister he had left behind, and I had thought then: *But you weren't worried enough, were you, Gary? Not worried enough to stick around.* No, because he had his own survival needs and his own life to live, and when all is said and done, we have to look out for ourselves. An engineering degree and then multiple job offers and upper-middle-class paychecks and a move to another state altogether. He could voice them, but his worries stayed in the abstract. Then, after he made his escape, Janie sidled right in. What was I supposed to do? Send her back to the double-wide, with its no-lock hollow-core doors? I ask you: what was I supposed to do? She came to the apartment one night with a cardboard box for her clothes, and she slept on Gary's cast-off twin mattress until she slipped into mine several nights later, and there we were. One night I was snoring, the next night there were four legs where once there were two, and we made each other yip in the night without trying too hard. Did we experience rapture? Please. It was companionable, I don't mind saying so, but it wasn't like there had been any kind of discussion, much less a formal invitation.

You can believe me or not. We never really talked about what we were doing together, and I assumed the arrangement was temporary until it wasn't. It's not like I hadn't been seeing other women now and again up to that moment in time, and I assumed that she was seeing other men—boys, rather—closer to her own age. After all, she was just starting college complete with a day-pack and carrot sticks and juice boxes, all her tidy school supplies, and I had middle school papers to correct. She was a psychology major, so she had her insights, and then she was a religious studies major, so she could turn her big thoughts into epiphanies. But I had other plans entirely, most of which involved the Olivetti on the kitchen table. Romance, sex, love, sex, intimacy, sex. Sex and a little more sex, isn't that what we've been taught and conditioned to expect from our adult years? I cringe now to think of my naivete. But if such activities weren't on the page, I hoped to keep them siloed and secondary, like periodic rewards for the discipline of art. That was our "relationship" then, a term that, if it means anything at all, was simply a pooling of resources and the filling of mutual needs. And then a few months later, Janie mentioned marriage, and I saw a flash-forward of the next thirty or forty years.

"You could do better," I said, stalling for time. There had to be any number of arguments against marriage, convention, and a lifetime commitment, but my mind didn't go blank so much as vacant.

"Or worse. I could marry a violent drunk. I've seen those. I've lived with those. When you get drunk," she said, "you take a nap. You might get a bit snappish, but mostly your eyes glaze over."

"Quite a recommendation," I said. "How could I not be tempted?"

"Look," she said, "this is the best thing for both of us. Trust me."

"Oh, I should trust you now. College girl that you are."

"Yes, you should. You know that girls mature more quickly than boys. Your brains don't develop until you're dead, and then it's too late. You need help in the right-here and the right-now.

I'm right, you know, and I'm right-here. I'm right about this, and we've gotten to know one another well enough. You know it in your heart."

"You think we ought to get married. You think we ought to play house together. You think you're right about everything, and you can help Mr. Know-Nothing function. Is that it?"

"Yes. I know I can. And you know it, too."

What I knew—even then—was that I was no great shakes and had little enough to offer except a middling income and a selfish preoccupation that few would tolerate. If she was insistent upon getting married to me, her insistence was masking her own desperation, one that had more to do with her mother and her mother's trailer and those boyfriends that served as a constant and high probability of threat. Even someone as oblivious as I could see that it wasn't fair: I had a job, a ratty apartment, and a plan for the Great American Something. I also had my set of middle-class assumptions, borne of genial if indifferent parents, all of which she lacked, so here she was: living on the kindness of someone who was little more than a stranger, when she was without much in the way of options. If my plan for writing and my prospects for success have turned out to be just so much insubstantial vapor, then I suppose I should be glad that the marriage I stumbled into turned out to be so long-lasting, if not without its blemishes. Even if its foundations might have seemed inexplicable at the time. I've heard about rescue fantasies and those men who harbor illusions about saving the damsel from various forms of danger and distress—violent, economic, or sexual—but if I am to be honest, my good deed was done wholly without deliberation or intent.

◎ ◎ ◎

I told Janie at the time that marriage was one thing and writing another, and that the two activities were not always compatible.

Over the years, we had our share of such conversations, Janie and I, about the garage and what I did out there, and she came to call the Olivetti and then the succession of word processors and laptops "Clarissa" because in her mind, the implements of the trade were nothing more than wild women staking their claim.

The conversations were not always pleasant. Testy, maybe, would be my best characterization. One of the worst happened early in our marriage, when Janie was still in seminary and interning at a Presbyterian church, one of the old-school variety. You know, the "Frozen Chosen" folks who don't brook a lot of nonsense or tomfoolery. This was back when I still felt obligated to go with her on Sunday mornings, when I tried to find common ground with people who would, in the future, write her letters of recommendation.

She brought me into an adult Sunday School class and introduced me as the middle-school English teacher that I was and a "budding young fiction writer" with whom she rarely had a conversation, my distraction so prevalent and my eyes so often focused on the blank sheet of paper rolled around the platen. In retrospect, I suppose that "budding young fiction writer" comment was as accurate a descriptor as English teacher, even if I was pushing thirty, and to my ears felt dismissive and, as metaphors go, misleading if not dead, since no one would ever confuse me for a flower.

The room was filled with white-haired women over the age of seventy. The leader of that group, an angular and caustic old Scot named Agatha Reid, proceeded to interrogate me regarding my publication record, to which I could only reply that there wasn't one. Not yet.

To which, she said, "Then I guess you're not really a writer, are you? Not yet."

"I can show you all the paper that I've spoiled," I said, "if you need proof of activity if not accomplishment."

"He's great," Janie said in my defense, although in those years, she was also reluctant to read anything I'd written, and I can't really say she rushed to my aid. "Really. Great."

"I guess we'll have to take your word for it," Agatha said, "and wait for the book launch."

"Sure," I said, "we'll have a party. I'll send out the invitations."

"Okay," she sniffed. "God willing and I'm still alive, I'll be waiting by the mailbox."

Janie managed to shift the discussion then from my lack of publication to the Gospel of Luke and the parable of the Good Samaritan. And from there, she managed to make a transition to Bonhoeffer, whose martyrdom managed to eclipse everything of our previous discussion. I couldn't have felt smaller unless Agatha Reid had told me to stick to teaching, which was a sentence I dreamed often enough.

But later, when we were at home in our latest crappy apartment, we went at it for an hour or more, and I told her that in the future, she could leave me out. "My name enough is fine," I said. "No need for explanations or titles."

"I was only trying to include you," she said. "Was that so awful?"

Over the years we had something like this same argument, about my choices and the worth of my time in the hours I spent after school. About how I spent that time. We never did get it quite right. But if I had Agatha Reid, I took no small satisfaction some years later when Janie gained Georgette Cartwright, which only seemed fair and comeuppance enough, since she had been so willing once upon a time to feed me to the wolves.

◎ ◎ ◎

To my mind, Janie's certainty about our future together was just a good guess. On the other hand, her way of talking about me was a little less assured and open to acrimony and interpretation. On my *other* other hand, Orwell had it right about so many other things, small as well as large, and because of that, he has been something of a hero to me. Maybe 1984 isn't exactly the way we're living now; then again, maybe it is, and we just can't see the dictators for the despots. Or systemic bias for the policies that perpetuate inequities. Blah-blah-blah economics, blah-blah-blah politics. Forests and trees and global politics aside, Orwell might have been even better at recognizing those small gestures that betray the irony and absurdity of our humanity: the condemned man avoiding a puddle on his way to the gallows so as to keep his bare feet dry; a policeman who shoots an elephant not because it presents a danger to the local community, but because he doesn't want to look like a fool. What would he have done with a writer whom no one wants to read?

It is his elephant that haunts me now when it no longer matters. If I continued to write—novel after novel, story after story, through marriage and fatherhood and the day after day after day of middle school hell—only because I was afraid of being the butt of a joke, so what? Does that constitute a waste of a life? To my mind, stopping would have been the true admission of failure, an admission of how foolish I had been all these years. I might as well have written Agatha Reid a note of apology for wasting her time. Speaking of whom . . . I ran into Sister Reid years later, long after Janie had migrated from the Presbyterians to the Methodists and from there to the Open Door. Miss Reid was as acerbic as ever, even if she was noticeably slower, moving from her aging Volvo to the automatic door of the Food 4 Less. I was coming out holding a discarded whiskey box with its bottles of cheap red blends, the accompaniment to afternoon storytelling.

"It's the bard himself," she said, spotting my box, "or the drinker, as the case may be."

"We are what we do," I said. "At the moment, I'm the shopper, and in another moment, I'll be a driver. The drinker doesn't show up until after five."

"Indeed. It's five somewhere, I hear tell." She stood in front of me, so that both our paths were blocked, so close that I could see the pills in her sensible cotton pants and the pulls in her acrylic sweater, none of which were noticeable from a distance. Her scalp gleamed pink through the shellac of her hair. "Tell me," she said, "after all this time: have you found a publisher yet?"

I shook my head, and the glass bottles tolled their presence in their box.

"I guess that explains why I never received an invitation."

"That's it," I said.

"Maybe," she said with her hard Presbyterian starch, "a little less of the sauce might be advisable. And then I'll be able to stop praying for you. Your wife worries, you know."

"I work hard," I called after her retreating back.

Without turning, she threw her hand up in a wave of farewell or dismissal or judgment, maybe all three.

"I work hard," I called again, "and you can stop praying for me anytime you like."

She waved again.

"You can pray for me all you like," I yelled, "but I've never heard a prayer yet that beats the declarative sentence."

Take that, you dried-up old cow.

You and your Volvo and your bank-account standards of success.

◉ ◉ ◉

Oh, I talked a good game. But I had my suspicions that my perseverance was just stubbornness or delusion in disguise. What did I know? What did I know for sure? It's hard enough not being a joke to others without the fear of becoming a joke to oneself, and God knows, I lived long enough in the knowledge of how I must appear to the world at large: a pudgy middle-school teacher, a has-been of the might-have-been, a perpetual striver and failure.

But so long as I continued to write, I hadn't failed entirely, for there was always the next novel, story, paragraph, and sentence, and I could look the world in the eye, no matter how much it cost me to do so.

Janie, on the other hand, manages to be practical and clear-eyed, hard-headed and likeable until she's not, with one caveat: she's never not likeable around strangers or the congregations within her charge; it's only her family who has to beware, and then she can skewer us all. She can wither a cactus if she's in a mood. Never have I possessed such qualities of force with the possible exception of passive-aggressive stubbornness, and that was probably a matter of genetics and led to my own downfall anyway. Witness Dorothy.

All of which is to say, I admire my wife, even as I wish I could have offered something more for her to cheer.

⊙ ⊙ ⊙

The last time I talked to Janie, I was on a gurney in a hallway on the non-COVID side of our local emergency department. I was surrounded by sounds and images that could only be summoned by Dante, and if I could have raised my hand to go home, I would have made myself the most eager of students. Hall pass? Please?

One ninety-year-old woman was lying on a gurney with her wrists strapped to the side rails by gauze restraints. She would tear off her clothes and her face mask otherwise. Even so, she was moaning about the abuse she was suffering, asking Mathilda to take her home. Who was Mathilda? Maybe a sister, long since dead. Maybe a nurse, a caretaker, or a child. Another woman, much less elderly, sat ramrod straight on her gurney, demanding she be seen. Now, if not immediately. Her hair was permed into a blue helmet, she wore a housecoat with creases, and she spoke imperiously to each nurse who walked by.

"This is not right," she said. "I've been here two hours already."

"I understand," one nurse said. "But we're very busy. I'm sure you understand."

"I do not understand," the woman snapped to the nurse's retreating back. "I would like to speak with your manager."

"Lady," I sighed, "we all have to wait our turn."

"Well, I never!"

"Of course you haven't." I wasn't proud of myself, but I did want some peace and quiet.

She huffed and sputtered, and somewhere, around the corner and beyond my sight, a man was screaming. What was he saying? Who knows? If nobody seemed to care, that was only because he was one of so many who were suffering and afraid.

I dialed Janie. "You wouldn't believe this place," I said, before she could say hello. "I will never need to experience an asylum."

"Maybe you'll think twice about having a heart attack," she said. "If that's what it was."

"I had all the signs," I said. "And it knocked me out of my chair."

"Okay," she said. "Okay."

Janie had found me on the cement floor of the garage because the dog was going bananas, barking and jumping at the doors like a maniac. Dorothy was that attuned to the fact that something was wrong, even if my wife didn't believe it at the time or for several hours after the fact, for that matter. I had felt a pain, as though someone had hit me in the chest with a hammer and then squeezed with a chest-size C-clamp, revenge for all my dismissals of tools and materially productive behavior. Against all middle-class protocols, I had turned our garage into an office and replaced pegboard tool holders with bulletin boards and power tools with a computer, and this is what I got for my troubles. Then I must have passed out because the first thing I knew, I was on the floor, my cheek pressed against the cement, and Dorothy was acting as if she were having a seizure, and Janie was standing over me and asking what in the hell was I thinking.

"Writing isn't that hard," I seem to recall her saying, "without you turning it into self-flagellation."

I mumbled something to the effect that she shouldn't compare sermons to stories because then we'd have to talk about truths and lies, and Sundays wouldn't fare as well as the other days of the week. At least that's what I should have said if I could have made any sense out of what was happening.

"What?" she said, but I knew enough to leave it alone.

After the EMTs loaded me into the back of the ambulance, they stuck a nitro patch on my chest and did an EKG and then said that they couldn't really say anything, not being doctors or nurses, but the hospital was the place to go, and now was the time to do it.

"If we could say something, we probably wouldn't anyhow," one of them said to Janie, "because it's really not the time for discussion."

Now, as I waited in the hallway, the C-clamp was loosening, and my chest felt less constricted.

"Have you walked Dorothy?" I asked. I knew she wouldn't have since our history of dog ownership has revolved around passive-aggressive stare-downs: the person who blinks first has to get the leash, and I blink a lot.

"I'll get to it," she said. "I've been a little busy, with you-know-who getting a thousand-dollar motorcade to the hospital."

"Sure, bring that up."

"I called the boys," she said. "That took a while."

"And?"

"Cole fell apart, if you can believe that. And Josh gave me an inventory of symptoms. You would have thought he had the questions written down."

"What do you know?" I said. "Children are always surprising. Even as adults."

And a reminder that even those closest to us are as mysterious as the universe in which we live.

"Look," I said, "I'm feeling better already. Maybe it was a panic attack, after all. I've never had one, so I wouldn't know, but then I've never had a heart attack either. On the other hand, nothing beats being in hell to lift a person's spirits."

"You stay there," she said, "and you let them figure out what's wrong. Don't you dare come home and then fall over dead."

"That would be a lesson for you, wouldn't it?"

"Like I need more lessons. A lesson for you more like it, old man."

"You'll be lucky to be so old."

"Cranky, retired old man."

"Just tired in perpetuum," I said. "No need to do it twice."

Our conversation petered out after a time, and since the background soundtrack consisted of so much ambient and unrelieved suffering—those unearthly shrieks and heartbreaking groans—I found it hard to stay focused. Anyway, she said she was going to walk the dog. But then not long afterward Janie sent me a text about a story I'd written years ago as a kind of joke, a toss-off parody, a satire about a female minister and a church filled with Agatha Reids and Georgette Cartwrights and the cruelty of those who mean well. It had won a prize. Well, second place, which is winning by rejection and creates a less exuberant, more ambivalent celebration. *Shh, keep the excitement down*, and *amen, brother*.

She accused me of having stolen her life, although I think she meant that kindly since everyone's life is out there to be used. What do I know? She gave me the good news in a text without a single emoji, which is so unlike her usual style as to be ominous. Then again, if I had stolen her life, she had also taken my voice and made it irrelevant, and whenever she answered her phone as Reverend Peterson, another piece of my skepticism and cynicism was leeched away. As though the residue of my nature was just so much dryer fluff.

I put the phone next to my leg, conscious of how little battery life I had left, and fatigue overtook me with a sudden certainty. A weight descended, and I closed my eyes against the crush and the blue burn of the fluorescent hallway lights.

Which was when Hilda Upton pressed her thumbs against my eyelids. Hilda Upton! My nemesis! Of all people!

"What?" I said or tried to say. She was wearing a nurse's blue uniform smock with those Precious Moments angels as a pattern, and she was waving a pen light in front of my eyes. "What are you doing here? I've heard of career changes, but this is too cute by half. What happened to anger and black-on-black?"

"Shut up," Hilda said.

But it wasn't Hilda after all—*how did I know this?*—and she wasn't talking to me. She was an older, overweight woman in those campy scrubs and plastic gloves, with a mask behind a face shield, and she was wielding paddles linked to a machine on wheels, and it was a scene from a movie I didn't want to see. Or one of those television hospital dramas, in which the doctors might as well be models and have more sex than they do medical obligations, except in the middle when they lose the cranky, late-middle-aged writer, who's been stuck in a forgotten hallway with the rest of the misfit toys.

That was enough to make me float away, so that I could see it all, this little tableau of desperation and failure and too-lateness. I could see the story—nothing but a piece of flash—unfold.

The ninety-year-old woman was still moaning, although she had gotten one hand free, and was even now working mindlessly on the buttons of her housecoat. But the other woman was no longer issuing her commands, so transfixed was she by the commotion surrounding the gurney to her left.

This is how you get seen, isn't it, Regis?

This is how you get attention.

◉

ACKNOWLEDGMENTS

I would like to thank the editors of the magazines and journals in which these stories first appeared, some in different versions: *Manoa* ("The Garden"); *Witness* ("Words from Another Time Zone" and "Financial Planning for the New Millennium"); *Mid-American Review* ("[The] Only Lie"); *Book of Matches* ("Shop Tools"); *Christian Century* ("Theologians, 1959," under the title "Prayers and Miracles"); *In the Grove* ("Monopoly"); *The Packinghouse Review* ("Lost"); *Idaho Review* ("The Soul of the Gorilla"); and *Storyglossia* ("The Secret Life of Engineers").

⊚ ⊚ ⊚

I'm going to go out on a limb here and make a horrible generalization (entirely self-based, of course): most writers are introverts who spend their working hours in dark rooms with the doors closed. Sound is only welcomed after hours, preferably accompanied by an open bar. We might be mistaken for misanthropes but for those moments on the page when joy and love intrude, experiences that no one seemingly sees otherwise in life. That said, I am indebted to two longtime friends: fellow writers and fellow football fans/obsessives/sufferers, Steve Yarbrough and Ric Dice, whose periodic phone calls and emails have kept me—a dour, chronically depressed Czech—in tune enough with what passes for cheerful. (*Roll Tide . . .*)

I am likewise grateful for those friends, readers, and colleagues who have read and responded to my work while reserving judgment for the writer's character defects and emotional foibles. My thanks to James Coffey for reading everything when he could have been walking the dogs on the beach; to Deb and Greg Lapp, who remind me by the practice of their lives that not all who write need be confined to a chair and dark rooms; and to Nancy Spiller, whose professionalism is always balanced by an appreciation for cake.

For thirty-six years, I was blessed to have worked with the kindest of folks at Reedley College; even six years after retirement, my gratitude is not diminished. Thank you, friends. Likewise, my online students and colleagues in the Writers' Program at UCLA Extension—you rock.

I am once again grateful beyond measure to all at Johns Hopkins University Press: series editor Wyatt Prunty, who said *Yes* to this manuscript with his usual encouragement, support, and advice; executive editor Matthew McAdam, who has gracefully guided this book through the publication process; Anthony Blake, for spreading the word; and Hilary Jacqmin, whose copyediting prowess has once again made for a wonderful online conversation.

My family of women puts up with all manner of petulant nonsense. Thanks to my wife, Deb Everson Borofka, as well as our daughters and their partners, Katie Borofka and Mara Burmeister, and Krissie Borofka and Amanda Dewey. Your good humor—not to mention your willingness to overlook my default mode of grouchy—is appreciated. And for our grandson, Everson Philip Dewey Borofka—dude, I have a few cautionary tales to tell you, some of which, at the age of three, you already know . . .

ABOUT THE AUTHOR

David Borofka's first collection of stories, *Hints of His Mortality*, was selected by Oscar Hijuelos as the winner of the 1996 Iowa Award for short fiction. His novel, *The Island*, was published in 1997.

His short fiction has appeared in *Image, Massachusetts Review, Southern Review, Black Warrior Review, Missouri Review, Manoa, Gettysburg Review*, and *Shenandoah*, among other places. He is the winner of the *Missouri Review* Editors' Prize, the Charles B. Wood Award from *Carolina Quarterly*, the Emerging Writers Network award, the *Prism Review* fiction prize, and *Jabberwock Review*'s Nancy D. Hargrove Editors' Prize.

His most recent collection, *A Longing for Impossible Things*, was published in 2022 by Johns Hopkins University Press and was the winner of an American Fiction Award for the short story from the American Book Fest. *The End of Good Intentions*, his novel of Evangelicalism and academia gone sideways, was published in 2023 by Fomite Press.

A member of the faculty at Reedley College from 1983 until his retirement in 2019, he continues to teach on assignment for the Writers' Program at UCLA Extension.

FICTION TITLES IN THE SERIES

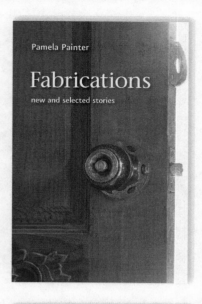
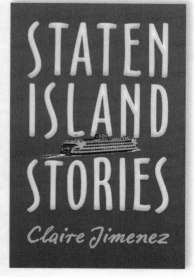